The Gall

CW01657824

T M Goble

The Gallery and Murder

First paperback edition printed in 2021 in the United Kingdom

A catalogue record for this book is available from the British Library

ISBN
Paperback 978-1-915742-21-6
Kindle 978-1-915742-20-9

Published by The Creative Peak(TCP)

Book Design: T M Goble
Cover Image: Copyright Shutterstock

T M Goble's Website

www.tmgoble.com

Action Thrillers
Detective Murder Mysteries
Standalone Murder Mysteries
Historical Fiction
Contemporary Fiction
History of Peak District Literature
Seasonal Recipes
I occasionally send newsletters with details on new releases, special offers and other bits of news relating to my books.

01

The aggression in the voices outside her window sent a shiver of unease through Jenny. She tweaked the frayed old curtain a few inches. Foul language delivered in a screaming shout came from nearby. Two men stood in the Market Square facing each other. Although she had only been in the village for a week, she had met both.

Lionel, the taciturn butcher's huge frame filled the doorway of his shop on the opposite side of the Square. He waved a large knife tinged with blood. Red with rage, he shouted abuse at the other man. Tony, a local farmer, screeched invectives as he stepped from his tractor and snatched a pitchfork from the trailer, waving it in Lionel's direction. Tony, much smaller than Lionel, red-faced with temper, strode towards the butcher's shop, brandishing the pitchfork. 'I'll park my tractor where I want!' The smell of manure from Tony's trailer wafted across the square.

Since moving into the village, Jenny had appreciated the quiet ambience and sleepy nature of Market Square. The angry altercation shattered the peace of the morning. The aggression between Lionel and Tony could escalate into a serious incident.

She had no intention of intervening, but would they calm if she became a witness? Pulling on her jacket and tutting with irritation at the boyish exploits of two grown men, she opened the door into the square. With a deliberate movement, she slammed it behind her. Both men glanced in her direction but took no notice. The shouting and aggression continued unabated. Tony continued to advance towards the butcher's shop, thrusting his pitchfork in a menacing and curving arc above his head. Lionel had stepped from the doorway into the square carrying the bloody knife. The two men stopped a few yards apart.

'Gentlemen!' shouted Jenny as she strode across the square, her eyes fixed on the hostile pair. With no preconceived idea of what action to take, she could not standby and observe a potential deadly fight between them. They glanced in her direction. Jenny grimaced with consternation as she drew closer, while her eyes remained riveted on the pair. Would they hurt each other? What could she do to stop their aggression escalating? She stopped a few yards away, ready to give them a piece of her mind. They were behaving like truculent teenagers.

A man waving his arms strode into Market Square. He bellowed, 'Tony, Lionel! For goodness' sake. Stop arguing! I can hear you at the other end of the village. How many more times!' With this intervention Lionel glanced at the man and brandishing his knife in the air, he stomped back to his shop. Tony frowned, shrugged, and loped back to his tractor. The man hadn't finished and marched towards Tony. He pointed an accusing finger towards the trailer. 'Get that smelly thing out of the Square. Have some sense, man!'

Tony glared but remained tight-lipped since the

appearance of the man but jumped onto the tractor and within seconds the engine spluttered into life and he pulled away. The man didn't acknowledge Jenny, but stood motionless until Tony had left the square. He entered Lionel's shop. Jenny sighed with relief.

Quietness had returned, but what would happen if they met without witnesses? Anxiety swelled through her for the first time since her arrival in the village. With a grimace, she returned to her door and tried to push the thoughts of violence from her head. Over the many previous years, she'd become used to hostility but had become adept at controlling the disquieting and terrifying pictures from that period, which often unwillingly filled her mind. The two men's behaviour had been unacceptable. Yes, she'd witnessed far worse, but it had surprised her to observe the aggression in an idyllic setting. She wished for a future with no more violence.

02

The sun shone brightly on Market Square and warmed her as she took in the vista of her chosen village of Peaklow. A smile came to her lips, as there would be no more terror and living in fear. The quiet village represented a transformation from the happenings of the past.

She had surprised herself a few months ago by buying a disused shop on the corner of the Square. Rubbing her finger along the rough paintwork of the sill, she smiled in anticipation, as it would be transformed over the next week. The rough old curtains in the shop covered the internal redecoration. Before long, the outside would receive a new coat of white paint. She had fallen in love with the shop and the cottage, renovated into a single unit during the 1960s, at first sight. The small, rustic seventeenth century cottage would become her home. As she lived on her own, with no current man in her life, it suited her needs to perfection. A soothing rural retreat and a new focus in her life.

She strolled into the backyard, which housed a variety of stone outbuildings, most in a ramshackle state, but she would leave work on them until the summer months. Except for the recent local feud witnessed earlier, she enjoyed living in a village tucked into the rolling limestone landscape. The peaks and troughs of the hills and valleys presented an intriguing skyline, while the nearby fields, edged with dry stone walls, were filled with sheep.

Whether she would enjoy a restful and secluded life after the last turbulent twenty years, she couldn't be sure, but she had resolved to take the initiative, as her circumstances had changed. One problem had nagged at her throughout the week. Her friends didn't know her new address. She couldn't be bothered with emails and would be different by sending a letter through the post. Therefore, a stroll across to the post office for the stamps, paper and envelopes had become a necessity.

As she crossed the Square her concentration settled on the empty run-down shop next to the butcher's. No one had offered her a reason for its neglect. Paint peeled from the battered bolted door. The boarded windows were buckled from the damp. The old stone walls stood firm, though partially obscured by a rampant ivy, which reached the roof of the two-storey building. It seemed a shame to allow the decay and it spoilt the picturesque square where she would soon open her shop. With a shake of her head, she sauntered across the road.

The post office was more business-like than she expected for a remote village, but local enterprises attracted tourists, so they used it as a bank. Inside, the shop had two distinct areas. A brown painted counter with a glass screen provided the security for the business transactions and official Post Office matters. At the other end, an open counter functioned as the village newsagents. 'Good afternoon, Jenny,' came the friendly voice as soon as she stepped inside.

Elizabeth glanced at the clock as though checking noon had passed. Tall and slim, she had a precise and detailed manner, but always dressed in a rather frumpy style. She wore a cream blouse with a thin brown cardigan, which didn't match her thick straight skirt and dark heavy tights. Her shoes could best be described as sensible. With flushing cheeks, she bustled between the two counters in the shop. Her hair had been lifted imprecisely into a bun. She pushed a strand of hair away from her face.

In the first conversation she'd had with Elizabeth, she revealed herself to be forty-four years old. Jenny, the same age, hoped she didn't look the same as Elizabeth, who she'd assumed to be in her mid-fifties.

Leaning against the counter, Elizabeth huffed out a weary breath. 'It's been so busy today.' Jenny glanced around the empty shop, giving an inward smile. Busy didn't conjure up the right image, as no other customers had arrived. With her former friends, she would have laughed, but Elizabeth lacked a sense of humour. Perhaps the phrase had become ingrained over the years. She gave the impression of a woman set in her ways, but she had been most welcoming since Jenny had arrived in the village. The friendly approach of the locals had surprised her. Many had lived in the village all their lives, but there had been no animosity towards a newcomer.

'Spring is flying past.' Elizabeth handed Jenny the local newspaper, her selected stationary and a book of stamps. 'The caravan site opens this week after the winter closure. It will make my life much busier.' Her shoulders slumped and her expression slid into a frown.

As Jenny left, she guessed Elizabeth would repeat the conversation with the next customer. Perhaps she led a dull life and had little imaginative conversation to offer.

03

With her curiosity aroused by Elizabeth's reference to the caravan site, Jenny strolled towards the edge of the village, passing her own shop and the George pub. The displayed menu caught her attention. Several dishes appealed to her, so a visit one evening would save the effort of cooking.

She had become immersed in the charm of the old village, with its limestone buildings, many dating back to the sixteenth century. The ruins of a castle, silhouetted against the sky, stood on the edge of a steep crag, high above her. The forlorn and crumbling walls remained in proud defiance to the elements, its glory days long since passed. What changes it must have witnessed over the centuries?

Turning away, she ambled through the village. The twists and turns of the High Street, coupled with over-hanging buildings, had persuaded the council to build a by-pass, allowing the road to become a peaceful haven, with only a distant rumble as vehicles sped along the new dual carriageway.

Her efforts of moving in over the past week had made the days exhausting. On the plus side, she had enjoyed a series of restful nights, but they wouldn't last. The horrors which plagued her in the dark hours always returned. When they did, early morning or late-night walks were the only remedy which helped to calm and eradicate the horrendous images. She considered owning a dog, as then it wouldn't seem strange to be wandering around the village at such bizarre times. Hopefully, she would settle into life in the village and the nightmares would dissipate. It would be a relief if they did.

In an unhurried manner she ambled along the track of the High Street, enjoying the fresh air, the solitude and the picturesque landscape which surrounded her. The caravan site was wedged between the old and new main roads and on one side had an avenue of trees, which, when in full leaf, would obscure the site. The neat caravan pitches complemented the freshly painted shower block, and once open for the season it would be a hive of activity. She dawdled on the bridge, peering into the gushing water of the river. Resting her arms on the solid stone parapet, she gazed at the ever-changing lights and shadows playing on the surface. The large boulders in the stream pushed the flow in different directions, which caused the rushing water sound, so typical of the countryside.

She day-dreamed, which allowed her mind to wander. It careered into those dark places and the chilling thoughts of an ambush by gun wielding militants. Grimacing, she wrestled the disturbing images of violence back into the recesses of her mind. The burbling stream soothed her tortured thoughts and, with a positive effort, she returned her concentration to her village affairs. The enjoyment of the local topography could come later, as she had many important tasks to complete before she could settle into her new life.

04

After a brisk walk back to Market Square, she panted, while sweat beaded her forehead. Her former fitness had gone. More pressing matters than a healthier lifestyle required her attention for the next couple of weeks. As she arrived at her shop, the transformation during her brief absence gave her a warm glow of satisfaction.

The old curtains had vanished. Kevin, the local builder, worked inside, putting the final touches to the redecoration. Fresh and white matched Jenny's requirements. She smiled as Kevin, in a loud baritone voice, sang along with a song on the radio. Rounding the corner into the narrow side street, she almost collided with a couple strolling arm in arm.

She recognised him. He had intervened earlier between Tony and Lionel. Dark-haired and handsome, he apologised for the near collision. Removing his sunglasses, 'Have you moved in?' He pointed towards the shop and the cottage with a questioning expression.

Jenny gave a vigorous nod and grinned.

'Welcome to the village. I'm Nicolas and this is Amanda. We live in Victoria House along the road, where the scaffolding is being erected.' She'd passed it on one of her walks and it stood out as one of the larger houses in the village. They impressed her as a perfect couple as they stood together, exuding charm. Amanda's long blonde hair had been perfectly cut and Nicolas was the most handsome man she'd seen in the village, apart from Kevin, the builder.

With smiles of farewell, Nicholas and Amanda strolled away hand in hand towards their house. Jenny passed along the side of the shop and the outbuildings to turn into a small gate at the end of her yard. Alongside the back entrance, a rickety five bar farm gate hung at a strange angle on rusty hinges. It led to a track between the houses and then to an open green field.

Entering the cottage, she placed the stamps, notepaper, and envelopes on the kitchen table, intending to write tonight to inform her friends of her new address. A smile of amusement crossed her lips, as she imagined their faces when they opened the letter and discovered her new location. Many would visit as they wouldn't believe she had settled in a remote village. The contrast to her past life would come as a shock to many of her former colleagues and friends. But for her, the difference held an invitation to a peaceful future.

'Kevin, it looks great! What a brilliant job!' Jenny stopped in the doorway and stared at the shop with wide-eyed delight, as the former dingy space had been transformed. Kevin perched on a stepladder, touching up the entrance door frame, and grinned his satisfaction at the compliment. He balanced his brush on the paint tin and climbed down. 'It's come up well, bright and white.'

Kevin had impressed her since they'd first met. He worked to a high standard which extended to his personal presentation, as he dressed smartly, regardless of the type of work. The monogrammed t-shirt and functional work trousers gave him a professional appearance, and his tool bag, which went everywhere with him, had been organised to perfection. Clean shaven with short black hair, he looked immaculate. An impish grin, paired with a good sense of humour, created a charismatic character.

He slipped a tiny object from his pocket and pointed it at several places around the shop.

Jenny was curious. 'What are you doing?'

'I always like to take pictures of my work.'

'That's a tiny camera.'

He handed it to her. It appeared an anonymous piece of plastic, the type that was a lucky charm on a key ring.

She handed it back to him with a grin.

It had been luck that several months ago, when she had visited before buying the property, she had met him. One morning, while standing in Market Square, peering up at the building, and wondering if this might be the perfect location for her new enterprise, he had come whistling around the corner, tool bag in one hand and paint pot in the other. Not recognising Jenny, curiosity had won, and he'd stopped for a chat. Like all good business owners, he had given her his card before departing, with a cheery wave, across Market Square. It had made moving easy, because he had re-decorated and repaired the cottage before she arrived.

Forcing herself back to the present, 'Can I borrow one of your tall step ladders, please?'

'I'll do it.'

Jenny laughed. 'You don't know why I want the steps?'

'Never mind.' He chuckled as he eyed her with curiosity. 'Tell me.'

'I want to check the work required on the outbuilding roofs.' In one swift movement, Kevin picked up a pair of steps and, with long strides, set out for the yard behind the shop.

He placed them next to the outbuildings, and with ease and confidence, stepped up three rungs and peered at the roofs. 'Several tiles missing and I can't see any felt.'

'Let me have a look.'

Dropping to the ground, he eyed Jenny up and down. 'Do you think that's wise?' But a broad grin crossed his face.

'Don't be cheeky!' She batted him playfully on his arm. 'And don't you dare peer at the weight restrictions on the label.'

With a throaty laugh, he grabbed the steps to steady them, as she climbed to examine the work required.

'Look, none of the treads have bowed from my weight!' Laughing, she returned to the ground. Another rumble of laughter erupted, and he put his arm around her shoulder and gave her a gentle squeeze.

'I'll give you a price. It will be a good one, because I've only work for the next few weeks.'

'Thanks for the offer, but I intend doing it myself during the summer. It's not complicated, and it gives me a sense of satisfaction to achieve simple jobs.'

A serious expression crossed his face, and his forehead wrinkled with concern. 'Promise me you will get a tower scaffold to work from. With any building jobs, safety first. I'm serious. Far too many accidents happen with building work because people don't pay attention to detail and take unnecessary risks. It only takes a moment of lapsed concentration for a life-threatening accident to happen.'

'Thanks Kevin, that's sensible advice.'

The noise of a tractor distracted them as it arrived from across the field. Tony, who had argued with Lionel earlier, cut the engine and quietness returned. Jenny checked, but he no longer pulled the trailer full of manure. He waved, 'Afternoon Jenny.'

She crossed to meet him and expected Kevin to join her. 'I'll finish painting in the shop.' He returned inside. Jenny thought his manner bordered on abruptness, especially as they were fellow villagers and both enjoyed talking.

'Good afternoon, Tony.' He clamoured from the tractor to open the farm gate. Slightly shorter than her, but a wiry character, he always wore a hat. Today a standard flat cap, in keeping with a thick checked shirt and jeans, along with a pair of green Wellington boots.

'I can't stop for long; I need to check the field next to the caravan site before I finish this afternoon.' Advancing towards the gate, he untangled the piece of rope that kept it closed.

'What's wrong with it?' Jenny wasn't sure why a field needed checking.

'Because of the pleasant weather, if the caravan site is busy, and the field has dried out, I can use it as a temporary overflow.'

'Do you own the caravan site?'

'Yes, I received a good grant to diversify away from standard farming, and it's worth far more than grazing sheep or cattle.' His eyes gleamed. Returning his attention to the gate, he used his muscular arms to haul it up and heave it to one side. 'I'm lifting a good crop of root vegetables this afternoon so they will be in my farm shop by early morning. You haven't been to visit us, so if you pop along, I'll introduce you to the missus.'

'I'll come tomorrow.'

Nodding his approval, he climbed back into the tractor's cab, then with a roar and a great deal of shuddering and rattling, he drove into the Square. Tony had been one of the first people she had encountered when she had moved in, because of his use of the Market Square gate. Although he had lived in the village for generations, he had shown no reluctance to welcoming a newcomer. A warm and contented glow spread through her as she peered around the ancient Market Square. Convinced she'd made the right decision, her new life in Peaklow would be a wonderful challenge.

05

A week until her big day. Jenny chuckled to herself as she ate her breakfast the following morning. Most women considered their big day to be walking down the aisle. Jenny didn't have a man, so no wedding would occur next Saturday, but she had planned the important event with care and detail. The crucial crates and signs would arrive in the afternoon.

Pushing aside her excitement, she would take up Tony's invitation to visit the farm shop. Healthy vegetables and good walks might help her waistline. For the past twenty years, she had gone long periods without tasting fresh food. While improvements had come in recent times, crops straight from the ground had no equal. If she used the footpath at the back of Market Square, Tony's farm shop would be about a mile away. A pleasant morning with an early cloud cover greeted her as she left the cottage. Ambling along the well-trodden footpath, she revelled in the fresh air and solitude of the countryside, with only the noises of nature breaking the peace. For Tony's farm shop, she had built up an image of quaint rustic stalls or barrows in a dark and draughty barn.

As she entered the immaculate farmyard and

glimpsed the renovated building, the farm shop seemed an inadequate label. The large glass doors and surrounding woodwork showed quality craftsmanship. She stepped inside and her eyes widened in amazement. A tiled floor, bright subtle lighting which highlighted chiller cabinets and next to them were a mixture of cane weaved baskets, set in rich wooden frameworks, with a wonderful array of vegetables. Open tread stairs led to a mezzanine floor with signs to the coffee shop. Speechless at such a superb shop, only Tony's voice brought her back to reality. 'Do you like it? Not bad for a farm shop, is it?'

Tony weaved his way between the cabinets, with his leather cowboy hat set at a jaunty angle, and a huge grin on his face. Her eyes darted around the amazing variety of foods on offer. 'It's wonderful, and I intend having a good look at the vegetables and the delicatessen counter.' Several assistants waited to serve, but no customers had arrived, apart from her.

Tony waved his hand towards the mezzanine floor. 'Jacqui and I have a coffee together before the business of the day starts. Come and join us, as she's upstairs.' Jenny smiled in agreement and followed Tony. A smart woman, the only one not in a shop assistant's uniform, stood behind the counter pouring coffees. Tony called out, 'Make that three, Jacqui. Jenny has arrived.'

Jacqui waved and called out, 'Cherry scone?'

No, jumped onto the tip of Jenny's tongue, but then she spotted them on a stand near the till. 'Yes please, but let me pay.'

Tony waved the offer away with a flap of his hand. As Jacqui went to pick up the tray and bring it to the table, he moved towards the counter, 'Let me do that, luv.' Jacqui smiled in acknowledgement, and walked towards the table empty handed, leaving Tony to pick up the cutlery on the way.

Elizabeth, at the post office, had briefed Jenny about most people in the village. It had meant nothing to her because she hadn't met them. Elizabeth had mentioned that Tony was fifty-five and his wife ten years younger. He looked sixty, but Jacqui could pass as mid-thirties. Tony placed the tray on the table, and allocated the coffee and scones, ensuring they had cutlery and serviettes, before seating himself.

The large cherry scone must have been baked that morning. Jenny's mouth watered in anticipation as she spread the butter onto its warm, crumbling surface. Tony piled three spoonfuls of sugar into his coffee and stirred it vigorously. He glanced at his wife with a smile of satisfaction, 'I work on the farm and Jacqui works in the shop. The arrangement works well for us, doesn't it, love?' Jacqui nodded as she buttered her scone. Jenny took a thoughtful sip of her coffee as she studied the smart, attractive woman.

The long nails and immaculate clothes didn't look like someone who did a full-time job in a farm shop. With annoyance, she mentally reprimanded herself. What right did she have to cast opinions about Tony's wife?

Jacqui, after a brief search of the table, put her serviette to one side, 'I'll grab some more butter from the counter.'

Tony sprang up. 'I'll fetch it.'

Jacqui gave a small blush of embarrassment, 'He won't let me do anything. You can see what he's like.'

Too over possessive for my taste, but keeping these

thoughts to herself, Jenny allowed a small smile to creep across her lips. 'He seems thoughtful and attentive.'

As he returned to the table with the extra butter, Tony's mobile rang. He answered it. 'You girls have a chat. A delivery lorry has arrived in the yard.' Gulping down the rest of his coffee, he grabbed his hat from the table and turned away. 'I will see to it. Be back in a mo!'

Jacqui smiled, but didn't start a conversation.

Jenny filled the silence with an obvious comment, 'Looking around your shop, I'm surprised you haven't a meat section as you have cattle on the farm.'

Jacqui gave her a quizzical look, 'It's something we've mulled over, but you are new to the village, so won't know the background.'

'Go on.' This sounded intriguing. Every small village had gossip that lay under the surface.

'You must have met Lionel, the butcher.'

'Yes, his shop is across the square, so I buy my meat there.'

'Tony offered him a good deal to sell our beef and poultry before we opened the farm shop, but Lionel is stubborn and set in his ways and will only take meat from the wholesaler. Tony became livid with him and they had a big argument. Once Tony has argued with someone, he will not let the matter drop. Did you notice the small derelict building when you arrived next to this barn?'

Jenny could recall a small ramshackle building that contrasted to the immaculate farm shop.

'After the argument, Tony applied for planning permission to turn it into a butcher's shop.'

Jenny raised her eyebrows. 'What happened then?'

'We're still waiting on the outcome of our planning

proposal. When Lionel found out about our scheme, he wanted to retaliate, so he came up with his own development. The old guy at the big hall owns the empty shop next to Lionel's in the Market Square.

Jenny nodded as she'd studied its dilapidation a few days earlier. The neglected building spoilt the picturesque Market Square.

'It's rarely been on the market and he's done nothing with it. Lionel approached this old guy and made him an offer.' She pursed her lips. 'After all these years, Lionel has decided to expand his business to the shop next door. He's told people he intends opening a deli with fresh vegetables and a coffee shop.' With a huff of indignation, she pushed her coffee cup aside and leant forward, placing her folded arms on the table.

Jenny gave a small cough to suppress the smile of amusement. The two men's behaviour smacked of one-upmanship, but village politics intrigued her, and her curiosity had been aroused. It accounted for the animosity between the two men in Market Square.

'Tony has made a counter offer for the same derelict shop. He wants to extend the business from here. And that's not all,' Jacqui huffed out a noisy breath and a faint flush appeared on her cheeks.

'Isn't it?' Jenny once again resisted the temptation to smile, because Jacqui appeared so serious. The whole scenario seemed more appropriate to headstrong teenagers than grown men.

Jacqui paused and drew her eyebrows together in a frown, 'To make matters more complicated, Kevin has put in a third offer. He wants to open a builder's merchants, as the shop has a good size barn at the back for storage.'

The sound of footsteps coming up the stairs attracted their attention. Tony approached them with large, swaggering strides. Panic came to Jacqui's face. 'Perhaps, I've said too much.'

'I promise I won't say a word,' whispered Jenny as she came to terms with the background of the first piece of village politics. It brought a smile to her lips but gave her the explanation of the argument she had witnessed yesterday.

It was easy to imagine that in such a picturesque village, everyone would be friendly towards each other. A naïve assumption. She should know better. In any society there would be conflict, sometimes apparent, but at other times bubbling beneath the surface, waiting to explode. Would more old feuds and resentments come to light as she settled herself into village life?

06

Could the wrangling and gossip of this tranquil village disrupt her plans? Emerging into the car park of the farm shop, she gazed with interest at the small stone building which Jacqui had hinted would become a butcher's shop. Would it ever happen? She couldn't guess.

Despite the chill wind that blew, she chose a longer route back to Market Square along a quiet, wide lane flanked by low limestone walls. The views across the patchwork of fields towards the hills enchanted her, as the shadows of the scudding clouds changed the colours and textures of the grass and rocks. Before reaching the village, she stopped to catch her breath and took in the tranquillity of her surroundings. No traffic noise and no people. A sense of wellbeing and contentment drifted over her as her anxieties floated away.

In the distance, the village's oldest pub, a former Elizabethan manor, caught her attention. It had been converted into a small hotel with a popular pub-restaurant. Making a mental note to visit it for a meal, she resumed her stroll along the lane to the outskirts of the village. Turning along the old main road, she passed a row of traditional cottages, and then a single detached house. The lintel with 1870 inscribed on its weathered surface contrasted with a newly erected sign, Victoria House. It was where Nicolas and Amanda, who she had bumped into the previous day, lived. It had been built into a small hill with the ground floor at street level, but the first floor extending further back, and opening onto a sloping garden.

Scaffolding, which hadn't been there a couple of days ago, had been erected across the front and sides of the house. Shielding her eyes from the sun, she stopped and peered upwards. Kevin stood on the roof above the scaffolding, taking off the old tiles. He waved.

Jenny waved back. 'Be careful up there!'

'Perfectly safe!' he caught hold of the rope attached to the harness he wore. He flicked it so that Jenny could see that the rope had been securely wrapped around the chimney breast. Once more impressed by his safety conscious attitude, she waved goodbye and continued her walk.

A narrow footpath ran along the edge of the side garden of Victoria's house. A small wooden footpath sign lay on its side, half covered over by a tangle of weeds. The path appeared well used, although walking boots would be required in wet weather to negotiate its rutted muddy surface. It would be worth an explore when she embarked on a walk.

As she approached Market Square, the sight of the small hairdressers reminded her that before her big day she wanted her hair cut. She had never been fussy with her hair and had accepted the first specks of grey that had appeared in the brown and had no wish to colour them out. Short and tidy, but it required a trim.

The hairdressers, an unusual building of corrugated

metal, had been set back next to a garage. On impulse, she would make an appointment. Entering the bright and welcoming interior of Peaklow Hairdressers, Jenny stared in amazement, and came to an abrupt halt with her hand still resting on the handle of the open door.

Amanda, sitting behind a small desk, greeted her with a smile. 'Come in.' Her immaculate appearance must come from owning a hairdressing business.

'I'm after a wash and trim. Can I make an appointment?'

'I could wash and blow dry it now if you wanted?'

After Jenny's hair had been washed, she sat waiting for it to be trimmed and dried. Amanda busied herself selecting scissors and comb to prepare for the trim. 'You've been revamping the old shop. We expected a conversion to living accommodation.'

'No, I want it as a shop.'

'The entire village is intrigued.' Amanda smiled and curiosity flashed across her face. 'Even Elizabeth at the post office hasn't been able to extract the information from you. Some locals are worried you might open a rival business.'

Jenny grinned with a hint of wicked amusement. 'I've been keeping it under wraps, but no one in the village needs fear competition from me. While I'm not a secretive person, some villagers might develop the wrong impression, so I'm telling no one.'

Amanda blinked with surprise and obvious disappointment. Seconds ticked by while Amanda snipped away at Jenny's hair. To avoid any more probing questions, Jenny changed the direction of the conversation.

'This morning has been my first trip to the farm shop. I'm impressed with the vegetables.'

Amanda gave a little laugh but didn't reply.

'What's so funny?' Jenny eyed her with curiosity.

'It's interesting to find a person outside of the politics of the village.'

Could this be the second snippet of village gossip in one morning? Jenny had only mentioned vegetables. A slow smile spread across her face. 'You will have to explain because I don't understand.'

'Two men in the village often argue.'

Jenny laughed. 'I know the answer to that one. It's Lionel and Tony.'

Amusement glinted in Amanda's expressive blue eyes. 'You are learning quickly. Lionel is my dad.'

'Oh,' Jenny's eyes narrowed as she searched her face.

'I've not much time for the dispute. Why they can't agree is beyond me. They have known each other most of their lives. My husband, Nicolas, has no time for such squabbles.'

'I can understand his reasoning,' Jenny glanced at Amanda to make sure she hadn't taken offence. As she snipped away at Jenny's hair, Amanda continued to chat. 'Nic isn't from the village but owns an extensive business in Birmingham, and so we also have a house there. The major thrust of his company is import and export, so he travels extensively. He maintains that in business you must work with everybody, there is no point in becoming petty.'

Jenny nodded her agreement but didn't comment any further. She would be wary of making another mistake elsewhere in the village until she'd uncovered all the outdated feuds.

Changing the topic onto safer grounds, 'Are you his only child?'

'No, I've a brother, John. He helps dad in the shop and works at the George. That's the small pub along the road here, not the big one on the edge of the village. Have you heard about the dispute over the empty shop next to dad's?'

Jenny nodded. A pause occurred while Amanda, having finished the cut, plugged in the hair dryer and reached for her styling brush. Using a small soft brush, she flicked the discarded hair from Jenny's shoulders before continuing the conversation. 'It makes it difficult for John, because he serves behind the bar at the George, and that is the favourite place for both Tony and Kevin, who are both competing for the empty shop. Kevin wants to open a hardware store, while Tony wants the shop just to annoy my dad.'

A question sprang into Jenny's mind, but she decided not to ask. If Kevin was a rival for the unused shop, it must create a difficult atmosphere, so why had he been asked to work at Amanda's house? Nicolas must make the decisions.

07

Jenny, fizzing with excitement, opened the doors of her Watercolour Gallery on a wet and gloomy Saturday morning. She had been up early and fixed the external signs in the pouring rain, wanting to leave the disclosure of her shop's purpose until the last possible moment. How would the villagers react? Would they visit out of curiosity?

The tight closing blinds had shielded the inside of the gallery from anyone trying to peep in from the pavement, so no one would have discovered the shop's purpose in advance. Art had been her passion since a child, and about ten years ago, she chose her preferred wash style of painting.

Standing in the middle of her gallery, she surveyed the interior with satisfaction. As she had travelled the world in the last twenty years, she had painted many landscapes. The paintings had often been shipped home and stored until she returned. Crates full of them had arrived during the week. She had picked the best of the landscapes from places she had visited. They were arranged into a gallery which people could meander at leisure. A small section had the title, The Landscape of Peaklow, but that display remained empty, though before long, she hoped to fill it with local landscapes.

She strolled around the displays, stopping before certain pictures as she recalled the time and place where it had been painted. They represented a journey through her life. Interesting and varied. She'd made a lot of friends and travelled the world. But it had become necessary to leave that part of her life behind, put down roots and enjoy a more settled life. Her friends would visit when time allowed. A smile spread across her face as she expected to make painting trips around the local area.

Where to paint first? There were many local spectacular views. The idea of opening a gallery had assumed the persona of an adventure. The most difficult problem had been pricing her work. As she didn't need the money, she had made the most expensive ones less than one hundred pounds. She hoped to sell a few, which would encourage her to paint more often.

The previous weekend had been pleasant, when she had walked up to the farm shop, but today the usual March weather prevailed. Since the middle of the night, it had been raining hard and the cold strong wind would deter all but the most hardy souls. She preferred to paint on location but would often use a photograph.

Last week, she had taken a dramatic photo of a large local viaduct that had once taken a railway line over both the river and the road. Near the edge of the village, she could set up there when the weather improved. While in the gallery, she wanted to be busy, so she positioned herself in front of her easel and began the wash background for the viaduct, using the photo as her guide. The finishing touches would come on location.

While she hoped for visitors, she doubted the locals would come in, and the tourist season hadn't yet started. The rain had abated, and about half an hour after opening, Nicolas and Amanda peered through the window and then stepped inside.

'May we look?'

'Of course.' Jenny appreciated the visit. Using hushed voices, they moved around the gallery, taking a long time examining each picture.

Nicolas smiled across at her and pointed, 'I recognise this painting, as I go to Hamburg regularly, so it stood out for me.'

On the first day, someone had recognised one of her pictures. Jenny bubbled with pride and a grin of pure pleasure appeared.

Nicolas studied the picture with intense scrutiny. 'You are a fine artist. Are they for sale today?'

'Yes.' Jenny swallowed, trying to ease the sudden dryness in her throat.

'I will have the one of Hamburg, it will look perfect in my office at work.' As he spoke, he took out his wallet and withdrew eighty pounds. Jenny gave him a broad smile, as with shaking hands, she sealed the picture in a large thick plastic bag.

How amazing! She'd been open less than an hour and had sold one of her paintings. Amanda walked over and stared at the easel and the photograph of the local viaduct. So far, Jenny had only managed a background wash and had painted no detail. Returning to her husband, she leant in close and whispered, so that Jenny couldn't hear.

He nodded his approval and pointed towards the easel. 'Amanda would like the first option on the one you are painting. The river and the viaduct are favourite locations of hers and she has the perfect spot for it in the salon.'

Jenny grinned from ear to ear. 'I would be pleased to offer it to you first.'

Amanda bounced from foot to foot and her blue eyes sparkled. 'I'm sure I shall have it. Your style is so consistent. It will be delightful.'

'Do you paint portraits?' Amanda queried, her blue eyes twinkling even more vividly.

'I do,' nodded Jenny, 'but only from photographs. I find it too difficult to paint with a model sitting in front of me.'

Nicolas put his arm around Amanda's shoulder and nodded his head. 'Do you take the photos? If so, will you take one of Amanda and paint it?'

'Yes.' Jenny's face lit up as pride flashed through her at obtaining a portrait commission. A beaming smile spread across her face. Turning her attention to Amanda, she took a quick steadying breath to calm herself. 'You look beautiful in your blue top today. Would you like me to take the photo now?'

Amanda nodded, and within a few minutes, Jenny had positioned her against a white screen and had the photos she required. She thanked them and as they turned to leave, 'With all this rain, I hope your roof is finished as Kevin removed the tiles the other day.'

Amanda flicked her long hair away from her face. 'Yes, he's finished the roof. Today he is painting the window frames on the scaffolding.' She gave a quick glance towards the rain hammering on the shop window. 'He's undercover and can work without interruption.'

Nicolas rested his hand on Amanda's shoulder. 'I want him to finish, as the scaffolding and its plastic covering are blocking the light.'

'It shouldn't affect you.' Amanda grinned. 'Nic's going abroad this afternoon for a week.'

Pulling their jackets around them, they took their new purchase and left as another couple entered. They were tourists and chatted at length about the pictures and the B & B they were staying in for the weekend but didn't buy.

Jenny, wanting to keep busy, settled herself at the easel and continued with the painting of the viaduct. Light classical music played in the background, competing with the rain which lashed against the windows. A calmness descended over her as she absorbed herself mixing colours and applying the wash to the canvas with steady sweeping strokes.

About lunchtime, Kevin came in. The rain on his black jacket glistened in the brightness from the halogen spotlights. 'Just popped off the job at Amanda's to pick up a sandwich from home.' He glanced around. 'It looks impressive.'

Standing with his hands on his hips, he smiled and scanned the pictures. 'It never occurred to me you were an artist. I saw the shop signs this morning. When you wouldn't divulge the type of shop you were opening, I'd speculated on different themes, but an art gallery had never occurred to me.'

Jenny appreciated his good nature by popping in to support her. 'Working at the weekend?' She set her paintbrush down, twisted on her chair, and gave him a questioning look.

'Nicolas asked me to finish as soon as possible. I didn't want to work today, as I've little on next week, but the customer is always right.' He gave a loud over dramatic sigh and adjusted his baseball cap.

'Have you much more to do?'

'Finish the window frames and then the front door. That's it, so I'll complete by Monday lunchtime, unless someone pinches my paint again.' His face crinkled into a frown of exasperation and he shook his head.

'All of it?' Jenny's eyes widened in disbelief.

'Only one can and a brush. Last night, I'd cleaned up the brush, closed the can and put it near to the window for the morning. When I arrived, they had disappeared, along with my empty flask.'

Jenny raised her eyebrows and Kevin grinned. 'I checked everywhere, but they have gone. Disappeared without a trace.' Then with a cheery wave of his hand, he twisted away. 'Must go, work to do. See you soon.'

08

Long before dawn the following morning, Jenny rose following a restless night. Rubbing the disjointed sleep from her eyes with one hand, she stifled a yawn with the other. No sounds reached her from Market Square as she sat wrapped in her soft, warm dressing gown. The fire in the grate no longer burned, so she shivered in the coolness of the early morning.

It had been a good opening day in the gallery. After the early sale to Nicolas and Amanda, it had remained quiet, but she'd had a few visitors later in the afternoon, so overall a good day, with her first sale and commission.

While she had been reading on the couch yesterday evening, she had dropped off to sleep, but had woken a few hours later with a gasp as her head pounded. The horrors and nightmares had returned with a vengeance. Even on waking from the nightmare, the images continued to haunt her by coming to life as they twisted and twirled in the room. The frightening scenes she had lived through revisited her with vivid clarity.

Her method of coping was to give up on sleep for the night. From experience, a long walk would help to erase most of the graphic horrors. Although it had been ten o'clock at night, she had put on her outdoor clothes and gone for a walk through the village and along its tracks. She had not returned home until after midnight and then settled by the cosy fire once again with her book. Going to bed had remained out of the question. From experience, it would be a restless night with little sleep. With luck on her side, she managed to doze in the chair for a few hours.

After a warming cup of tea, she once again donned her walking clothes, and at five o'clock in the morning, she set off again. Walking alone in the dark in Peaklow gave her little concern. Despite the tension between Tony the farmer and Lionel the butcher, she enjoyed the tranquil village which was so different from other places she had lived.

Leaving the dark Market Square she headed along the old road towards the caravan site. As she passed by, the ghostly outlines of several caravans loomed in the darkness. No one moved. Silence enveloped her, and she marched on, following the twisting lane to the huge Victorian viaduct. Then she turned onto a rutted narrow footpath flanked by dense undergrowth with trees arched overhead that sloped down and finished under the viaduct. She peered up at the huge brick pillars towards the arches, which appeared so drab in the semi darkness of early morning, compared to the scene she was painting. Later today she might continue to paint, which would lift her spirits.

A jolt of panic zipped through her as something moved overhead. Flattening herself against the wall of the arches, she held her breath and listened. With an exasperated sigh, she breathed out and reprimanded herself for such stupidity. There would be no snipers lurking in the shadows today. No doubt a bird flapping around the arches, perhaps searching for shelter from the cool wind that whipped along the valley. Easing herself away from the wall, she pressed onwards towards the old mill.

Picking up her pace along the track, the brisk walk helped to dissolve the terror of the nightmare, and a sense of calmness infiltrated her thoughts. In a more positive frame of mind, she stood for a while, enjoying the solitude, peering at the rushing waters of the weir. In the darkness, their inky blackness was barely visible.

Her mind wandered over the challenges of painting moving water as she listened to it gushing over the weir. From her previous observations, she had to be aware of the ground over which the water flows. Where the stream bed is level, the water takes on colour from the sky, but at the weir, it would appear much lighter. The faster the water moves, the whiter it becomes.

She pictured returning to the weir to paint the swirling gushing water. A smile crept across her face as she expected the challenge. With a spring in her step, she followed the wide path of the old railway track. When she reached the former station, which now housed a cafe, but not open at this time of the morning, she headed for home.

Unsure of her route, she followed the first footpath sign back to the village. The path would take her towards the church spire, which rose in a ghostly silhouette into the lightening sky. She deduced that her route would lead her past Victoria House.

The narrow footpath became overgrown and muddy, but Jenny's thick trousers and sturdy boots eased any problems. The dawn extended across the fields, devoid of colour in the early light, appeared in shades of grey. Switching off the torch she popped it into her pocket and gazed around, absorbed in the techniques required to produce the monochrome picture. Although interesting, its eeriness didn't appeal as colourful landscapes developed her best painting.

As she progressed along the path the dawn light seemed to lift with each step. A distant view of Victoria House was blocked by a small hill. Plodding up the path towards the top hadn't been as easy as expected. Annoyed with herself for being so unfit, she panted, even though only a gentle slope.

On reaching the summit, the extensive garden at the back of Victoria House came into view, surrounded by a large stone wall topped with a small fence, no doubt to keep out the prying eyes of people walking along the path. Village rumours had revealed Nicolas wanted to divert the path to the other side of his house. No one could glimpse the garden from that route, as the terrain was low and level.

The path descended following the edge of the stone wall and blotted out any further views of the garden. It narrowed as it approached the gap between the garden wall of Victoria House and the cottage next door. Kevin's scaffolding remained, the dark poles glistening in the dim light. The early morning dew made the ground slippery, so she picked her way carefully.

A low-level gate from the path led into the side garden of Victoria House, so she glanced in. The grass and the borders caught the early morning light in the tranquil setting. With a jolt of apprehension, she stopped and stepped back to the gate. Leaning on the gatepost she peered into the shadows under the scaffolding of the side garden to the front of the house. It took a few seconds for her eyes to be accustomed to the shadows.

As she leaned on the fence post and peered into the dim light, a cold tremor ran through her body. Her initial glancing perception had not deceived her. Someone lay face down in the front garden. It had been a cold and wet night, so no one would volunteer to lay there.

Instinct took over, and she moved swiftly and sure-footedly. A flight of garden steps took her down the side of the house to the front garden. Her eyes remained fixed on the shape sprawled on the ground with limbs at awkward angles. No movement came from the person. Kneeling, she checked for a pulse on the neck, but couldn't find one. No body warmth emanated from the still form, meaning that death had occurred many hours ago.

Although the body lay face down, the head rested sideways. As the rays of light flicked across the face, she gasped. Kevin, the builder. His skin pale. Lifeless eyes staring. Instinctively she raised her eyes because he lay at the bottom of a ladder. A gap in the scaffolding above her had pieces of rope dangling over the edge. He must have fallen. She checked again for a pulse, but he had been dead for a long time.

Studying the body, she sighed, as she had liked Kevin. Cheeky and full of fun. Touching and seeing a dead body gave her no qualms, as she had seen so many before. She took her mobile phone from her pocket, turned it on, and calmly waited for a signal. She dialled 999. Early morning at the weekend might not result in a quick response from the police, so it could be a long wait.

A noise above caught her attention. She guessed the wind in the scaffolding, caused the plastic sheeting to vibrate. Although not nervous, she would check the surrounding garden. Was there anyone else here?

She wouldn't leave the body unattended for long but walked back up the steps to the back garden. From there she opened the gate at the end of the scaffold and walked with care along the planks, her boots clumping on the bare boards. At the end she stopped to look down at Kevin's crumpled body. No gate had been fixed so she gripped onto the scaffolding to ensure she didn't slip.

Several pieces of rope and various tools lay scattered around on the boards. The tarpaulin flapped, which accounted for the noise. Further along the scaffolding at the front of the building, near to one window, stood a paint pot with a brush carefully balanced on top of it. Next to it stood a flask with its lid removed. Walking along the front of the house on the wide scaffolding boards she touched nothing.

Retracing her route, she waited near the body. Ten minutes later a distant blue flashing light sped towards the house. Jenny positioned herself on the pavement and waved. The police car pulled into the kerbside. After taking them to the body and proving her identity, they let her return home. To recover from the shock of finding Kevin's body, she needed a cup of tea and to sit down. A mixture of sadness and confusion swirled within her as she sat in silence.

09

A few days after finding Kevin's body, Jenny plodded through the Market Square and along the High Street. The police had not returned to interview her, so his death must have been judged accidental. Her mood did not match the brightness of the spring morning.

The time had come to offer condolences to his widow. Even though she would be a stranger to Kevin's wife, Jenny intended to speak with her because she had found his body and had a connection with his death. The image of his lifeless form came to the forefront of her mind. She wanted to remember him alive and full of fun with cheeky mischief.

Elizabeth at the post office had supplied her with the name of Kevin's wife and her address. Taking a deep breath and unsure of what to expect, Jenny knocked on the door of a cottage opposite to the George pub.

Sounds of movement came from inside and the door opened to reveal a slim woman in her early thirties wearing a white tee-shirt and jeans. Her dishevelled short, cropped hair hadn't been brushed, and red eyes stood out from her pale face. Clutching the door frame, she stared at Jenny in bewilderment.

'Lindy?' Jenny gave a cautious smile. 'I'm Jenny from the gallery on the corner of Market Square.' After a moment's hesitation while she seemed to process this information, she opened the door wider and with a slight gesture of her hand, 'Please come in.'

Leading Jenny from the hallway, she entered the small front room of the cottage. Like her own front room, it had a comfortable and cosy atmosphere. A dark blue three-piece suite occupied most of the space. Only a little light filtered into the room through the small cottage window, so a bright table lamp glowed in the corner. Lindy dropped into a seat next to the empty fireplace and pointed to the other armchair.

Jenny settled herself and then fixed her gaze on the sad face of the woman opposite. Keeping her voice gentle, 'Please accept my condolences. Kevin was the first person I met when I arrived in the village and he re-decorated my gallery.'

Lindy nodded in a mesmerised manner, but then fixed her gaze on Jenny's face. 'Didn't you find him? Her voice sounded determined.

She answered the question with a small nod.

'I can't believe it.' Lindy's eyes filled with tears as she scrabbled in her pocket to retrieve her crumpled handkerchief.

Jenny waited while she dabbed her eyes and regained her composure. 'Sudden deaths are the most difficult to comprehend.' Jenny kept her voice quiet and hoped her words would be comforting.

Lindy's piercing brown eyes focused on her. 'Kevin and I talked about the dangers of his building work. My father lost his life in a building site accident. When the police informed me of what had happened, I struggled to believe it.'

'What did they say?' Jenny eyed her thoughtfully. She didn't want to pry, but if Lindy wanted someone to listen, she would be willing. She remained curious about how the police viewed the accident.

Lindy slumped back in her chair and her chin trembled. 'They maintained that Kevin had been drunk and they considered the scaffolding dangerous, because it did not follow the safety requirements. The health and safety man reported an accidental death. The police believe he died the previous evening, by tripping on a rope laying on the boards and then fell through the gap in the scaffolding.'

Silence permeated the room. The only sound was laughter from someone outside in the High Street. Jenny waited while Lindy stared down at her hands in her lap and smoothed her fingers over her golden wedding ring.

'That evening I visited my mum,' her voice quivered. 'I assumed he had finished work and gone to the pub. He liked his beer and often stayed late into the night for heavy after hours drinking. When I arrived home about ten that evening, I went straight to bed and to sleep. When he had a late night session he would often sleep in the spare room. By the time I had dressed the next morning, the police had arrived.' Using her crumpled handkerchief, she mopped up the tears that ran freely down her cheeks.

Jenny searched for words. 'He was safety conscious when he worked on the roof of Victoria House.'

'Yes,' Lindy sniffed and stared at Jenny with wet eyes. 'We've been married ten years, and I have never known him to go on a job after drinking alcohol.'

Jenny searched her memory. He had emerged from the pub at lunchtime when he had been decorating the gallery. Perhaps because of the low-level painting, he had been happy to have a drink. The gallery was small, and he only used a pair of short steps to reach the ceiling. No scaffolding or long ladders had been necessary when he worked for her.

As though reading her thoughts Lindy continued, 'On days I worked, he would go into the George for his lunch, but he only ever had lemonade at lunchtimes.'

That might be his story, but did he say it to keep everyone happy and to reinforce the idea of his safety conscious image?

Tears formed again in Lindy's eyes.

Sadness welled in Jenny, as she could do little to ease Lindy's grief. 'I'm sorry Lindy, I didn't want to renew your anguish.' She was lost for words so a long silence followed.

As Jenny went to stand and take her leave, Lindy leaned forward with an air of exasperation, 'Whenever he had scaffolding, he would insist there were gates at the gaps in the bars.' Lindy's forthright voice caught her by surprise. 'My dad died because building sites didn't have gates in those days. A rotten scaffolding board broke, and he fell down the ladder.' Lindy groaned, flopped back in the chair, and gazed at the ceiling.

Anxiousness coupled with frustration filled Jenny, but there was nothing she could do to help. 'Two similar tragedies in the same family must make it hard to bear.' Jenny wanted to distract Lindy away from the details, as they would keep the death fresh in her mind. Not wanting to outstay her welcome, she readied herself to leave. It seemed appropriate to make a positive comment before she departed. 'I thought him a good man. He was charming whenever we met.'

10

As Jenny walked back to her cottage, her mind ran through the confused conversation with Lindy. Everything she had seen about Kevin's work had been safety conscious. Tools were never left untidy, ready to be tripped over and he never worked dangerously from a stepladder. When she had seen him on the roof of Victoria House, he wore a safety harness. She couldn't ever recollect a roofer wearing one before.

Her mind dwelled on the problem as she entered the front door of the gallery, which was closed on a Tuesday and Wednesday.

Attempting to return to a sense of calm after the visit to Lindy, she settled with her brushes. As the viaduct picture had been commissioned, she would work steadily until completion. With the blinds raised, she had a full view of Market Square. An elderly man crossing the square headed towards the gallery. Although upright for a man of his age, he had a stick and limped heavily. He stumbled and prevented himself from falling by catching the side of a nearby waste bin. He tottered as he struggled to recover.

Jenny abandoned her painting, left her gallery, and

trotted across to offer her help. 'Come on sir, take my arm. Let's go into my gallery so you can sit down to recover.' Clasping Jenny's outstretched arm, he steadied himself. Pulling his shoulders back and straightening himself, he eyed Jenny with bright, alert eyes. 'I wanted to visit, but it's closed. My wife's in the post office. My leg has failed me this morning, so I must return home, but I wanted to look at the paintings.'

Making slow progress, she helped him limp across to the gallery. With care, she guided him to a seat near the window. He eased himself down with a frustrated groan and rubbed his leg with a grimace.

'Sit and relax, please,' Jenny smiled. 'Would you like a cup of tea while you are waiting?' A smile of relief crossed his face, and he nodded his acceptance. She handed him a painting from the display so he could study it without standing. Nodding his appreciation at the painting, he grimaced from the pain in his leg. He had become pale, with beads of sweat on his forehead. A woman came from the post office. She stopped and glanced around the Square. Jenny popped outside and waved. As she arrived in the gallery's doorway her forehead creased with concern.

'He stumbled because of his leg.'

'Damn thing!' muttered the man. Struggling to rise from the chair, the man winced in discomfort. He crept towards the door, leaning heavily on his stick, taking care with every step. As he reached the exit, he paused. 'They are excellent pictures. I'll return for a detailed look.'

'Thank you.' It pleased Jenny that someone else had taken an interest in them.

Finishing the viaduct picture, she mulled over her approach to the portrait of Amanda. The shop phone rang. She had been practising her response, 'Watercolour Gallery, Jenny speaking.'

'Hello Jenny. This is Gwendoline. We met this morning, after you helped my husband. 'As you are closed today, we wondered if you were free to drop in for tea. Gerald wishes to discuss your work.'

The invitation took Jenny by surprise. 'I'd be delighted.'

'We live at Stanton House. The entrance to the drive is near the viaduct. Would three o'clock be convenient?'

'Yes, perfect,' Jenny beamed, intrigued by the invitation to visit the historic house.

When she'd been walking, she had passed it on many occasions and had wondered who lived there. Today she wouldn't walk, as she couldn't turn up covered in mud as she wanted to create the right impression.

Five minutes before her appointment, she turned her white Ford Ka up the drive. A huge semi-gothic mansion with arched windows and huge turrets stood before her as she pulled up. Precisely on time, she pulled on the elaborate brass handle next to the front door and the distant jangling of a bell sounded.

Gwendoline answered the door, 'Come in. Gerald is by the drawing room fire. I'll take you to him and then I will make the tea.' Jenny followed Gwendoline across the marble expanse of the hall. She opened the first door and Jenny entered a small room for the size of the house, although her front room would fit into it about four times.

A cosy room with huge bookcases dominating one wall, although they were too far away to read the titles. Her eye lingered on a huge painting of a battle scene on the opposite wall. Painted in oils, full of vibrancy and colour, it depicted cavalry on white horses charging with swords raised. Gerald sat by the fire with his bad leg raised on a cushioned footstool. He smiled and attempted to stand.

'Please stay seated,' Jenny flapped her hand at him, but he still pushed himself up. Tall and slim, wearing smart well-tailored dark trousers, a white shirt and tie. A tweed jacket rested on a chair nearby but wouldn't be needed as the log fire roared in an ornate fireplace. He indicated the chair opposite and Jenny settled herself in a comfortable wing backed armchair.

With no preamble, the man eyed Jenny through bright alert eyes. 'I like your paintings and wanted to talk about them but can't travel to the gallery until my leg is better.' He rubbed the offending leg with a grimace of displeasure.

'It's a pleasure to come here.'

A knock on the door came. 'Come in.' A broad-shouldered, tall man carrying a basket of logs with ease entered and placed them by the fire.

'Is that sufficient for today, Colonel?'

'Yes, thank you.'

The man left and Jenny's eyes lit. 'What regiment, sir?'

'Coldstream Guards. Family tradition as we herald from the Scottish Borders.'

She sat straighter and squared her shoulder as she was in the presence of a senior officer.

'I've recently left the Army.'

Surprise swept across his face. 'What role?'

'A Matron in the Queen Alexandra's.'

His eyes lit up, 'So you were a Major.'

'Yes sir.'

'We'll have no ranks in this house. I'm Gerald and I know you are Jenny.'

Gwendoline appeared with the tea and, realising they had moved to army talk, she left them.

While Jenny enjoyed talking to the Colonel about the army. For twenty years, she had been a dedicated nurse but had started a new life in Peaklow. She wouldn't look back and had a determination to focus on the future.

11

As Jenny pulled the blinds to prepare for closing her gallery on the day after Kevin's funeral, Lindy, his widow, arrived. Jenny had attended the funeral and had expected to stand anonymously at the back, expecting the church to be packed, but to her surprise few had attended. The church usher had encouraged her forward to join the thirty mourners.

Lindy gave a grim smile. 'I wanted to catch you at closing time.'

'Let me lock up.' With a friendly smile, Jenny led her to the parlour behind the gallery.

Two large armchairs dominated the room on either side of the empty fireplace. Lindy refused a drink and dropped into an armchair.

'Thanks for coming to the funeral. I want your opinions about Kevin's death. When we spoke before, you seemed surprised about the details of his accident.'

Jenny chose her words carefully. 'When he worked for me here at the gallery, he had a safety conscious outlook. It didn't matter, as he worked on the ground floor and mainly low-level painting.'

'He always took safety seriously.' Lindy pressed her

lips together.

Where would this conversation lead? Why did Lindy want to talk?

'When you found him, did you examine the site?'

She became wary, as Lindy's line of enquiry could lead her into difficulties. Although she would explain her observations, she would not offer opinions.

'I checked no one lurked nearby.' Lindy's eyes opened wide. 'After confirming I was alone, I tried to find signs of life, but he had been dead for many hours.' The wide eyes continued to examine her. 'I worked as a nurse so could perform the necessary medical checks.'

Lindy nodded.

'Movement came from the plastic sheeting blowing in the wind.' Jenny omitted the details of the paint pot and flask.'

'Was the gate closed at the top of the ladder where he fell?'

'There was no gate.'

Lindy shuffled in her chair, 'That's something about his death which is not right.'

Jenny agreed but wouldn't voice her opinion. It had surprised her that the police hadn't returned to interview her. She would have explained her concerns to them, but they must have concluded that Kevin's death had been accidental. Why would Kevin put emphasis on safety and not follow his own advice?

Lindy stood with an attempted smile. 'If there's anything else you saw or remember which might help the coroner, will you let me know?'

'Of course.' But she remained uncertain about her approach to any new information, as the most obvious course of action would be to inform the police.

Lindy, after mumbling a few words of appreciation for her help, left. Jenny gazed out the window.

Had Kevin been a person to say one thing and do another? If so, then the conclusion of the police investigation could be correct, but if he had been true to his word, then what had happened that night on the scaffold?

Jenny crossed to the post office to discover if Elizabeth had further information about the death. She pulled on a thick jacket as a brisk wind howled around the village. As she left through the back gate, Tony arrived in the square on his tractor, apparently on his way home.

When she'd first arrived in the village, it appeared unusual that he constantly used the gate. But she had become familiar with the area. It would be the quickest route from the village to his farm. They nodded greetings. Jenny's mind could not leave the poor attendance at the funeral. 'There weren't many at Kevin's funeral yesterday, which surprised me about a close-knit community.'

'It's not my normal policy to speak ill of the dead, but he was a conman and I had no time for him.' He started his tractor, touched his black plaid cap and drove away. The tractor bounced across the field, leaving Jenny with a frown of confusion. What had happened between Tony and Kevin to generate such a reaction?

Tony appeared to be a volatile and argumentative man. She'd witnessed his vitriolic disagreement with Lionel. But he wasn't friendly with Kevin either. Did he have any friends in the village, or did he argue with everyone? How long ago had they fallen out? Wouldn't it be easier in a small community to patch up their arguments? What other intrigues lay beneath the surface of this peaceful village?

Jenny strolled across the square towards the post office, intrigued by underlying village animosities. Fortunately empty, Jenny wanted to discover other people's opinion of Kevin. 'Hello Elizabeth, I'm intrigued as you closed for the funeral but didn't attend the church service.'

Elizabeth tugged her brown cardigan tight across her chest and checked the newspapers on the counter. Her welcoming smile had vanished and her face flushed. 'I'd rather not talk about him.'

What an unusual reaction. Elizabeth always wanted to air her views. Normally she enjoyed a good gossip sharing any scandalous information with relish. It didn't worry her whether her stories were true or false.

As she continued to stare at the papers on the table, her hand clutched a biro so tightly that her knuckles had turned white and her face became taut.

What an interesting reaction. Why was she behaving in such an uncharacteristic manner?

Curiosity grabbed Jenny. 'Kevin must have frequented the post office regularly to deal with his business transactions.'

'Yes, he did,' her eyes narrowed to crinkled slits, 'but I rather he'd gone elsewhere. Originally, I thought him an honourable man, but one time he suggested...' Jenny waited, but Elizabeth busied herself with rearranging the already neat newspapers. Elizabeth's flush deepened. 'Definitely not a gentleman, and even less after he became a married man.'

She had a venomous edge to her voice. Snatching papers from the counter, she twisted away and stomped off into the store. The loud sound of boxes being moved around filled the air for several minutes. Then, with hard staring eyes, she stormed back into the shop and served Jenny without speaking another word.

Elizabeth's unusual behaviour, coupled with the flash of anger in her eyes showed a different side to her. Had Kevin made a pass at her? Surely not. He had been a handsome man. Elizabeth's frumpy clothes and plain face wouldn't have attracted a man like Kevin.

Arriving back at the gallery, she installed herself in the back parlour with a steaming cup of coffee. The lilting sound of background music enabled her to organise her thoughts. One option would be to let the whole matter drop, as she'd only known him for a few weeks.

The police and the coroner didn't think his death was worth investigating, so why should she? But a shred of doubt festered. There were strange anomalies that hadn't been resolved. On the other extreme she could become a sleuth, the image of a young Miss Marple appeared fleetingly in her mind.

With a chuckle, she dismissed the idea as too ridiculous as that only happened in books. Sitting back in her chair, the ideas flowed freely as she searched for the best solution. An intermediate line took shape in her mind. Although close to doing nothing, it would relieve the nagging doubt that had entered her head. She nodded approval with her plan and relaxed back in the chair. Instead of cooking her own evening meal, she would let the kitchen at the George pub prepare it for her.

Closing her eyes, she allowed the background music from Grieg's piano concerto to float through the air, calming her mind and shutting out the problems and trivialities of village life. As she drifted off to sleep, she mused that this sleepy village had little idea of the conflicts, hatred, and turmoil of the outside world.

12

Refreshed from her nap, and with a growing sense of determination, at six o'clock Jenny took the short walk to the George. A few customers were dotted around the bar. The dark varnished wood gave a subdued atmosphere, which appeared dismal after the outside daylight. The corner lamps gave a weak light. The identity of the man behind the bar became obvious, although they had not met before. He had the same facial features as his father Lionel.

Perching on a bar stool, 'Hello John.' A bemused expression flashed across his face at the use of his name from a stranger, but he made no comment. 'I'll have a large gin and tonic please, and the food menu.' As he poured her a drink, he studied her carefully.

She grinned at his anxious face. 'I had my hair styled with Amanda who explained you worked here. And don't you look exactly like your father!' she kept her voice light and friendly.

Recognition dawned on his face. He laughed, 'I hope I do not look that old!' but his humour disappeared. Like his father, he had a dour expression. 'I'm guessing, but have you opened the gallery in the Square?'

Jenny nodded. 'I wanted to catch Amanda to express my sympathy to her, after the fatal accident at her house.'

'It hit her hard, so she has closed the house for a week and moved to their house in Birmingham, while the workmen clear the scaffolding.'

Pressing her lips firmly together, 'Kevin's death must have come as a shock to people, as Lindy told me he was a regular in this pub.' No smile came, and he turned his attention to wiping a cloth across the already pristine bar. Jenny waited. Why had he delayed his response?

Finally, he faced her and gave a dismissive shrug. 'Yes, a regular,' he paused, his fingers clenching and unclenching around the cloth in his hand, 'although I never liked him.'

Jenny allowed the words to register. Another person who didn't like him. Why was everyone negative about him? Strange, because she'd found him a helpful and cheerful man. He'd been good at his job with a professional attitude and attention to detail. A direct approach seemed the best way to elicit any information. 'Is that because of the dispute over the derelict shop in Market Square? My gallery is opposite, so I've heard of the situation.'

'No.' He resumed his polishing of the glasses. 'I never liked him. We were at school together but were never friends.' He turned away, folded the cloth and placed it carefully on the surface at the back of the bar. After a pause, he faced her once again with a forced smile on his face.

A perfect opportunity to put her plan into action. Leaning forward, she rested her elbows on the bar and concentrated on keeping her voice casual. 'If he came here regularly, he must have been a heavy drinker. I'm sure I could smell it on his breath one afternoon when he worked at the Gallery.' The lie rolled effortlessly off her tongue. She folded her arms and waited for his response.

Confusion flooded his features. 'You'd be wrong there. I didn't like the man. At lunchtime, he always had a lemonade. In an evening he would tuck them away, but never at lunchtime.'

The simple statement from John corroborated Lindy's information. It also confirmed that Kevin had been true to his word when he stated he never drank while working on a job. If he didn't mix drinking with work, why had he been drunk when he fell from the scaffolding? No obvious answer presented itself.

As other customers arrived, John became busy serving, so she moved to a small table. While she tucked into her meal, she watched the activity in the bar. Jenny had finished her pie and stared down in dismay at the empty plate. It had been delicious. In the future, she would have to resist the temptation to pop over to the pub for her tea.

The door swung open for Tony and Jacqui to enter. She hadn't spoken to Jacqui since the morning they first met at the farm shop, although occasionally they'd acknowledged each other from a distance.

John, who had been smiling as he talked to customers, frowned at Tony. These petty village feuds were unbelievable. She wanted to bang their heads together and tell them to grow up. John's frown never lifted as he served Tony.

Jacqui waved as soon as she spotted Jenny and within a minute had settled down next to her. Tony brought a drink over for them, which surprised her. 'Thank you

Tony, please join us.'

'I'd love to, but I want to catch the guys over there about business.'

When he reached the far end of the bar Jacqui whispered, 'Thanks for not saying anything the last time we met in the shop, I shouldn't gossip, Tony would have been cross with me.'

As she sipped her drink, another small plan settled itself in Jenny's mind. When she'd asked Tony about the funeral, she had received a brief reply. It was an ideal opportunity to quiz Jacqui and discover her reaction. Keeping her voice casual, 'I didn't see you at Kevin's funeral.'

Jacqui peered around to check who was nearby as a flush of embarrassment spread across her cheeks. She leaned in closer and lowered her voice. 'I would have attended, but Tony wouldn't have allowed it, so I didn't even ask.' A mixture of curiosity and amazement settled on Jenny. The village was inundated with quarrels and secrets.

'I shouldn't tell you, but several years ago Tony applied for a grant to diversify. He came up with the idea of the caravan site, but it took time for the council to agree over the proposed design of the shower and toilet building. The planning committee insisted on a certain type of building block. At the time, Kevin completed building work for Tony. The blocks seemed in short supply, but Kevin got them. They were expensive, but Tony had no option.'

Jenny could guess what would come next.

'Tony found out that Kevin charged him four times what he paid.'

'Did the blocks start a feud, which has not been resolved?'

'That was not the only issue.'

'Something else?' Jenny probed, determined to elicit as much information as possible from Jacqui.

'Yes, it became public knowledge, so there's no harm in telling you. Although it involves me, so it's embarrassing.'

Jenny gave her a smile of encouragement, not that she needed an invitation to talk.

'At the same time as the problem over the bricks, Tony, myself and Kevin were on the annual village carnival committee. Kevin had always paid me a lot of attention, but one night he became over familiar. I sat next to him in the meeting. He kept putting his hand on my knee and leaning in closer to look at my papers. I tried to resist as Tony had noticed his antics and didn't look pleased.'

'What happened?'

'The meeting ended, but Tony insisted we followed Kevin as he wanted to speak with him. I pleaded, but to no avail. We caught up with him in a quiet area and Tony hit him without warning. Kevin, a younger man, retaliated, and they punched each other a few times. Although a silly thing to do, I jumped in between them. Tony accidentally hit me, allowing Kevin to run away. I had an amazing black eye.' She giggled in embarrassment.

'Were there any other witnesses?'

Jacqui shook her head, 'The argument resumed anytime they met when they would hurl verbal abuse at each other.' She gave another furtive glance around the bar to make sure no one else listened to their conversation. 'They never hit each other again, but everyone in the village knew about the dispute between them. It went on for months and then gradually became a silent feud. So, I couldn't go to the funeral, although I had liked Kevin when we first met. It's such a pity that Tony and Kevin didn't resolve their differences.' A flicker of irritation lit her eyes, but in an instant, it disappeared to be replaced by a small smile. Picking up her glass, she slipped from her seat. 'I must go. It was good to talk to you.'

Jacqui skipped to join her husband, leaving Jenny to read a magazine as she finished her drink. Although she gazed at the words on the page, her mind wouldn't focus on reading, but went over the conversations with both John and Jacqui. John and Tony had disliked Kevin. Was the dislike mutual? Bearing grudges over a long period didn't present a healthy approach to life, as it allowed them to fester and assume too much importance. Words like spiteful, pointless, and callous came to her thoughts.

A notice on the wall gave the timing of a dart and dominoes match that evening and the bar was soon filled with noisy chatter and laughter.

A man entered, who she'd seen at Stanton House when she'd been chatting with Gerald and he had brought in the logs. Recognising her, 'Welcome to the village, ma'am.'

She recognised the tone of voice, but replied, 'It's Jenny.'

A smile of acknowledgement appeared. 'Colonel mentioned you were an officer.'

His short cropped hair and smart appearance prompted her, 'Which service?'

'A gunner before being invalided out. I would have stayed, but they made me leave.' His shoulders drooped and a frown of frustration swept across his face. 'The colonel has been good to me.' He paused, turning away to check that the darts matches hadn't started yet. 'I notice you live on your own. My wife and I live along the road, Oak Cottage. Anything you want done, let me know.'

Before he went to join his fellow dart players, he held out his hand, 'My name's Clayton.'

Jenny finished her drink and walked back to her cottage. Bleary eyed and drained, she hoped the horrors wouldn't return tonight. She slumped down in the armchair by the fire, acknowledging that while her body ached with tiredness, her mind whirled with conflicting thoughts and ideas.

With nothing on the television that appealed to her, she tried to read, but couldn't concentrate. Her thoughts about Kevin and the conversations she'd had during the day kept returning. There had been more to him than first appeared. The ladies had liked him, even Elizabeth, although unhappy with what he had suggested to her. The thought brought a smile to her lips.

Kevin hadn't been liked by the men. There might be several reasons. He had been successful with the ladies. Alternatively, he might have been a business conman and overcharged. His charges for her had been good, but why had he risked his reputation over those bricks for Tony's caravan site?

As only a handful of the villagers had attended his funeral, they must harbour a poor opinion of him. Perhaps she had only picked up the nasty rumours about him, but one question came to her mind. If he would never work after drinking alcohol, how could the verdict be an accident while he was drunk? And why had he been there? Why was he on the scaffolding? Why wasn't a safety gate in place? Her mind leapt forward on a course of its own. If not an accident, he must have been murdered. She shivered. Murder didn't happen in a quiet village.

13

On a blustery morning, after a night free of the traumas, Jenny met Lindy as she crossed the square to Lionel's butcher shop. Lindy, with a serious expression on her face, beckoned her to one side.

'The inquest has been opened.' Her voice was laden with emotion and tears welled in her eyes. Jenny didn't comment, sensing that Lindy had more to say. 'I spoke to the Coroner's officer. As Kevin's death occurred while he was working, they would get information from all interested parties. I'm allowed to make a statement as a direct family member.' She clutched Jenny's arm and drew in a deep breath. 'Would you make one if I told the Coroner about you?'

Jenny expected such a request but would have preferred a more formal appeal from the Coroner's Office. Not wishing to commit herself, she attempted to diffuse the request with a bland statement. 'I expect they will contact me, as I found him, and I will make a statement then. How long could the inquest take?'

'It is agonisingly slow,' she groaned, 'between three and six months.'

'A long time, but it will be thorough, and you can raise your concerns.'

Lindy nodded somewhat distractedly, 'There's something wrong as he paid strict attention to safety.'

Jenny's tenuous plan of investigation involved collecting background information. Her meeting with Lindy would be an ideal opportunity to get another view of the argument between Kevin and Tony. They stood in Market Square outside the disused shop between Lionel's and the post office. She waved her hand towards the dilapidated shop. 'I suppose you will abandon your interest in developing this shop into a hardware store.'

'No, I shall be bidding.'

She stared at Lindy with wide-eyed amazement, who leaned close and placed her hand on Jenny's arm while she gazed at the old shop with a gleam in her eye. 'For many years, I have worked for a builder's merchant in Braxton, but Kevin and I had planned to open our own shop. He would continue with his building company and I would organise and run the shop. My current job will not last long, so I still intend setting up my business. It's ideal, because of the big barn at the back with a road entrance near the garage. I'll need it more than ever now as I'm on my own.'

'What about the rivals? Tony and Lionel seemed keen to gain it intending to expand their own businesses.'

'They will both back out,' she raised her chin in defiance. 'Lionel only showed an interest because he wanted to annoy Tony, but he and his son John are too mean to pay out the money needed for conversion.'

'What about Tony?' Jenny pulled her coat tighter to keep out the chill breeze that swept across the Square?

'He invests in property. He's not interested in a shop in the village. His only intention is to extend his farm shop with a butchery. He will concentrate his efforts on developing his business on his farm and caravan site. Also, there is a rumour that he has put in planning permission to extend his caravan site. A spy in his camp told me he wants a shop with a cafe, besides the one he already has at the farm. He can attract walkers from along the trail. He won't want a business in the village.' By the time Lindy had finished her explanation, a faint flush tinged her cheeks and she huffed out a breath while taking a surreptitious look around.

The confident gleam in Lindy's eyes encouraged Jenny to keep her talking and ask more questions. Lindy didn't appear to be in a hurry and was keen to chat this morning. Taking a blunt and direct approach, 'Your Kevin and Tony didn't see eye to eye, did they?'

'No,' Lindy's chin trembled with emotion, 'Tony believed Kevin conned him over building blocks for the caravan site. You've probably heard the rumour that he ripped him off at four times the rate.'

'Yes, that's the rumour.' Jenny looked at the intensity in Lindy's eyes.

A tight smile crossed her lips and her hands balled into fists. 'Tony found similar blocks, but of inferior quality and the planning authority wouldn't have approved them.'

Jenny smiled back in a friendly manner and ended the discussion for the time being. 'Look, there's no queue in Lionel's, let's buy our meat.' Allowing Lindy to go first, she watched the exchange between Lionel and Lindy. No smiles or greetings came from either of them. Lindy used the minimum number of words to order her meat and Lionel replied only with the price: Neither a please nor thank you came from either. Jenny had expected him to show some sympathy.

With a nod of farewell to Jenny, Lindy left the shop. Jenny greeted Lionel in a friendly manner, which he didn't return. Irritation bubbled up in her. As a customer, she expected a smile of welcome. He should be able to coerce a grin onto his face. It had become her policy to smile and engage in eye contact. Her years as a nurse reinforced the idea that a positive attitude went a long way. On some days Lionel forced a smile, but on other occasions his dour face never changed.

Totally the wrong attitude, she huffed but remained silent. She hankered to question him about the shop next door. His perspective on the matter might be interesting, but in his current mood he would be tight lipped and uncommunicative. Even if she couldn't drag the information from Lionel, perhaps she could elicit the current situation from John at the George.

As she waited for her purchases to be wrapped, her mind drifted. Her shop and cottage had stood empty for some time before she put in an offer. Was there a local rivalry about hers? It wouldn't be suitable for a builder's merchant and Lionel would only want the shop next door to his own. That only left Tony, but she thought that Lindy's rationale about him not wanting to develop in the village made sense.

14

Jenny pulled up the blinds on the gallery. After finishing the viaduct landscape painting, she would concentrate on Amanda's portrait, which with hard work could be completed within a week.

Paying a visit to Amanda and Nicolas with the finished pictures would afford the opportunity to discover if the police had provided them with a sequence of events. Although she had been enjoying her small investigations, she expected them to end soon. Talking to people and asking questions had given her a sense of purpose, though it unsettled her to discover the amount of long-standing hostility and resentment that simmered beneath the surface of what had appeared a tranquil village. Soon the legal process would take over and then she would transfer her full attention back to her gallery.

A few visitors drifted in during the day and she sold another painting. Summer could be a pleasing prospect for sales, but she would have to consider extra publicity. Nestled in her usual comfortable chair, she relaxed in front of the television. The documentary, while interesting, didn't hold her attention and her mind drifted over recent events. With an effort she attempted to organise her discoveries. The warmth from the fire and her whirling thoughts made her eyelids droop and her head lolled back against the chair.

She woke with a jolt as the frightening images filled her mind. Hot and bothered, her heart pounded. She gripped the arms of the chair, forcing the remnants of the nightmare from her mind. The barrel of the gun pointing at her persisted. Shaking her head, she stared wildly around her cosy room. Her eyes came to rest on the vase of bright yellow daffodils.

Staring at them with unswerving intensity, she focused on their sunshine colour and their arrangement in the pottery jug, as she rid her mind of the distorted violence. She forced herself to concentrate on the pleasure she'd experienced in buying them and then finding the perfect location in her little cottage. Gradually her breathing returned to normal and the familiarity of her surroundings soothed her. If she closed her eyes, even for a moment, the images would return with startling speed. Remaining by the warm fire, her eyelids would droop again.

Tired after a long day, she didn't want to leave the cottage, but experience had taught her nothing else would save the nightmare images. One nightmare was enough, she didn't want two. Should she seek a professional to consult about the recurring images? She had resisted when in the army, but as she had settled in Peaklow, it would be a consideration. Tonight, however, it would be fresh air and a good walk.

Within ten minutes, she had donned her anorak and waterproof trousers as the weather had turned showery and she could be out for hours. As the church clock struck ten o'clock, she locked up and strode along the road, meeting a couple of dog walkers, who nodded but didn't speak.

Passing The George, the muffled noise of laughter and conversations reached her, and she hesitated, almost tempted to join them. Dismissing the idea, she plodded on and reached the edge of the village, where she selected a simple walk along the disused railway track. Built on an embankment, it had a wide path and in the moonlight she didn't need a torch. Her feet crunched on the gravel as she walked with a rhythmic stride along the flat surface. A cool windy night and the swaying of the trees and the rustling of leaves filled the air. She enjoyed the solitude as the darkness swirled around her. Calmness reluctantly returned.

After midnight, tired and wanting her bed, she returned along the High Street. The outside lights of the George had been turned off, but the inside glow edged the blinds. The locals would indulge in late night drinking.

Intent on taking her normal route in the back door, she headed towards Market Square. Her mind had left the ghastly images behind and focused on the next local landscape she would choose to paint. If the weather held, she would venture towards the large nearby reservoirs. The possibilities for painting were endless. Views across water with the moorland hills in the distance. With the resolution, an inner peace descended on her. Time to shelve her plan of finding out more about the village feuds and Kevin's death. She'd concentrate on her painting and organising adverts for the Gallery. Amateur sleuthing had lost its appeal.

As she passed the front of the gallery, a flash of light along the edge of a blind caught her attention. Had another source of light caused a reflection in the window? Nothing. Moving with caution to ensure her walking boots made no noise, she crept closer to the main door into the gallery. Allowing her eyes to become accustomed to the light, she peered through a small gap between the blinds and the edge of the window. She had insisted to the blind company she wanted no gaps as it might affect her pictures so she could see little through the minute gap. No more flashes of light came, but several changes in the shadows inside the gallery were clear. Had someone broken in?

The noise of a chair moving and another small sliver of light gave her confirmation. Somebody moved around the gallery. Her heart pounded and her fingers curled into a fist as a mixture of fear and indignation swarmed through her. How dare someone break in? She paused, hardly daring to breathe, as she weighed up the pros and cons of what action to take. Safety first, in case there were several burglars. Ringing the police would take too long as the intruders would have left. Walking away wasn't her style and although fear knotted her stomach, anger and determination had the upper hand. Surprise was in her favour. She had her torch at the ready both as a weapon and to discover what was happening.

Dismissing negative thoughts, her muscles tightened in readiness as she prepared herself for action. She shoved the key in the lock of the main gallery, kicked back the door, and swung the full beam of the torch around the room. The noise of the key in the lock caused inside panic. One of the darkened figures pushed a display screen towards her, but she stepped back and shouted as loud as she could. The other figure had reached the doorway to the house and Jenny's torch followed the second intruder as it disappeared in the same direction.

Common sense prevailed, and she didn't follow them through the house in case they waited for her. She rushed up the pavement along the back of the outbuildings. In the moonlight, two figures ran away across the field, keeping close to the wall along the line of the back of the nearby cottages, and disappeared into the darkness.

Jenny ran swiftly to the front of the gallery as she dialled 999 on her mobile. Although they had gone, she would still be wary. Her shouting had attracted the attention of a man who had come from the direction of the pub. Standing nearby, he waited, listening while she spoke rapidly into the phone and told the police the details. As she disconnected the call, he approached. 'Have you had a break-in?'

'Yes,' she grimaced, 'but I'm sure they're gone. I must have surprised them.'

'You stay here, luv. I'll turn the lights on. Where are the switches?' Jenny shone the torch on the far wall. The gallery suddenly filled with light. A couple of his friends also came from the pub and were quickly informed of the situation. The man called back, 'Do you want us to check the house out?'

'Yes please,' Jenny's voice shook. She leaned against the doorway as her knees buckled. Why had they broken in? What were they hoping to find? Had they left a terrible mess? She'd never contemplated the theft of her pictures.

Stepping inside, she braced herself. In the gallery bright red spray paint in foot-high letters read, 'GO

AWAY'. The paint had covered some of her pictures and the display board underneath. Some pictures had been trampled on. The viaduct painting had been slashed with a knife and the paint powder near her easel had been poured on the floor.

She had never been at the end of a senseless act of vandalism before. With a chilling sense of bewilderment, she stared at the message on the wall. Someone didn't want her here. But who? Everyone had been friendly. Was it someone she hadn't met, or more disturbingly, was it someone she knew who had only pretended to be friendly? A shiver of apprehension chilled her as she closed her eyes to blot out the message on the wall.

The men returned and reported the rest of the house hadn't been touched. What would the intruders have done if they hadn't been interrupted? Would they have spoiled all the pictures and then wrecked the house as well? A police car with flashing blue lights pulled up outside.

15

'It's not acceptable!' growled Lionel with vehemence as Jenny entered the butcher's shop the morning after the break-in. Throughout the night her thoughts had spiralled as she attempted to unravel the implications of the graffiti sprayed in her gallery. The explicit message on the wall had upset her. Someone didn't want her in the village. With a jolt, she focused on the present. As she was the only customer, Lionel had spoken to her. 'What's not acceptable, Lionel?'

'The break-in,' he stood with his hands on his hips and stared at her with what appeared to be a mixture of disbelief and condemnation. 'On behalf of the villagers I can say that you are most welcome to be here. Your shop had been empty for years. You have given the village a feature shop that can be extolled with pride.' His teeth glinted in a brief smile.

Taken aback by his sentiments, a broad grin crept across her face. 'Thank you, Lionel.'

'I'm prepared to come over after work and help you clean up.'

His suggestion gave her a warm glow. 'A kind offer which I appreciate but I've completed the cleaning as only a quarter of the gallery had been affected.'

'Have the police made progress?'

'No,' she gave a small shake of her head, 'and they didn't sound hopeful. 'There were no fingerprints or footprints. The only description they have is my brief glimpse of them.' The image of the perpetrators escaping across the field flashed through her mind. 'There were two intruders. Both wore dark clothing and balaclavas which covered their faces. They could run, but I couldn't even decide whether they were male or female.'

After she left the shop, she reflected on Lionel's staunch defence of her. Given his normal surly attitude, his reaction had come as a surprise. As Jenny entered the Post Office, Elizabeth came out from behind the counter and gave her shoulders an encouraging squeeze. 'You poor woman. It must have been terrifying to discover two burglars.' She drew her eyebrows together in an anguished expression. 'It's something I dread. I wouldn't know what to do. Were you frightened?'

'Wary.' Jenny frowned with a sudden shiver of apprehension. 'I stayed out of their way so they couldn't attack me. But although scary, I've had worst happen to me.'

A quizzical look came to Elizabeth's face, but she didn't respond to Jenny's remark and busied herself rearranging the bars of chocolate on a stand behind the counter. Pushing a stray wisp of hair from her face, 'I spoke to Lionel early this morning before we opened. We agreed that the shops and key people in the village should rally around so we can defy whoever did this to you.'

Elizabeth's supportive words brought her a sense of calm. Her friendly concern helped to ease the negative thoughts which swirled in her mind.

'That's thoughtful of you, Elizabeth, but I cannot see why someone wants me to leave the village. I have upset no one.'

Elizabeth looked pained. 'Will you leave?'

'No, I'm staying, but I shall be cautious.'

Jenny wandered back to her gallery in a thoughtful mood to work on Amanda's portrait. She hadn't left it on the easel. As it was in a cupboard, it hadn't been vandalised. Standing in the doorway of the gallery, she surveyed the tidy space. The damaged paintings had been boxed, awaiting disposal. The smell of fresh paint still lingered in the air. Although the offending words had been removed, her mind's eye kept repeating those two words in her head. Go away, go away, go away.

Who wanted her to leave the village? With a resigned sigh, she refocused on the future for the gallery. The damage to the other paintings annoyed her, but she had a large number stored in the spare bedroom of the cottage not on display. On many occasions, she had painted the same scene more than once. Often, they were at a slightly different angle or she'd chosen subtly different colours. She had virtual duplicates of all, except one that had been ruined by the spray paint. With an acute sense of purpose, she moved away from the door to reorganise and unpack her boxed paintings to fill the gaps on the wall before she opened. As she turned to lock the door, Amanda and Nicolas came in her direction. She re-opened the door and let them in. They both looked with interest around the gallery, perhaps hoping to see the extent of the damage caused by the break in.

Amanda gave her a hug. 'You poor woman, what a terrible time you've had recently. Finding Kevin's body and now a break in and the damage to your paintings. Why would anyone want to damage such beautiful pictures?' Spreading her arms wide in a gesture of bewilderment, she glanced around as though searching for an explanation.

Jenny grimaced, 'I'm afraid that one of the burglars took a knife to the viaduct painting and it's ruined, so I shall start again.'

'That's terrible,' Amanda's tone sounded soothing, 'but please take your time. We are willing to wait.'

She appreciated the concern shown by people from the village. 'Luckily, I find painting therapeutic and as I'm not busy, I'm happy to finish the portrait and repaint the viaduct picture.'

Nicholas patted her hand and smiled indulgently, 'We wanted to have a quick word with you.' They glanced as though not wanting to be overheard. Jenny pulled down the blinds, locked the door, and organised two extra chairs near to her easel. Once they were all settled, Jenny waited in silence. What did they want to discuss?

Nicolas opened the conversation with a solemn expression on his face. 'I believe you had the misfortune of finding Kevin.'

She nodded as the image of Kevin's body appeared in her mind. 'He was dead when I found him. Nothing could be done for him, so I waited until the police arrived and left.' She deliberately kept her comments brief and the details to a minimum.

Amanda eyed her with concern, her face pale despite her immaculate make up, 'The police mentioned you found him early in the morning.' Something in her tone of voice and the emphasis on the word early suggested that she found this unusual.

Jenny would not explain about her nightmares. 'I often go for walks early and I had turned towards home from the old railway track. As I enjoy walking, I have been exploring the local tracks and paths. It surprised me when I discovered it came out near your house.'

Nicolas frowned. 'It's a bit intrusive, to be frank. We applied to move the path to the other side of the house. The problem is that the adjacent land belongs to Tony, so it requires his agreement. It wouldn't make any difference to him, as it would be an alternative route across his field. We offered to pay for the new stile, but he saw no reason to move it and wouldn't even consider the idea. We have no resolution, but it will be on the agenda for the next parish council meeting.'

Forgetting her earlier intention to stop asking questions, Jenny spotted an opportunity to turn the conversation to Kevin. 'I can't believe he continued to work there into the evening. When we spoke earlier that day, you mentioned that Nicolas planned to be away, but as no curtains were drawn when I discovered Kevin, I assumed you had gone as well.'

Amanda lowered her gaze to her lap. 'Did you go up the ladder?'

Jenny let out a long deep breath. 'I walked to the back garden and on to the scaffolding to ensure I was alone.'

Amanda shifted in her seat. 'Nic's meeting in Germany was cancelled, so I joined him at our house in Birmingham. We had a long weekend because I don't open the salon on Mondays. Once the news came through, I rang everyone to cancel my appointments for the week.'

Her voice wavered, and she folded her arms tightly across her chest. 'I couldn't face returning until the police had completed their work, and the scaffolding had been removed.'

16

The day had passed with surprising speed. Jenny had rearranged paintings and unpacked new ones to fill the gaps. She then settled at her easel and continued with the portrait of Amanda. The smell of the freshly painted wall constantly reminded her of the break in, though her work forced her to keep her mind focused.

After closing the shop in the late afternoon, Jenny thought about the evening. The horrors had forced her to walk late the previous evening and after she'd disturbed the burglars; she hadn't been able to sleep. Once the police had departed, she'd tidied the gallery and then dozed for a couple of hours in her armchair. During the early morning, she'd busied herself painting over the red letters on the wall. Feeling tired, she tidied the gallery and crossed to The George.

'Good evening, Jenny,' John stood behind the bar. 'I'm so sorry to hear about the break-in. As you are on your own, it must make you nervous.'

She perched on a bar stool. 'It was an unpleasant experience. I'm not sure why someone wants me to leave the village. Would you have any ideas?' He raised his eyebrows. 'You might have heard comments in the pub or your dad's shop.'

'Just the opposite. People have been positive about you. You're cheery and have settled in well,' his teeth glinted as he flashed a friendly grin. 'Even my dad is impressed with your gallery and he's a hard man to please.'

Jenny ordered a gin and tonic and couldn't resist the steak and kidney pie. As John poured her a drink, 'The lads that come in here have mentioned seeing you out late at night, on many occasions.'

Jenny didn't want to go into the details so kept her answer short and to the point, 'Yes, I often walk late at night.'

John gave a knowing smile. 'To do with your artistic tendencies, no doubt.' She didn't contradict him.

'There are four evenings when I don't work or I finish at nine o'clock.' Why had he given her this information? Tilting her head to one side, she gazed at him in confusion. He produced a piece of paper from under the counter and wrote a number on it. 'If you feel like company, then I'm willing to accompany you. After I've finished work, it takes time to wind down, so a walk and chat would be good.' He handed her the paper and added, 'Call or text me and we can take it from there.'

'Thanks.' His thoughtfulness had come as a surprise. She tucked the paper in her pocket intending to take him up on the offer, as she would be apprehensive on her own. The same as this morning with his father, tonight John had an entirely different approach to her. John went to serve another customer, and she moved away from the bar to a small table near the window. With its usual speed, her meal appeared, and she focused on people watching as she tucked into the delicious meal with enthusiasm, realising that hunger had crept up on her as she'd forgotten to have lunch.

She had just finished her pie and sipped the last few drops of her gin and tonic while a group of young lads joking and laughing with each other downed their pints of lager. John cleared away her empty plate. 'Another gin and tonic?'

Jenny nodded. Taking a new magazine from her capacious bag, she spread it on the table and settled to read. As she opened the first page of the Artist's Illustrated, she recognised a voice at the bar. Lindy stood waiting to be served.

'Hello, Jenny.' Her voice was bright and her manner bubbly. 'On your own, may I join you?' Jenny put the magazine away. Removing her coat, she settled herself on the wooden chair opposite. Smiling and relaxed, she took a sip from her large glass of red wine. 'I didn't realise you came in here. I work late one day in the week at the builder's merchants, so I pop over for my supper. Kevin would often come as well.' She gasped slightly. Tears came into her eyes, but she blinked them away. 'Why don't we meet up on those evenings? Company is better than sitting alone.'

'I would like that.' Although she had become used to being on her own, she expected to enjoy Lindy's company. Lindy and her association with Kevin made her mind drift. Was the break-in at the gallery connected to her amateur sleuthing about past incidents? She dismissed the idea as ridiculous as she'd only asked a few general questions. 'Lindy, did anyone else have an interest in my shop before I bought it?'

'No genuine interest.' Lindy laughed.

'What's funny?'

'We have a festival week in the village near the end of August. It involves well-dressings, a carnival and other charity events.'

Jenny nodded. 'I've seen old leaflets.'

'There is a committee.' Jenny didn't comment but a small voice in her head whispered, no chance. 'Some months after the festival week, we convene for a meal. It's when the takings and charity donations for the year are revealed.'

'Go on,' Jenny frowned, 'although I'm not sure what this has to do with my shop.'

'I'm on the committee, along with John over there. At last year's meal, we spoke about the village and how good it would be to see the closed shops re-opened. Kevin and I hadn't come up with opening a hardware store in the square. That occurred to us a few months later.' She paused, sipped her wine, and her eyes took on a faraway look. 'Anyway, as the beer and wine flowed, people made suggestions for your shop and cottage, with light-hearted ideas.'

'Can you remember any of them?'

'One stood out. It was unusual that Nicolas could devise a scheme so quickly.'

'Sounds interesting.' Jenny picked up her glass and studied the ice and lemon as it swirled around in the colourless liquid before taking a sip.

'The main shop would become a wine bar with bistro food aimed at the summer visitors. The cottage would be an exclusive salon for Amanda. The outbuildings were big enough for a coffee shop extension to the bistro. Also, from his international trading he could supply gifts, so it could double up as a gift shop.'

'What a grandiose plan.'

'Yes, a couple of months later we found out that you had bought it. Most of the village didn't even realise it had been offered for sale.'

Jenny leaned back in her seat as she absorbed Lindy's story. Were Nicolas and Amanda still interested in her shop?

As Jenny wandered home along the High Street, having left Lindy in the pub, she considered this new piece of information. Nicolas and Amanda had been welcoming. They had been her first visitors to the new gallery, and they had shown her no animosity. Perhaps she would have her hair styled and introduce the topic into the conversation. As she approached the gallery, her steps slowed. Although sure there wouldn't be another break in, she approached with caution. With quiet precision, she turned the key in the lock, opened the door and listened. Unaware that she had been holding her breath, a long sigh escaped. No noise came from the gallery.

17

'Come in, it's good of you to come,' Gerald welcomed Jenny to Stanton House. He led the way across the imposing hall towards the same room she had visited last time. With his hand resting on the door handle, he hesitated. 'It is an informal dinner. My brother is visiting from Scotland and likes to meet more than me and Gwendoline, so I've invited a few guests.'

Despite Gwendoline insisting on the phone that the dinner would be informal, Gerald, as a former officer, would always follow the correct protocol. She raised her eyebrows when she entered the room, quickly counting nine other guests. With a silent chuckle, she guessed there would be a single man.

It amused her to work out whether she had been the add-on for an even number, or whether that label applied to the single man. By the time the introductions were complete, the sherry had been finished, Gwendoline suggested they went through to dinner. Gerald offered his arm and Jenny accepted as the large heavy pair of doors to the dining room were opened by Gwendoline and a maid. The young girl looked familiar, but Jenny couldn't remember where she had seen her before.

Jenny's eyes opened wide. The table had been formally set and crammed with every silverware item that could be required on a table, including a large and elaborate candelabra, at its centrepiece. Everything sparkled in the light shed from the crystal chandelier. The plates and other crockery on the sideboard contained an elaborate crest which she recognised from the front of the house. Jenny paused. 'An impressive display, sir.'

'The dinner is informal, but with my brother here, we have to prove we have not sold the family silver and crockery in Chesterfield market. A gentle laugh came from behind at one of the usual family jokes. Jenny had been used to elaborate formal dinners in the officer's mess. As part of her role, she had visited many regiments where she had been richly entertained, so the set table didn't daunt her. She glanced at the cutlery which suggested several courses.

Clayton acted as the butler, 'I hope you enjoy your dinner, ma'am.' As he poured the wine he whispered, 'My wife is cooking dinner and my daughter is the waitress. After the last guest has left, we will drive to the village. If you wish to have a drink, please do. I'm sure the Colonel won't mind you leaving your car here and you can come back with us.'

'Thank you, Clayton, I will accept your kind offer.'

It did not surprise her to be seated next to the single man, who had been introduced as Henry. On her other side, she had Gerald's brother, Fergus. Her stomach rumbled in anticipation as the aromas of the food reached the dining room. Clayton's wife must be in the kitchen as Gwendoline remained seated.

Gerald took his seat at the head of the table. 'It's

been deliberate to sit you three together,' he pointed at Jenny and the two men on either side with a mischievous grin on his face. Henry grinned. 'I'm guessing we must have something in common.'

Fergus with a good-natured smile, but in a strong Borders' accent, 'You're probably right, but what is it?'

Jenny started with the most obvious question. 'Were you in the military?'

Fergus replied, 'Good grief, no! One gung-ho in the family is enough, and he nodded at Gerald. 'I'm an accountant.'

'And I'm a solicitor,' added Henry.

'It can't be them,' Jenny laughed, 'As I know nothing about the law or finance.'

'May we presume you have left the military?'

'Yes, earlier this year.'

Fergus wrinkled his brow in mock concentration. 'The mystery deepens, but it's typical of Gerald.

What are you doing now?'

'I've opened the Watercolour Gallery in the village.'

'You're an artist?'

'Of sorts.'

Fergus nodded, 'I love to paint. What about you Henry?'

'I'm not good, but I've painted since I was at school.'

They heard Gerald's voice. 'I can see, by the expression on your faces, you've made the connection. It took time. I expected little from a solicitor and an accountant, but I would have expected a speedier connection from you Jenny.' He laughed with a devilish glint in his eye.

The many courses had been delicious. Jenny had

particularly enjoyed the richness of the beef en croute. Angus and Henry had been good company throughout the meal, keeping her entertained with amusing tales. At the end of the dinner, they moved back into the drawing room for liqueurs, brandy and coffee.'

Jenny had been relieved that the break-in had not been mentioned. It would not have made a suitable topic for the dinner table. As she poured her coffee on the large sideboard, a man to whom she hadn't spoken during the evening approached.

Tall and elderly, he leaned heavily on a walking stick but stared at Jenny with twinkling slate grey eyes. She poured him a coffee.

'I believe you have recently moved into Peaklow?'

'Yes.' She didn't recollect seeing him in the village. 'Do you live in Peaklow?'

'No, our house is several miles away, but we have always been friends with Gerald and Gwendoline.' With a thoughtful expression, he leaned towards her and lowered his voice. 'Please be wary of some people in the village.'

Jenny's curiosity surfaced. 'That's a strange comment.' The man was in his eighties. Had he lost focus in his life? She dismissed the idea as the grey eyes were alert but had a worried expression.

'I don't want to be indiscreet about my former pupils.' She frowned and studied his face, looking for clues. 'You look confused. I thought Gerald might have explained the background of the guests, as you are new.'

Jenny shook her head.

The old man's brow knitted together. 'I was the headteacher of the local comprehensive school for more years than I care to remember. I joined the school as a young teacher and stayed to eventually become the head, which allowed me to teach several generations of the same families. Please be wary of dealing with two families from the village, that is all I ask.'

Jenny tilted her head to one side, more confused than ever by this strange conversation.

'Do carry on, but I probably don't know them.'

'I'm sure you do. There is a butcher's shop and a post office.'

'Lionel...'

He interrupted, 'and his family.'

'Elizabeth?'

He nodded. 'I shall say no more. Shall we join the others?'

Jenny picked up her coffee cup and made her way across the room, while she thought through the man's revelations.

As the evening ended, much to her disappointment, she hadn't quizzed the former headteacher for more information. When she next visited the butchers or the post office, she would keep her eyes and ears open.

Clayton oversaw the last guests leaving. His wife Tanya and daughter Millie waited to go. 'I'm sure I've seen you before, Millie.' Jenny tilted her head to one side quizzically.

Millie giggled. 'I work at the butcher's on a Saturday and I served you a couple of weeks ago.'

'That's right you did. I remember now.'

As Clayton drove along the high street, 'I'll park outside my cottage and see Millie and Tanya in. Then I'll walk you back to your house.'

‘Thank you,’ Jenny suspected he wanted to speak with her. He lived close to Nicolas and Amanda. He ushered his wife and daughter safely into the house and they waved as they closed the door. Walking along the deserted pavement towards Market Square, their footsteps echoed in the still night air.

‘The break-in the other night concerns me, as you live on your own. I didn’t want to alarm Tanya and Millie, but here is my number.’ Clayton handed over a piece of paper. ‘Text or call me and I’ll come immediately.’

‘Thank you, Clayton. I’ve seen you out late at night with your dog.’

‘Yes, he doesn’t want to go, but I do, which I’m sure you understand.’

‘Did you notice anything suspicious the night of the break in?’

‘No. I must have arrived home about the time it happened. If I’d seen lights on or the police, I would have come, but nothing caught my attention. The only people I met were Elizabeth and Amanda coming back from the Manor pub where they informed me they’d enjoyed a lavish meal.’

18

Jenny had been tired as she had entered her cottage the previous night after the dinner at Stanton House. Clayton had come in with her to check the cottage and gallery had remained secure. Thankfully, she'd had a good night's sleep with no horrific dreams to disturb her. In her usual style, she rose early and had already breakfasted before the first rays of dawn broke over the village.

Lingering over her second cup of coffee, she allowed her mind to wander over recent events, but it kept drifting to the persons responsible for the break-in and graffiti. It made no sense to her why someone wanted her to leave the village. Perhaps the reason would become clear, but for now she intended carrying on as before, although she would exercise caution. As the gallery would be closed today, painting on location would be a good idea. It might help to distract her from dwelling on all the unsavoury happenings.

The weather forecast predicted a calm and sunny day, making it perfect for location painting. Finding a new local scene occupied her mind as she packed her equipment into her car. Planning to leave, she picked up her jacket and her eye caught the ready packaged parcel sitting on the small side table. Tutting with annoyance at her forgetfulness, she picked up the box, which contained a birthday present for her niece.

She had left it to the last moment, making it essential to catch today's post. Checking her watch, it was before eight, but she was keen to leave. A simple solution to the problem formed. Elizabeth arrived in her shop well before the opening time of nine o'clock. Perhaps if she nipped to the back entrance, she could leave the parcel with money and ask Elizabeth to post it when she opened for the day.

She scribbled a quick note to Elizabeth and placed the money in an envelope. The parcel would arrive on time and she would have a full day's painting on location. Jenny nipped to the back of the shops where a rutted old track led her towards the barn at the back of the disused shop. The back door of the post office came to her left. Stepping from the track, she passed wheelie bins, and a stone shed. The back door, made of solid metal, necessary security for a post office, had no bell. If Elizabeth didn't respond to a knock, she would leave the parcel on the step and telephone her when she had found a location for painting. She tried the door handle, which to her surprise yielded to her touch.

Despite it being a large, heavy door, it opened silently. As she stepped across the threshold, her eyes widened in amazement. Stunned, she froze to the spot. Lionel and Elizabeth kissed passionately on the far side of the storeroom. A slight movement caught her eye. Lionel's hand was up Elizabeth's skirt and Elizabeth's hands raked across Lionel's head in a frenzied movement. They hadn't heard Jenny. She didn't make a sound but the sudden influx of cooler air made them break their kiss and look towards the door. All three stood staring at each other for several seconds in stunned silence.

Lionel responded first, 'I'd better return to the shop.'

Jenny mumbled, 'I'll leave you,' and promptly closed the door. Breathing deeply, she made her way back to the gallery, still clutching her parcel. There were always likely to be relationships hidden in a village, but they made an unlikely couple. She would never dream of mentioning this morning's discovery to either of them. She revised her plan for the day and would find another post office to post her parcel. As she reached her car to drive away, Lionel and Elizabeth stood at their shop doors watching her. It had been unfortunate timing.

Did they meet there every morning before they opened their respective shops? Was it just a fling or a serious affair? A small smile creased her lips as she would never have paired those two together. She assumed the surprising encounter would never be mentioned again. To avoid awkwardness, she resolved to buy meat from the supermarket on her way home and to avoid the post office for several days.

19

It had been a productive day of painting in a small village on the edges of the moor with stunning views and, along with the photographs she had taken, she had the basis for several pictures. As Jenny drove home at the end of her day out, her early morning encounter with Elizabeth and Lionel sprang back into her mind.

She remained intent on avoiding them for as long as possible, in that way she hoped to avoid embarrassment. It had been such a surprise, especially after Elizabeth's comments about Kevin's suggestions. Perhaps she said one thing but did something else? The warning from the former headteacher came to her mind, although his comments probably related to poor behaviour when at school. Perhaps he'd forgotten how many years had passed and that she was now a grown woman.

A police car had parked outside the gallery. She pulled up behind it. As she had her painting equipment with her, she unlocked the gallery door. Before she unloaded, two policemen emerged from the parked car and approached her. 'Jenny Maltravers?

'Yes.' She expected a progress report on the break-in at the gallery.

'Would you accompany us to the police station?'

'Now?'

'Yes, please.'

Polite, but they didn't smile. 'May I ask why?'

'You discovered a body in the garden of Victoria House.'

'The constable, who took my statement, maintained that I might be asked further questions, but that someone would visit me.'

The policeman showed no interest in her reply, 'The Sergeant would like you to come to the station, to fulfil the formalities.'

'Okay, let me lock up.'

It took thirty minutes to reach Chesterfield police station. Neither of the policemen spoke. As the journey progressed, Jenny's irritation with the situation increased. It hadn't been a convenient time to drop everything and travel to Chesterfield. Tired from her busy day out, she had expected a quiet evening with a long soak in the bath to relieve her aching limbs. It had been a surprise that she couldn't attend a local station. She would make her displeasure known when she spoke to the Sergeant.

On arrival, the officers led her to a small room with a table, four chairs and some recording equipment. They informed her that the Sergeant would be with her soon. A constable remained standing by the door but didn't speak. The blank white walls and the potent smell of cleaning fluid did little to appease her irritation as she waited. Glancing once again at her watch, a sigh of exasperation escaped her lips. They had already kept her waiting for ten minutes. She had never been involved with the police before, even as a witness, so she didn't know the procedure.

Feeling uncomfortable, she guessed they had methods to follow, but how much longer did they intend to keep her cooped up here in this stark uninviting place?

A man strode authoritatively into the room. 'Detective Sergeant Smith.'

She received no welcoming smile, no handshake, or an apology for keeping her waiting. The lack of good manners didn't quell her rising annoyance. Tall and slim, Jenny guessed him to be mid-thirties. He wore a white shirt, dark tie and blue suit trousers, but no jacket and appeared relaxed and confident. Settling himself into the chair on the opposite side of the table, his expression remained solemn while he shuffled the papers.

Having adjusted to the situation, Jenny remained silent and waited for him to speak as the quicker he started the interview, the quicker she could go home.

A woman constable entered. 'Mrs Maltravers, for the process of elimination, we wish to take your fingerprints.' Although this request sent a shiver down her spine, she nodded, as she hadn't expected this procedure.

With effort, she regained her composure. The young constable took them and gave Jenny a cloth and tissues to wipe her hands. The Sergeant fiddled with the recording equipment and inserted a tape.

The silence weighed heavily. 'For your information, it is Miss Maltravers.' After the last twenty years, saying her civilian title seemed strange. The Constable left with her fingerprints as the Sergeant started the tape.

'So we are clear about the details of the answers you give. I am recording the conversation.'

Jenny nodded. 'For the benefit of the tape, please confirm your name, date of birth and address. I have not issued a caution, but you are required to tell the truth to the police.'

Jenny's surprised expression brought a frown of confusion, causing his forehead to furrow. The Constable returned with a piece of paper, which he read and raised his eyebrows. The interruptions were irritating. Tired and hungry from her day out, she wanted this meeting finished so she could return home.

The Sergeant tapped a piece of paper on the desk in front of him and his blue eyes impaled her with a glower of disapproval. 'We could not trace your background. We know you bought your current residence with the attached shop earlier this year.' His fierce expression didn't waver. 'I want you to give me your addresses for the past ten years.'

The arrogance of the man caused her irritation to bubble to the surface. She didn't wish to have this conversation and delayed her answer. Then a tight smile flicked across her face. 'I am prohibited from telling you where I have been and lived by the Official Secrets Act.' Even to her ears, her voice sounded stern and rather pompous.

The Sergeant's expression darkened. 'I require more information than that. You are obliged...'

Jenny gritted her teeth and snapped, 'I have been a member of her Majesty's Armed Forces. Until the thirty-first of January this year, I was Major Jennifer Maltravers.'

'We will check.'

'Please do!'

'You will wait while we confirm through various channels.'

Jenny pushed back her chair and stood up. Resting

her hands on the edge of the table, she leaned forward. 'Sergeant, I will not wait!' She huffed out a breath of annoyance and glared at him through narrowed eyes. 'Now please take me back to my house in Peaklow.'

'We have not questioned you.' A twinge of anger laced his voice.

She ground her teeth and clenched her jaw so tight it hurt. 'You will find that in twenty years' service in the army, I had an unblemished record. I have no intention of answering any further questions until I have taken legal advice.'

He shoved back his chair and stood to face her. 'I believe that we have enough evidence to arrest you.'

'For what?' She gave him a look of disdain as she folded her arms across her chest.

'The charge would be uncertain until we have questioned you.'

'Sergeant,' she treated him to a look of unmitigated annoyance. 'You have bungled the investigation into Kevin Cartwright's death from the beginning. You have let many days pass without determining your inquiry. I shall be most willing to assist the police, but not now. I wish to return home. You may make an appointment with me at the convenience of my solicitor. For your information, I shall not be travelling away from Peaklow, but I may be out on location painting.' The Sergeant hesitated. Jenny spotted his uncertainty and, seizing the opportunity, continued in a commanding voice, 'That is all I shall say on the matter tonight. Now please arrange my transport!'

Within twenty minutes, Jenny travelled home. Before she left, the police had confirmed her identity. Although annoyed at their attitude, a slither of nervousness had wriggled its way into her mind. Readjusting her position in the back seat of the police car, an icy shiver spiralled down her spine. She replayed the words of the interview over in her mind. Were they thinking she had more involvement than as a witness? Did they suspect she had killed Kevin? Or perhaps pushed him off the scaffolding in the middle of an argument? Some serious consideration was required about how she could be implicated. Although she was innocent of any wrongdoing, how could she prove it? In the morning, a solicitor would be her priority. Did Henry, who she had sat next to at dinner, do legal case work?

20

After the police car had dropped her off, she unloaded her painting equipment from her car and dumped it in the middle of the gallery. In no mood to cook herself tea and close to nine o'clock, she walked to The George.

'Just in time, if you want food,' John from behind the bar called out with a glance towards the wall clock. She nodded, placed her usual order, and took her drink to a corner table. The food arrived promptly as there were few customers in the pub. As she finished her meal, John came over to take her empty plate away. 'Another gin and tonic?'

'Yes, please.'

The large plate of steak and kidney pie and the first gin and tonic had helped her to regain a sense of equilibrium. Tomorrow she would engage a solicitor. With that resolution in mind, she relaxed in her seat.

As John returned with her drink so he also carried a pint of lager, 'Do you mind if I join you?'

'Please do,' Jenny waved a hand towards an empty chair with a surprised expression. Having someone to talk to might help distract her and stop her mind from dwelling on her encounter with the police.

'It's a night when I finish at nine o'clock, so I often have a drink before I leave.' He settled his muscular body into the chair opposite, took a large gulp of lager, and he leaned back with a loud relaxing sigh. Since the break-in, there had been a contrast in Lionel and John. Their morose faces stayed, but they now started conversations and seemed genuinely at ease in chatting about everyday matters.

As he finished the last mouthful of lager, he placed his glass back on the table and wiped his mouth with the back of his hand. He stretched and leaned back in his chair. 'I've plenty of time on my hands,' a melancholy frown flitted across his features and a faraway look came into his eye.

'Aren't you busy as you work in your dad's shop and here?'

'I've more time because I have recently separated from my long-term girlfriend.' John's brow furrowed, and he shrugged. 'She gave me the boot. At the time, I was disappointed, as I had expected to marry her. As I have more spare time, I might resurrect my interest in painting. It was the subject I enjoyed most at school.'

Jenny rubbed a weary hand over the back of her neck. 'Come to the gallery anytime, if you want to talk about painting.'

'Thanks.' He blew out a breath. 'That will be a great help to get me started again. If you are walking tonight and don't mind company. I would be happy to accompany you.'

Jenny doubted if she could sleep, so she had considered a walk, but had become apprehensive about being on her own. She could text Clayton but didn't want to impose on him. She flashed him a smile of acceptance, 'I'll need to fetch a better coat and change into boots.'

A small cheeky smile appeared on his face. 'Can we talk more about painting?'

'Yes, of course,' Jenny chuckled. 'It has been my passion since I was a young girl. I not only love painting but enjoy discussing it as well.

They left the pub together, walking the short distance up the shadowy deserted road, lit by only a few old street lamps. Jenny entered and left John in the passage that led from the gallery past the parlour. He already wore a heavy coat. After Jenny had picked up her anorak from upstairs and put on her walking boots, she locked up, and they agreed that the old railway path would be the best as they could easily walk side by side. Narrow footpaths did not lend themselves to having a sensible conversation. As they left the village, it was a pleasant and calm night.

Tilting her head upwards, bright stars were scattered across the inky blackness of the sky. Their boots crunched rhythmically on the gravel covered trackway as they strolled along, using the torch to check the way ahead. As they moved away from the village, the pinprick lights from distant houses vanished. The dark night surrounded them, robbing the world of the daytime details.

'Do you see much of your sister, Amanda?'

'Why do you ask?' Jenny didn't detect any resentment in her question. He sounded curious.

'While you live in the same village, you work early in the morning and in the evening, whilst she works during the day.'

'I visit her most days. She mentioned you had been to her salon to have your hair cut. Were you pleased with it?'

'Oh yes.' Jenny's hand instinctively patted her hair. 'I shall make a regular appointment.'

'That's good news. I shall tell her in the morning.'

'Are you a little older than her?'

'I'm about eighteen months her senior, so she's my little sister and I've always looked after her.'

Jenny smiled at the seriousness of his voice. 'Did she need looking after?'

They opened and closed a gate, which rattled on its hinges and closed with a resounding clank. A short path led them onto a narrow lane which would take them back towards the village. The inky darkness surrounded them. In the distance, an owl hooted, soon a second owl joined in answering the call.

'Neither of us performed well at school. I don't know why, but we were bullied. As I became stronger, I learned to protect myself.'

'It's unusual for a girl to be bullied, isn't it?'

'You've seen how pretty she is.' He let out a long sigh, and the words seemed to convey a wealth of emotion as they reached Jenny through the darkness. An image of Amanda appeared in Jenny's mind. Long blonde hair, blue eyes and a perfect figure. He carried on, his voice deliberate and unhurried. 'The other girls were jealous, so I had to protect her.'

The image of a knight in shining armour charging off on his trusted white stallion to rescue a damsel in distress leapt into Jenny's mind, making her grin. 'But she doesn't need protecting now, as she's married.'

'Not true.' She couldn't see his expression because of the darkness. But his tight and scathing voice pierced the night. 'I'm friendly with Nicolas, but he has a nasty streak in him. He upsets Amanda terribly, so two or three times since she has been married, I've had to have a word with him.'

Jenny made no comment about this piece of news.

After this morning's sight of Elizabeth and Lionel locked in a passionate embrace, appearances could be deceptive. Lionel was a brusque man and Elizabeth prudish, but Nicolas and Amanda seemed the perfect couple. As she discovered more about people in the village, matters were not dull or straightforward. Secrets seemed to appear at every corner.

21

As the silver-grey Vauxhall approached, a bubble of excitement made Jenny jiggle up and down. Standing on the pavement, she waved her arm with enthusiasm, as the car drew to a halt outside the gallery. The tall man unfolded himself from the driver's seat. Jenny threw her arms around his neck and hugged him tightly. 'This is such a surprise,' she gasped. 'How wonderful to see you!'

An hour previously, he had rung to inform her he was on the outskirts of the Peak District with the sole intention of visiting her. It was the diversion she required as she had risen early, unable to sleep, while her mind twirled on the previous day. The police interview had made her uneasy. The hostile attitude of the Police Sergeant had unsettled her. Releasing each other from the enthusiastic greeting, he stood back and with twinkling eyes and a theatrical wave of his hand, 'So this is the famous gallery.'

Jenny had always liked Dan, and this morning in his jeans, tee-shirt and trainers, he looked handsome. She pushed him playfully on the arm. 'It's not famous, Dan, and I'm sure it never will be.'

'That's where you are wrong.' He scanned the gallery with a wicked smile and a laugh escaped his lips. 'It is now famous throughout the Colchester Garrison.'

Jenny's eyebrows shot up in surprise. 'How do they know?'

'Mainly because I told everyone. No one who has known you for years could believe you would do it. I've many comments and good wishes for you, even from the garrison commander.'

'I don't believe it,' Jenny giggled with amusement, 'but do come in. You will stay with me, won't you?'

'If you've space, yes, please.' He gazed across Market Square. 'What's the village like?' Jenny wanted to comment that it was not as idyllic as it seemed, but would leave those comments until later. She revelled in the idea of being able to tell Dan about the village intrigue plus her worrying involvement in an unexplained death. 'Let's walk around the village after a cup of coffee.'

As they turned towards the open door of the gallery, two cars squealed to a halt behind Dan's Vauxhall. One a marked police car. The other a black Jaguar with darkened rear windows. The Police Sergeant who she'd met at the police station, stepped from the Jaguar. Tall and sombre, he stood on the pavement clutching a piece of paper, while his watchful blue eyes followed her every movement. Jenny grimaced and her hand grasped Dan's arm.

Tension gripped her and her throat constricted in fear. 'I haven't told you. It could be a surprise!' Eying the Sergeant warily, she struggled to draw in a deep breath.

Dan smiled, but his dark eyebrows lowered questioningly. The Sergeant flanked by two constables, strode towards her. He passed her a document, but before she could read it, he pointed, 'That document is an arrest warrant issued in court this morning.'

The words and the bureaucratic tone of his voice cut through her and she trembled. Her hand tightened its grip on Dan's arm. 'Jennifer Maltravers, I am arresting you in connection with the suspicious death of Kevin Cartwright. You do not have to say anything, but it may harm your defence if you do not mention when questioned something which you later rely on in court. Anything you say may be given in evidence.' He huffed out a breath and took another step towards her.

Jenny's mind careered in circles as she tried to make sense of it all. Why were they arresting her? Why did they think she was involved? Did they believe she murdered Kevin?

Dan stared in amazement as his eyes flicked between Jenny and the Sergeant.

'This is a surprise,' he shook his head and ran his fingers through his short, dark hair.

'Will you come with me, Dan?' she blurted, her tone urgent and pleading. It was pathetic to be so needy, but she wanted support.

'Of course.' He gave a small smile and his intelligent brown eyes filled with a mixture of confusion and concern. Jenny cleared her throat and spoke in a commanding voice, 'Sergeant, this is a friend of mine and he will be my advisor.'

The Sergeant frowned with irritation but nodded while his face remained as grey and unmoving as a block of granite. He motioned towards the police car without a word. Once settled, they travelled in silence.

Jenny clutched Dan's hand throughout the journey while she grappled to understand why she had been arrested. Fear and anxiety settled on her while images of Kevin's crumpled form kept appearing in her mind. Could the situation become any more complicated? The village grapevine would be rife with the information that she had been arrested. How would the people of the village react? Would they believe her capable of murder?

On arrival at the police station, a policeman escorted them to the same room where Jenny had been questioned the previous day. They waited a few minutes before the Sergeant and another man entered. The Sergeant nodded, his lips tight and perched himself on a chair in the corner. The other man arranged himself with slow precision at the table and placed a tape in the recording machine. His salt and pepper grey hair was neatly combed, and his brown eyes were calm and untroubled. After arranging the paperwork into a neat, regimented pile on the table, he then gazed around with a solemn expression. Flicking the button on the recorder, he stated the date and time before adding, 'There are four people present. Sergeant John Smith, myself Chief Inspector David Robinson.'

He indicated to Jenny, who stuttered, 'Jennifer Maltravers.'

The Inspector then nodded to Dan. 'Captain Daniel Harrison, Royal Military Police, but I would add that I am here in a private capacity.'

The Inspector's expression stalled with astonishment. He stared down at his notes for one long moment and then continued in a business-like tone, 'May I ask which branch of the Military Police?'

Dan took his time, allowing the silence to lengthen. 'The investigation branch.' Once again, he paused as though setting aside time for his words to sink in. 'My role in recent years has been the investigation of unexplained and suspicious deaths.' Dan's words hung in the air and the Inspector appeared to hesitate. He eyed Dan through narrowed eyes filled with distrust.

Recovering himself, he addressed a smooth controlled voice to Jenny, 'because of the senior rank you held, until recently, I have now been assigned to this case. Your service record is impeccable, but we have evidence to suggest you may be closely involved in Kevin Cartwright's death. It surprised me to learn of your uncooperative attitude when you were last here.'

The final accusation about being unhelpful riled Jenny. Gasping for control, she glowered with disapproval across the table. 'Inspector, your Sergeant was uncommunicative. I am completely prepared to help your inquiry.' Her voice was icy and self-assured. Dan's presence helped, as she no longer had to fight this battle on her own. Cold dignity created a stony mask on her face. 'I have found it strange that it has taken so long to reach the conclusion that Kevin's death is suspicious.' She cast a quick glance at the ceiling in ill-concealed exasperation. Further remarks occurred to her, but for now she dismissed them as a mixture of astonishment and disbelief spread across the Inspector's face.

'Why do you say that?' he snapped with narrowed eyes and obvious resentment at her disparaging comment. Fixing her sharp gaze on his face, she answered without hesitation. 'If you speak with anyone in the village, you will find that Kevin put safety first. You only had to watch him work to know that he practiced what he preached. The scaffolding boards at Victoria House were untidy with ropes and a lack of a safety gate. A second point is that he never drank alcohol while working, but by the smell of the flask, it contained alcohol.'

The Inspector rested his elbows on the table and leaned forward, 'You admit to being on the scaffolding?' His expression held a hint of smugness and his tone was full of menace. Jenny stared at the Inspector intensely and exhaled with exaggerated patience.

'My military training comes to the fore when needed. Finding a man dead under suspicious circumstances requires the near vicinity to be checked for danger. I informed the young constable who took my statement that I ensured that there were no further casualties nor any danger to me while I stayed with the body. He did not ask me whether I went on to the scaffolding and therefore I did not tell him as it did not appear relevant.'

The Inspector levelled her with a long assessing look while his mouth tightened in annoyance.

His quiet, accusing voice broke into her thoughts, 'Did you climb the ladder?'

'No, Inspector,' she stared at him with a scornful expression before adding, 'please give me a little credit. A man is lying at the foot of a ladder. From the position of his body and the angle of his head, I guessed he'd broken his neck in the fall. So, I didn't disturb the body. The only place I could check for a pulse was his neck. I concluded from my brief examination that he had been dead for many hours and had probably fallen the previous evening.' Memories flashed through her mind at extreme speed as she spoke about the finding of Kevin's body.

A stillness came over the Inspector. Jenny found the silence oppressive. The only sound came from footsteps moving along the corridor outside. The Inspector tossed his head and with a sceptical expression snarled, 'That seems a quick conclusion under the circumstances. Perhaps you have more information about the death than you are prepared to let on.' His voice was icy and emphatic.

Riled with the inspector, her head tight with frustration, she went to reply, but Dan interrupted, 'Inspector kindly refrain from unsubstantiated hints.' His commanding voice echoed. 'If you wish to ask questions, then do so. You have made a veiled suggestion that is deemed to unsettle the Major.'

Both Jenny and Dan smiled. 'I correct myself, Ms Maltravers. If you continue with such an approach, then I shall report you to your senior officer for professional incompetence.'

The shock of the reprimand recoiled across the Inspector's face. It darkened with a mixture of annoyance and disbelief as he struggled to regain his composure. He snorted with impatience. 'I'm conducting this interview and will pursue it in the manner I choose.'

Dan, unperturbed by the Inspector's displeasure, continued, 'I wonder how you ever have successful cases if you approach interviews in this manner.' His authoritative tone was now cool and professional with an edge of abruptness. 'Why don't you ask Ms Maltravers to make a full statement about her involvement with the deceased and exactly what she did on discovering the body? Then you will have a solid basis on which to ask your questions.'

The Inspector glared with unguarded resentment, but a momentary glimmer of doubt flickered in his eyes as though he weighed up his options on how to proceed.

Dan added in a more friendly voice, 'Inspector, the Armed Forces have many restrictions on what we can say outside of the confines of our regiment and to civilians.' The Inspector nodded and shifted in his seat. 'However, I have had to give evidence many times in civilian courts. I can tell you that Major Maltravers was a matron who specialised in the running of field hospitals in war zones. One of her roles would be to assess people bought into those hospitals making informed but immediate decisions on whether they were dead, wounded or just ill.'

The Inspector paused for a few minutes as though absorbing this information. His mood was hard to judge. No smile appeared on his face. Silence once again filled the room, making Jenny nervous and unsettled, but Dan's comments had given her a glimmer of hope. What would happen next?

The Inspector puffed out his cheeks, sat back in his chair and his brown eyes narrowed and hardened as he glowered at Jenny. 'Are you prepared to make a full statement as the Captain suggests?'

'Yes, Inspector.' Jenny responded, without hesitation.

Dan interrupted, 'The statement will be written to ensure accuracy and avoid ambiguity.' Pausing, he pressed his lips together in a thin straight line before continuing slowly, emphasising each word, 'and will not be dictated into a machine.'

With a knock at the door, a constable entered and passed a message to the Inspector.

The Inspector grunted, 'Show him in.'

He faced Jenny with a scowl of impatience. 'Your solicitor has arrived.'

This came as news to Jenny, who had not engaged one. It had been her intention when Dan had arrived earlier that morning. Who could it be? With her eyes fixed on the door, she almost held her breath as she waited. A broad smile covered her face as, with a professional air, Henry strode into the room, clutching his briefcase. 'Good morning, Inspector.'

He nodded to Jenny and waited for an introduction to the man sitting next to her. After the formalities were complete, he lowered himself onto a chair next to Jenny. Then he turned his attention to the Inspector who looked far from pleased at his arrival. A frown of impatience flickered across the policeman's face as he stared at the trio before him.

'And now Inspector,' a brief smile appeared on Henry's face, 'where are we with this matter?'

The Inspector summarized, while Jenny listened with care.

It was a concise and factual account of their conversations this morning and the interview late yesterday afternoon. The Inspector hinted he had evidence of Jenny's connection to the death of Kevin but didn't reveal any details. Jenny's breath hitched, and she momentarily closed her eyes, wishing she could be transported away from this nightmare. When would it end? Would she be able to prove her innocence? Did her new friends in the village think she was guilty? Questions spiralled out of control in her head, but there were no answers.

Henry's matter-of-fact voice brought her spinning back to reality. 'With your agreement we will now leave. Ms Maltravers' statement will be with you by tomorrow morning.'

Colonel Stanton of Stanton House sends his compliments and says that he will guarantee Major Maltravers will attend on the police at a convenient time to both parties.'

The Inspector's scowl deepened, 'My investigations are continuing and I wish to hold Ms Maltravers for further questioning, he paused and pinched the bridge of his nose as though attempting to control a headache, 'but with the Colonel involved, who also is the Chairman of the Magistrates, I have little option.'

He pushed all the paper back into his folder and his lips flattened into an angry line as he shoved back his chair and rose to his feet, signalling the end of the interview.

22

Despite her rising concerns, Jenny left the police station in a more positive frame of mind as she had Dan and Henry to support her. Henry drove them to Peaklow. Arriving back in the village by police car could now be avoided. She settled herself in the back seat and heaved a sigh of relief as they pulled away from the police station. During the journey, Henry explained Clayton had seen her arrested and contacted the Colonel. Without delay, the Colonel had phoned him, as he is the family solicitor. As they neared Peaklow, Henry mentioned Gerald wanted an update, and suggested they visit Stanton House to prepare the statement.

Gerald was Chairman of the Magistrates, so it would be good to involve him in the drafting of a detailed account of her actions after finding Kevin's body. Within minutes, they pulled up in front of Stanton House and were ushered inside by Gwendoline, who had expected them. After the introductions were complete, Gerald led them into the small sitting room. 'Let's sit down. I want to hear the details of why they suspect you, Jenny.'

She settled on a large comfortable sofa and stared at the battle scene of the charging horses hanging on the wall. Each time she looked at it, another detail presented itself. Today, her eye was drawn to the perfect movement of a galloping horse. The familiarity of the room and the friendly faces who stared expectantly at her brought her back to the current situation. With a deep breath, she focused on giving an accurate account.

'I found him early one morning, but I would guess that he died on the previous evening. About ten o'clock that evening, I went for a walk. As I'm new to the village, I'm still exploring the local tracks and footpaths. My route took me past Victoria house where the body was found. The wind blew up along the High Street and as I reached Victoria House, my bootlace came undone. I tucked myself into the gap where the footpath emerges by the side of the house to re-tie it.'

Although it was windy, the plastic sheeting attached to the scaffolding only made a minimal amount of noise. The house was in darkness.

'Do you often walk late at night on your own?' interrupted Henry, fixing her with a bemused stare. 'It seems a dangerous time.'

Jenny didn't wish to elaborate on the nightmares disrupting her sleep. 'I have problems sleeping, so I often walk, as it helps me to relax. Both Dan and Gerald nodded in understanding. 'If sleep is disjointed, I often walk early in the morning as well. After arriving home that evening, I only had a fitful sleep, so I went out again before daylight. I walked via the old railway track. As dawn broke, I took the footpath from the track which leads down to the High Street, the one that comes out by Victoria House.' 'Is that when you found him?' Gerald's solemn face appeared anxious.

Jenny nodded, rubbing a hand across her forehead as the image of Kevin's crumpled form flashed into her mind. He'd been so vibrant and full of fun when he was alive. The more she reflected, the more convinced she became he had been murdered.

'As I passed the gateway, I glanced into the garden. A strange shape on the grass caught my attention. With poor light, it took time to identify the mound on the lawn from where I stood. Once I had convinced myself a person lay there, I hurried into the garden. As I arrived at the body, I assumed it to be an accident. He lay at the bottom of the ladder and had broken his neck.'

Henry interrupted, 'Did you ring the police?'

'Yes, immediately, but I confirmed there were no other casualties or dangers, especially as noises came from the plastic sheeting on the scaffolding. The morning was windy, and the plastic flapped where it had loosened. I walked up the steps and checked the back garden and moved on to the scaffolding. Because the garden slopes upwards, I didn't need to use the ladder, but could step straight onto the scaffolding boards. Jenny paused and scanned their faces.

'Then I became suspicious. The scaffolding boards were covered with tools, bits of rope, and the ladder didn't have a gate. I walked the entire length of the boards, which were placed at first floor level and stretched along the side of the house and across the front. Although I'd only known Kevin a short time, he emphasised safety to me frequently. He was meticulous about tidiness and followed strict and sensible rules to ensure he kept any dangers to a minimum.'

The three men remained silent, their expressions

grim, as they concentrated on Jenny's words. 'An open paint pot with a brush balanced across the top stood next to one. Next to the paint, a flask, which smelled of alcohol.'

Gerald scoffed. 'Is that their case? Do they think that because you went onto the scaffolding boards, that you were the cause of his fall?'

Henry interrupted; his face was serious. 'Jumping to conclusions at this point won't help. We don't know what evidence they have found.' Silence filled the room, broken by the sonorous ticking of the grandfather clock.

Dan rubbed his chin thoughtfully. 'Anything else which could incriminate?'

A sigh caught in Jenny's throat. 'After the interview at the police station last night, I guessed there must be more. Although they haven't mentioned me walking past the house the previous evening, someone might have noticed me. That knowledge would no doubt fuel their suspicions and they'd want to arrest me as I was near to the scene about the time that Kevin died. However, I've guessed what the damming evidence might be.'

'Go on.' Dan leaned forward and stared questioningly.

'You won't know this, but before the job at Victoria House, Kevin completed work for me to prepare the interior of my premises for opening. He finished decorating my gallery before starting work for Nicolas and Amanda.'

'Another coincidence,' Henry grimaced, 'nothing more.'

Jenny studied them carefully. 'On the last day he worked for me, he moved his tools and ladders into the hallway as a prelude to taking them to his van. He then took a phone call about future business and wandered outside. I wanted to retrieve something from the hall cupboard and moved his equipment out of the way.'

Henry sat straighter in his chair and gave a brief nod of understanding. 'So your fingerprints could be on the paint can, flask and brushes.'

Jenny nodded. 'I opened the gallery on the same day as he died. He popped in at lunchtime to offer his good wishes. In the conversation, he told me someone had stolen his paint pot, brushes and flask.'

'Perhaps he just mislaid them,' Henry suggested, 'and found them later.'

A frown of consternation creased her forehead. 'Kevin was neat and well organised. At first, I wondered whether he had been a military man. But I later learned that his father-in-law had been killed by falling from scaffolding, which prompted a tidy and safety conscious approach.'

Gerald tapped the arm of the chair with the flat of his hand and eyed the assembled group with a thoughtful expression. 'The most important matter is to have Jenny's statement written, so you and Henry go through to the library, while Dan and I put our heads together.'

23

After two intensive hours of concentration at a large table in the library, Henry leaned back in his chair and gave a satisfied sigh. 'The statement is finished. Before you sign it, I suggest our two experts in the other room read it through. Then I will arrange for delivery to the Inspector.'

Henry had been meticulous about the wording used in the statement. He wished to ensure there were no ambiguities. 'Thank you, Henry,' Jenny rubbed a hand across her aching forehead. The interview this morning at the police station and the writing of her detailed account had made her increasingly nervous about her situation. She'd never put a foot wrong in terms of the law. She still hadn't, but the pressure on her had intensified.

The police believed she had been involved in Kevin's death and had suggested that they had incriminating evidence. It had become startlingly obvious that she would have to rely on Henry to prove her innocence. Whilst those in the house today believed her, perhaps the police had other evidence they hadn't revealed yet. Would that make her friends doubt her?

'Shall we join the others?' Henry gathered up the

papers and put them carefully into his briefcase.

'Henry, before we go, can I ask you a question?' She pursed her lips and tapped her fingers on the table as she stared across at him. 'Why hadn't the unused shop in the Market Square been sold before I purchased it?'

Henry rested his elbows on the table and steepled his fingers. 'Gerald's family at one time owned all the shops in the square. His family goes back centuries. When Gerald inherited only two remained, the one next to the butcher's and yours. There had been no interest in them for years, so we had given up advertising and left them empty.'

'So why the change?'

'We were approached by a lady, the wife of the builder that you found. She asked for a price for the shop next to the butchers. Gerald put both on the market for a short time. Lindy appeared keen and was eager to buy the property as soon as possible.

'What happened then?'

He chuckled, 'Well, then you came along and with no problems bought the one on the corner. The other one is under negotiation between three interested parties. We are hoping to resolve the matter shortly, but there have been many delays. I would add there is nothing unusual about them, so we are making progress.'

'Did anyone else want to buy the one I bought?'

'We had one enquiry and a low bid, but I'm not sure from whom. You were keen and would pay the full price, so we went ahead.'

24

'I work here a couple of evenings a week,' Tanya, Clayton's wife, showed Jenny and Dan to their seats in the restaurant at the Manor. They weaved between the tables to a small window seat set for two people. The ambient background music mingled with the chatter of diners in the busy restaurant. As they settled down at the polished walnut table, complete with a small vase containing colourful narcissi, Jenny glanced across at her handsome companion.

His arrival this morning had been perfect timing for the disturbing events of the day that had been thrown at her. After returning from Stanton House, they'd chatted about old friends and Jenny had related gossip from the village, which had kept Dan amused. Knowing that she wouldn't want to cook, she'd booked a table at The Manor restaurant. Located at the north end of the village, they had walked the half a mile from the gallery. Jenny perused the elaborate menu with relish at the range of food on offer.

As soon as they had placed their order, Dan leaned back in his chair. 'Today was out of the ordinary.' A small smile appeared followed by a slow, disbelieving shake of his head. 'I suspected some surprises that you hadn't put in your letter, but I never expected you to be arrested on the morning I arrived.'

Jenny's stomach jittered as she recalled her trip to the police station, but being with Gerald, Henry and Dan had calmed her. She had nothing to do with the death of Kevin, but her concern was convincing the police of her innocence. Grinning across at her old friend Dan, she raised her eyebrows quizzically, 'What surprises were you expecting?'

Dan didn't answer immediately but allowed his eyes to wander around the bustling room as a smile played on his lips. 'I anticipated you were a Mrs Someone, and that your new husband came from the village, and that's why you located here.'

Jenny laughed. 'No, there is no man in my life. After I left the army, I travelled around the UK for a couple of months, drifting here and there as the whim took me. For the last twenty years I've travelled far and wide around the world, but it left no time to explore my native countryside. Also, I had to decide about my life. It took some time to accept I could do whatever I wanted and that it was my decision.

On a clear winter's day, I came to this village and found it delightful. The setting is perfect. Nestled at the far end of a beautiful valley with hills on three sides. The village appealed to me. The cottages built in traditional limestone make it so picturesque. I stayed in a small hotel overnight and the following morning, in the local paper, the shop and cottage were advertised. The idea of a gallery had constantly come to me, so on impulse I gave it a go.'

'That simple?'

Jenny nodded. 'The day I looked around the shop and cottage, the local builder Kevin had been called in by the estate agent because a window had been damaged. I met him for the first time. He gave me his card. Even though he didn't know me, he was friendly. Once the deal had been confirmed, I rang him and arranged for him to renovate the shop and cottage.'

Dan gave a small nod. 'He did a good job. What was he like?'

'I liked him. Lively, polite, although he made a few cheeky comments but with light-hearted humour. His work showed a high standard of vigilance towards safety, so it shocked me to find him dead that morning.'

'Did many people know he had been working at Victoria House where he died?'

Jenny paused for a sip of wine while she mulled over his question. The unexplained death seemed to recede to television drama rather than everyday life. Setting her glass down, she reluctantly refocused her mind, 'I can see your mind is ticking over whether it's an accident or deliberate. Everyone in the village would have seen him on the roof. He replaced the tiles before he started on the outside paintwork.'

'Did he work alone?'

'No, with two men, but they were not from the village. Nicolas and Amanda wanted a quick finish.'

The starters were cleared, and the wine was topped up. Jenny leaned back in her chair and allowed her gaze to wander around the restaurant. Two chandeliers glistened, sending shafts of light around the room and in the grate an enormous log fire crackled. The laughing and chattering diners and the opulent surrounding was not the place for a morose conversation. With a firm resolution and a show of positiveness that she somehow didn't feel, she turned to her handsome companion.

'Let's change the subject.' She tilted her head and treated him to a searching gaze. What have you been up to?'

'It must be a couple of years since we've met, but nothing has happened to me during that time. Unlike you, my life has been humdrum with no exciting stories to relate.'

Jenny mulled this over and, with exaggerated care, scanned her memory. 'When you rang to say you would visit, I guessed there might be some exciting news, as you had a girlfriend the last time we were together at the garrison.'

He shook his head and eyed her thoughtfully. 'It lasted for a while, but didn't work out, so we agreed to go our separate ways. When I received your letter about your new gallery, it prompted me to apply for leave, so I could come and say hello.'

Jenny tried to keep the question light, while inwardly her stomach tensed. 'You will stay more than a couple of days, won't you?' Her voice shook, which betrayed her anxiety. His timely arrival this morning had helped her through a difficult situation, and she didn't want him to leave. Facing the next challenge from the police would be easier with Dan. Was she being selfish, wanting him to stay and help her? Holding her breath, she waited for his reply.

'I'd love to Jenny,' he treated her to a soothing smile, 'apart from one trip to London, I can stay around until you become fed up with me.' His expression changed.

The smile vanished, and he leaned forward, and his eyes focused intently on her face. 'Before I leave, I want to see you out of this mess.'

Jenny exhaled with relief and a smile of gratitude filled her face. 'Thanks, I appreciate your support.' Her words sounded hopelessly inadequate. She could have hugged him. His support and belief in her meant a great deal.

Their conversation was interrupted by Tanya, who cleared the empty plates from the table. 'I'm afraid your arrest has spread around the village.'

Jenny laughed, 'I guessed it might, especially as it took place in the middle of Market Square.'

Tanya expertly balanced the plates and cutlery on her outstretched arm. As she picked up the last serving dish, she paused. 'Well, at least it wasn't the only unusual thing to happen in the village today.'

Jenny's interest was awakened, and she tilted her head in an enquiring gesture.

'Elizabeth was ill today and the post office didn't open on time. A temporary post office official arrived and took over.' Tanya shook her head in disbelief. 'Her absence came as a surprise.'

Jenny was becoming more curious by the minute. 'Well,' Tanya glanced over her shoulder and lowered her voice, 'Elizabeth appeared confused and disorientated yesterday. She seemed agitated; her face was pale, and her eyes were dull as though she'd had a shock. She couldn't concentrate, gave me the wrong change and had three attempts before I received the correct money.'

Jenny digested this information without comment, although she could guess the reason. Catching Lionel and

Elizabeth together yesterday morning must have caused her to react in such an uncharacteristic manner. Had it been a shock at being discovered or was she worried that Jenny would spread the details of the encounter around the village? Jenny had intended avoiding Elizabeth and Lionel, but perhaps it would be better if she talked to her.

As Jenny and Dan left the restaurant and strolled back to Market Square, the church clock chimed nine. The company of her old friend, coupled with delicious food in such elegant surroundings, had made it a memorable evening. Now that Dan had confirmed he would stay, she hoped they might have many more pleasurable evenings together. While he maintained he led a boring life, he always had an interesting story to tell.

On their way, they met Clayton leaving his house to walk his dog. After Jenny had introduced them, Dan accompanied him, having already made friends with the enthusiastic tail wagging black Labrador called Jet.

25

Jenny left Dan and Clayton to walk together and knocked on the door of Elizabeth's flat.

'Who is it?'

'Jenny. I've come for a chat.' A long pause followed when Jenny remained uncertain whether she could enter. Several bolts were pulled back, the door inched open, and Elizabeth peered out. Jenny stepped into the small hall before Elizabeth reacted. Once inside, she closed the door behind her with a resounding click. She had no intention of being sympathetic towards this pathetic woman but would encourage her out of this sudden change of behaviour.

'You look awful.' Jenny followed Elizabeth into the small lounge of her flat, where a standard brown three-piece suite dominated the room. A black television perched in the corner and a small electric fire glowed in the grate. The word drab came to mind, a lifeless room with no colour. Jenny was shocked by Elizabeth's pallor. With her hollow sunken eyes and dishevelled appearance, she could have passed for an old age pensioner.

'I'm ill, can't you see?' Her voice sounded high and tight. Jenny didn't wait for an invitation and sat in an armchair. Elizabeth perched on the edge of the couch.

Jenny forced a smile and compelled her voice to sound cheery. 'What's the matter with you?'

'I'm ill.'

'No, I don't think you are.' Jenny pursed her lips in disapproval and peered across at the dowdy woman. 'I think you are tearing yourself apart about yesterday morning, because I found you and Lionel kissing in the storeroom.'

Elizabeth cowered, as though withdrawing herself into a shell. 'No, I'm ill,' she whimpered. She jerked her head up, her eyes wide. 'Have you told anyone?'

'Don't be ridiculous, Elizabeth! Can you tell me one piece of gossip or rumour that I have passed on to you since I've been in the village?'

Elizabeth shook her head. 'But you might say something by accident.'

Jenny smiled, 'I've never mentioned my background as there is no reason for people to know, but it's no secret. During my last twenty years in the army, I have been in practically all the major war zones where there have been British troops. At such times, you do not speak inadvertently. In the places where I've worked, a misplaced word could cost lives.' Jenny paused, allowing Elizabeth time to absorb the information. 'However, please don't spread my military involvement around the village.'

'I wouldn't dream of spreading the information. When someone works in the post office, you respect privacy.' A prim smile appeared on her lips.

Jenny smiled, 'Now what's the matter? Come on, tell me?'

'It might ruin my reputation!'

'Elizabeth!' It might be deemed cruel, but she couldn't stop herself from the spontaneous laughter. 'You are a single woman and make your own decisions. If you wish to take a lover, then that is your choice. If the man is married, you might bring some troubles to yourself if his wife finds out, but beyond that it is up to you how you conduct your life.'

'Yes, well...' but her voice trailed away, and she puffed out her cheeks while her face clouded with concern. 'We've tried to be discreet.'

'I suggest you lock the door next time.'

'There will be no next time.' She crossed her arms across her chest, and her expression morphed into an indignant frown. 'Lionel doesn't believe you will tell anyone.'

'He's right, Elizabeth,' she gazed across at the woman huddled on the sofa and her eyes narrowed with determination. She didn't have any pity for her as she'd brought the situation on herself. Keeping her voice cool, 'So, sort yourself out, and open the post office as normal tomorrow. No one will know unless you tell them.'

Jenny became convinced that after a night's sleep, Elizabeth would be back in the shop the following day. A silence stretched between them. Elizabeth's eyes glazed as though deep in thought, and she rubbed a hand across her forehead. She lifted her head and in a quiet but steady voice, 'Thank you, Jenny. What a dear friend you are.'

Jenny patted Elizabeth's hand. 'Come on! Back to normal tomorrow, Elizabeth.'

A definite nod, and then a small smile appeared on Elizabeth's face. Jenny stood. 'Did I see a police car take you away this morning?'

'Yes,' she chuckled, 'it's no secret as I climbed into the police car in the middle of Market Square.' Supplying a little information presented itself as the best approach, as then no one would become suspicious. She squared her shoulders, and a resigned sigh escaped from her lips. 'As you know, I found Kevin's body. The police took a brief statement, but required a more detailed account.'

'Is there anything suspicious, then?' Elizabeth gasped and her hand flew to her mouth.

'Stop being so melodramatic. Kevin had been at work and fell from the scaffolding, so it counts as an industrial death, which means Health and Safety, police and the coroner are all involved. They need full statements.'

'I'm glad he's dead!' Elizabeth muttered as she stared down at the floor.

Jenny's mind whirled as the shock of the words took hold and she gaped in open mouthed astonishment. 'That's a terrible thing to say.'

'I hated him.' An animalistic growl emerged from her shaking body and she put her head in her hands. Jenny stared with disbelief at her outburst. Dropping her hands from her face, Elizabeth rocked slowly backwards and forwards, moaning quietly to herself.

Jenny waited.

Elizabeth raised her head and an intense, fevered stare covered her face. 'I didn't like him. He was a hateful, vindictive man.'

Jenny's mind raced. Something terrible must have happened.

'He tried to blackmail me.' She clasped her hands together in her lap and her face clouded with concern.

'Had he seen you and Lionel together?' She shook

her head and her shoulders slumped.

'Come on Elizabeth. Are you sure you're not blowing an insignificant incident out of all proportions? I find it hard to believe that you have done something that would warrant blackmail.'

Elizabeth hesitated, and her eyes darted around the room. 'It concerned me and Tony.'

'Tony the farmer?' Jenny's voice rose as she stared across in disbelief at the huddled female. Jenny had a problem believing Elizabeth could have two affairs. Her drab clothes and old fashioned approach made it seem farfetched.

She glanced up and must have noticed the expression on Jenny's face. 'Don't look like that, Jenny. I'm not having an affair with Tony.'

Jenny took a deep breath and rubbed a hand across her forehead as confusion swept through her. 'I don't understand.'

'It concerns the Village Players.' Elizabeth had a gleam in her eye. 'It's the local amateur dramatic group. Every autumn we put on a production and last year Tony and I played the leading roles.' Her jaw lifted and a proud smile played across her lips. 'As we were both determined to play the parts to the best of our ability, we spent a lot of time together besides the normal rehearsals. Our parts were those of two lovers and we had to kiss in the last scene, although by mutual agreement we intended leaving that to the dress rehearsal.' There was nothing to it. I don't like him, but he is a talented actor.

Every time Kevin came into the post office, he kept hinting he'd seen us in each other's arms. His choice of words became both embarrassing and suggestive. He kept hinting about the scandal that would spread through the village if information about Tony and me became news. In the end, I lost my temper and slapped him hard across the face. He had a nasty black eye afterwards, but told everyone he'd walked into a door on one of his jobs.' Elizabeth squirmed in her seat.

'Is that the complete story?'

'No, the following evening I came back from Amanda's house. I often visit when Nic is away. Kevin came out of The George, staggered across to me reeking of beer, then pinned me against the wall and tried to kiss me. He threatened that if I didn't go to bed with him, he would tell the village about me and Tony. That's blackmail.'

'Did you free yourself from him?'

Elizabeth nodded, 'Fortunately Clayton came out of his house with his dog, which meant that Kevin couldn't keep me there.'

'It sounds a nasty and unsettling experience. No wonder you didn't like him.'

'I hated him,' she snarled.

Jenny didn't want any further revelations from Elizabeth, so she would leave.

'Go to bed Elizabeth, have a good night's rest, and I will see you in the shop tomorrow.'

As Jenny walked back across the square to her cottage, she wondered whether Kevin had tried his tricks with other women in the village. Had he tried to blackmail Elizabeth? If so, did he try to blackmail anyone else? His behaviour seemed such a contrast to the fun loving and cheeky man she had known. Did he have a dark side? Perhaps he hoped to persuade Elizabeth into bed or inflict revenge on Tony, the person he disliked the most.

26

Jenny had gone to bed by the time Dan returned from his late evening walk, so they didn't chat until breakfast the following morning. Over coffee and toast, Dan revealed a snippet of information he had gleaned on his walk with Clayton the previous evening. 'A friend of Clayton's helped Kevin with the roof at Victoria House. Safety had been emphasised, and there would be an instant sack for anyone with a smell of alcohol. He confirmed Kevin would never have left bits of rope on the scaffolding boards and the ladder would never be without a gate.'

Jenny recounted the details of her visit to Elizabeth, emphasising the notion of blackmail, which to Jenny appeared farfetched in the bright light of morning, sitting in her cosy kitchen.

'What do you think, Dan?' Jenny stared across the breakfast table at him.

Munching thoughtfully on his toast, 'Blackmail is not something that's arisen about Kevin before, so we cannot jump to conclusions. Perhaps Elizabeth misconstrued his meaning. We need to keep an open mind. However, there seems to be enough evidence to conclude that he didn't drink while working. Also, with the scaffolding, he would have put safety first. The only conclusion can be a deliberate killing. However, that opens new difficulties and questions.'

He rested his elbows on the table and his eyes narrowed in concentration. 'Why was he there if not working? I'm assuming that the body hadn't been moved, and the fall killed him. Another mystery is the scaffolding gate at the top of the ladder. It could have been missing, but why wouldn't he replace it? Also, why would someone want to steal a paint pot and a flask?'

Jenny huffed out a sigh of exasperation. Too many questions, but no answers. She remained silent, mulling over the scene in her mind. 'The dangling ropes could have been placed after he had been killed.'

Dan's expression stalled and became serious. 'But how do you plan someone's death like that? Perhaps it was an opportunist killing rather than a planned murder?'

Jenny took another piece of toast. 'I presume the interest in me is because I was there, near the time of death, and then I also found the body.'

'Yes, but I can't see the police could make a case against you. They wouldn't be able to find a motive, and your presence would be circumstantial.' Dan paused and inhaled deeply. 'I'm convincing myself that it's most likely to be an accident and not a premeditated act of murder.'

Jenny pursed her lips. 'But he was meticulous about safety.'

'I had one case where stress caused the death.' He leant back in his chair and his brows knitted into a frown. 'A female business manager worked on a military site for a contractor, which is how I became involved. Well organised, she appeared to have a happy marriage with two kids. Then one day she'd found out her husband had been having an affair. The next day, she went to work as usual. She attended a colleague's birthday drink in the bar. A quiet woman she sat in the corner chatting. Her normal way. A little later, as she drove home, she hit a tree and was killed.'

'A tragic accident?'

'A long way over the limit. That morning she had bought two half bottles of vodka and had been drinking them at her desk.'

Jenny gave a small slow nod. 'So you think something must have happened in Kevin's life to cause him to abandon his normal routine.'

'Yes, that's certainly one line I would investigate.' Dan's expression became serious. 'I told you I had business in London. While the police are pursuing your statement, why don't I go there? I can return by tomorrow afternoon and I will stay until the matter is resolved.'

Although disappointed that he had to go, she could appreciate the logic behind his decision. She forced a smile as she piled the breakfast dishes. 'A good idea. It's a day for the gallery to be open, so I will carry on as normal.' Within ten minutes, Dan had left for Chesterfield to catch the train to London.

27

After opening the gallery, she settled at her easel. In between visitors, she had completed the portrait of Amanda and had made a second start on the painting of the viaduct. The sound of the door opening made her glance up as Lionel walked in. He nodded in greeting and attempted a small smile. Without speaking, he drifted around the gallery and had a brief look at the paintings but didn't comment.

Coming to a halt, he stared at Jenny. 'Can I have a quick word after your business is closed?'

Jenny guessed it would be personal. There would be no more customers today. She ushered Lionel through to the parlour and returned to lock the door and close the blinds. She joined him in the parlour. He hadn't sat but gazed into the yard. 'You could make something of those outbuildings.'

Jenny smiled at his back. Lionel wanted small talk before reaching his main reason for visiting but didn't have the aptitude for general chatter.

'What could I use them for?'

Lionel turned away from the window and settled himself into the vacant armchair opposite Jenny's. No smile appeared on his face, which had a stiff appearance with a gritted jaw and tired eyes. 'A teashop attached to your gallery. Let people sit to look at your paintings.'

'When I came here, I was confident that a gallery would not upset anyone in the village. A tea-shop would be a good idea, but might cause difficulties.'

'Only Tony would object, but he goes against anything that isn't his.'

'Rumours are that you wanted to open a coffee shop next door to you.'

He scowled with disapproval through narrowed eyes. 'I hope you only listen to rumours and do not pass them on.'

'I do exactly that!' Jenny responded in a confident voice.

His solemn dismal face didn't change. 'I've been trying to encourage John to take next door. As we do not need more space for the butchers, I've suggested several ideas. A delicatessen, coffee shop, bakery or even a fruit and vegetable shop.' Lionel chuckled. 'Fruit and vegetables would put Tony's nose out of joint.'

With an abruptness that surprised her, she asked without hesitation, 'You aren't friendly with Tony?'

'I've nothing against him. I've known him all my life, but he is such a pain-in-the-arse, I like to wind him up.'

Jenny hadn't expected that response. She had anticipated a reference to a long feud. Today was a different side to Lionel that Jenny had never seen before. 'What would you have done if Kevin had bought the shop?

He frowned in annoyance, but it didn't stay on his face and it returned to the usual deadpan expression. 'If he had wanted the shop, I would have outbid him. He was the only man in the village I disliked.'

Jenny ignored the venom in his voice and pushed ahead with her next question. 'Lindy still wants to go ahead, but you aren't friendly with her either. I could see that when we came into your shop together a few days ago.'

With narrowed eyes and obvious resentment, 'I didn't like Kevin. Lindy came under his influence too much for my liking. If she still wants it, that would be okay with me. She comes from a good local family and was a nice lass before she became involved with Kevin. I'd be prepared to meet her halfway.'

Once again, it hadn't been the response that Jenny had expected. A different side to Lionel had revealed itself.

She gave him a small grin. 'You didn't come to talk about the derelict shop.'

'No, I didn't.' His mouth tightened as if suppressing irritation.

Jenny didn't feel inclined to help him. He was a grown man and could deal with difficult situations.

He huffed out a long slow breath. 'You spoke with Elizabeth and promised you wouldn't tell anyone.'

'Lionel,' she shook her head bemusedly. 'It's none of my business! What people do between themselves, providing it doesn't affect me, holds no interest. I don't pass on rumours or speculation.'

Without acknowledging her response, he leant back in the chair and fixed his gaze on the ceiling. He laughed nervously. 'Elizabeth and I have known each other for years but it's only been in the last month or so...' His voice petered away. 'Ah... well.'

Shaking his head, he rose from the armchair. With his hand resting on the door handle, 'No one knows your background. I've been surprised that even Elizabeth has not persuaded you to reveal it. You're friendly with Clayton and have been to the hall to see the Colonel several times.' Jenny noted with satisfaction that Elizabeth had remained silent about her background and not passed it on to Lionel.

With a quizzical expression, 'So what do you conclude from that, Lionel?'

'You're probably ex-military.'

Jenny smiled, 'Has Millie told you?'

He shook his head. 'She is the most charming of girls. Polite and bright. The customers like her.' He gave another chuckle. 'She won't even tell me the time of day. No, she hasn't breathed a word.'

A ghost of a smile brushed her mouth. 'You are right, I'm ex-military.'

He waved his arm. 'That's good enough for me. You'll keep things to yourself if you want to.' He paused in the doorway. 'I've good quality pork chops in the shop. Why not pop over in the morning?'

Lionel didn't wait for an answer and disappeared out of the back door. Jenny drifted back into the gallery and mulled over the different side to Lionel she had witnessed. He didn't miss what happened in the village and seemed relaxed about being caught with Elizabeth. His comments about Tony showed no animosity.

A shiver ran through Jenny as her mind wandered away from the village politics to her own precarious position with the police. Keeping busy would help her nervousness, so she spen the remainder of the day on housework.

28

Jenny washed the windows of the gallery as she mulled over Lionel's visit and whether it would have any implications for her, but she could not think of any. As she finished and stood back to admire her gleaming handiwork, Lindy came along the pavement. 'Can I have a word?'

Jenny pointed towards the open door. 'Go through to the parlour. First right along the passage. Placing her step ladder and bucket in the gallery, she locked up, and joined Lindy, who had settled in an armchair.

'This room looks good. Your furniture is an excellent choice.'

'Thank you.' Jenny didn't make any further comments and waited. She didn't want to start the conversation, as she was curious to know the reason for Lindy's visit.

'Did they arrest you yesterday?'

Jenny smiled. 'Why do you think they arrested me?'

'A neighbour who crossed the Square had been convinced you were arrested.' Jenny went to dismiss it, when Lindy added, 'She used to be a policewoman, so she recognised the signs.'

Jenny's heart sank, as there was no point in prevaricating. A flush crept across her cheeks as the reality of the situation hit home. 'I'll be honest with you, Lindy. It is more than a witness.' Worry tinged her voice and her whole body tensed. 'How they have reached the conclusion that I'm involved is beyond me, but I've had to engage a solicitor.' Taking a deep breath, she fixed her gaze on Lindy's face. 'Although the police suspect me, I had nothing to do with his death, but if you want to leave, I understand.'

Lindy leaned back in the chair and gave a dismissive flap of her hand. 'I'd prefer to stay, as I cannot see how or why you could be involved.' Despite Lindy's words, Jenny wanted to offer some explanation.

'The night before his death, I went for a walk and passed Victoria House and then I found the body the following morning.'

Lindy shook her head. 'You've only recently arrived in the village, so what motivation would you have?' She gave a sudden gurgle of laughter.

Jenny couldn't fathom what she found amusing about Kevin's death and her involvement with the police. 'The police minds work in strange ways.' Lindy rolled her eyes skywards. 'Perhaps they think you offered yourself to Kevin, and he turned you down. So, you sought the revenge of rejection.' She finished with a theatrical wave of her hand.

Jenny laughed. 'It isn't true, but the police might think it is a reason.'

Without hesitation Lindy responded with a harsh edge to her voice, 'If they had known Kevin, they would not consider it a possibility!'

Jenny, intrigued by her remark, gave her a quizzical

look. 'What do you mean?'

'He would never turn down a woman.' Jenny studied her carefully, but didn't reply. 'I married him, although he had been a womaniser for years. In my youthful ignorance, I considered myself privileged when he picked me out and asked me to marry him. Although he promised me he would be faithful, he had another hidden aspect to his character.'

Jenny frowned in confusion. She was discovering more facts about Kevin, and most were not complimentary. What would she find out next?

Lindy's chin trembled. 'Kevin was highly sexed. His sexual appetite was insatiable, and he wouldn't leave me alone. In the end, it caused a lot of arguments.'

Jenny remained silent while she absorbed this new snippet of information as Lindy struggled to compose herself. A sigh escaped Lindy's lips, and she puffed out her cheeks. 'When his interest in me weakened, it usually signified he had started an affair. They didn't last long as he flitted from one flirtation to the next. We carried on normally, and I never mentioned them. I kept deciding to leave him, but then we would have a settled few weeks together and I pushed it aside, until the next time we argued.'

Jenny shuddered. How had Lindy coped with her marriage? It never failed to amaze her how people could be so deceptive. 'It's sad to hear.'

'If he had been discreet, it would have been bearable,' her mouth compressed into a hard line, 'but I'm the laughingstock of the village, because everyone knew about his affairs.'

'I'm sure it isn't as bad as that.' Jenny tried to make

her voice calm as a surge of pity for Lindy's obvious distress swept through her. 'I'm sorry about your marriage, but I presume you came to see me for a reason, and not just to find out whether I had been arrested.'

Lindy sniffed. 'Oh, Jenny, what must you think of me? I must sound like a scandal monger.' Scrabbling in her pocket for a handkerchief, she mopped up her tears and blew her nose. Then she straightened herself in the chair and fixed her eyes on Jenny's face.

'I miss Kevin a great deal, although he caused me many difficulties. But his death has given me a fresh start. It only struck me today that I'm on my own. I'm still young and healthy and I need to find a new direction for my life.'

Jenny gave her an encouraging smile. 'Are you still going after the shop over the road?'

'Yes, that's what I've come to talk to you about.'

Confusion surged through Jenny, 'I have no involvement with the derelict shop.'

She chuckled and her face lit up. 'I know you haven't. But it's obvious you are a clever woman who has set up in the village. There's no man about, so you must have set up the business on your own.'

A sense of pride that someone recognised her achievement gave Jenny a warm glow. 'Yes, I have.'

Lindy leaned forward with a bright-eyed expression. 'Since you came to see me that day, I took a liking to you and feel that we will become good friends.'

Jenny nodded, and her mouth crinkled into a smile. She couldn't disagree as she had also taken a liking to Lindy. Her positive attitude about moving on with her life impressed her. Today, her alertness suggested an air of firm determination to strive towards whatever goal she chose.

'Would you be prepared to give me help in organising the shop?'

This appeal for help came as a surprise to Jenny, and with an incredulous stare on her face, she gasped, 'I know nothing about building materials.'

Again, a laugh from Lindy, 'No, I understand all about them.' Her eyes twinkled with delight at Jenny's confusion. 'It's matters like the contract and what legal things are required that are a mystery to me.'

Without hesitation, Jenny responded, 'I'm most willing to help you with those issues.'

'Thanks a lot.' She clapped and a wide grin spread across her features. 'That's wonderful.'

Without warning, the enthusiasm slipped from her face to be replaced by a frown of concern. Lindy looked away, her face tight with anguish. Jenny waited, allowing the silence between them to lengthen. Lindy let out a short mirthless laugh. 'One problem about the shop is being next door to Lionel.'

After the conversation with Lionel earlier, Jenny could reassure her with confidence. 'Are you sure that Lionel has a problem with you? Wasn't his dislike just of Kevin?'

From Lindy's wide-eyed expression, she obviously hadn't considered the problem from that angle. 'See, I knew you would solve my problems.'

Jenny leaned back in her chair as her mind whirled through the complexities of Kevin's character. A sex maniac, a womaniser, and perhaps a blackmailer. The women fell for his charms, but the men detested him.

Curiosity bubbled to the surface. 'Why did Lionel and Kevin fall out?'

'Mainly to do with Amanda.' Lindy's expression stilled and became serious. 'Ever since they had been at school together, Kevin had been chasing after Amanda. They went out together for years in their late teens and gave the appearance of a couple totally besotted with each other. Everyone assumed they would be married one day. It then stopped, almost overnight, but no one found out why. I attempted to persuade Kevin to reveal what had happened, but he would never discuss it. After the break-up, Kevin and Lionel never spoke.'

Jenny mulled over Lindy's story. What had happened between Kevin and Amanda to have caused such a serious rift? Why would nobody discuss the cause of the problem? No obvious answer presented itself.

Turning her attention back to Lindy, she pondered about the best way forward to heal the rift between her and Lionel. Without doubt, they needed to talk to each other and attempt to resolve the differences between them. Keeping this in mind, she smiled at Lindy and concentrated on maintaining a calm and positive tone to her voice.

'I would guess that Lionel holds nothing against you. Would you be prepared to talk to him after the way he treated Kevin?'

Lindy paused for thought. 'Yes,' she gave an almost imperceptible nod, 'I can't think of any reason to hold a grudge against Lionel.'

'What about Elizabeth? Do you like her?'

Lindy studied her carefully, before replying and her face creased with confusion, 'Why do you ask?'

'Her post office will be your neighbour on the other side.'

Lindy didn't reply immediately and paused as though weighing up her response. 'She's a chatterbox, passes on scandal and has no sense of humour, but apart from that, she's okay. Although she is old fashioned and set in her ways. I wouldn't want much to do with her, but there's no hostility between us.'

Leaning forward in her chair, she rested her arms on her knees and her lips quirked up into a tight grin. 'You won't believe this Jenny, but I heard a rumour that recently Kevin had been chasing her. That I find difficult to believe.' She gave a throaty little laugh as she stood up and prepared to leave.

Once Lindy had left, Jenny busied herself with the last of the tidying up. All the while she mulled over village life, which kept producing mysteries and surprises. Each day brought a new revelation.

29

After a good night's sleep during which the horrors hadn't returned, she strolled across the Square to visit the butcher's and the post office. Both Lionel and Elizabeth were busy with customers. She received no special acknowledgement and they treated her as a normal customer. For Jenny, the relaxed relationship she'd originally established with them had returned.

When Lionel had been in her parlour, he was a different man. Jenny became convinced by his attitude that he had taken an opportunity with Elizabeth or that she had encouraged him. He had known her for years, but the affair had only happened recently. Elizabeth had become more of a mystery. She had been terrified of the news spreading through the village, but she had allowed him to have his hand up her skirt early in the morning in the stockroom.

Elizabeth's character worried Jenny, not helped by the former headmaster's warning. He'd advised her to avoid both Elizabeth and Lionel's family. What was behind his cautionary advice? Perhaps he lived in the past and referred to misdemeanours when they had been pupils at his school. It seemed the most obvious reason, so she dismissed his comments from her mind.

Emerging from the Post Office she bumped into Amanda with her brother John. 'I've finished the portrait and the painting of the viaduct. You can come and see them when you wish. I won't put it on display until you've had first viewing.'

'That's wonderful,' her blue eyes flashed with delight, 'can I come and see them now?'

'Yes, you are welcome.'

John leaned close to his sister's ear and whispered, but Jenny couldn't hear. Amanda nodded. 'When Nic is away I often have people to supper. Would you like to join us tonight? Elizabeth is coming. John is cooking. She smiled affectionately across at her brother and patted his arm. We can catch up on the news because we've hardly spoken recently.'

Normally, Jenny would have declined the invitation. Three women chatting wouldn't be her scene, although John would add a modicum of normality, but it presented an opportunity to ferret out a better insight into Amanda. Her curiosity had been aroused by Lindy's story. What had happened between Kevin and Amanda? If she'd been so close to him at one time, how did she react to his death at her house? Although now happily married, did she still hold any feelings for Kevin?

Had his death affected her more than she was prepared to admit? All these queries poured through Jenny's mind at lightning speed. Too many unanswered questions. With a discreet cough she attempted to suppress the chuckle of amusement which bubbled up at her over vivid imagination and her insatiable curiosity.

Also, it would be an opportunity to observe Elizabeth and discover whether she had calmed down.

She gave Amanda a wide beaming smile. 'I'd be delighted to come?'

John glanced at his watch. 'I'll see you later, sis. I must rush.' He wrapped his arms around her and gave her a hug. 'I'll pick up meat for tonight and see if dad wants help.' With a cheery wave of his hand, he strode away across Market Square.

Jenny and Amanda strolled the short distance towards the gallery. They turned down the track leading to the back door, Jenny paused at the gate, 'Your big brother is affectionate to you.'

Amanda smiled, 'He always has been since we were at school. Then he protected me, and nothing has changed.' A soft expression covered her face as she spoke about him.

Jenny concluded they had a close relationship. Twisting the key in the lock, she led the way along the short passage and opened the door to the parlour.

'Sit down,' she waved her arm in an inviting gesture. Make yourself comfortable and I'll fetch the paintings from the cupboard in the gallery.'

Jenny unwrapped them from the storage plastic. She then carried them with care and joined Amanda in the parlour, who stared out the window. Amanda took the portrait of herself and examined it in the daylight from the window.

Jenny fidgeted wondering what her reaction would be. Her stomach clenched in apprehension. Perhaps she wouldn't like it. After what seemed like a protracted silence during which Jenny almost held her breath. Amanda raised her eyes from the portrait. 'It is totally perfect.

I love it to bits. It will look good in my lounge.' Jenny smiled, and a sense of pride coursed through her.

With a large intake of breath, Jenny handed her the picture of the viaduct. Once again, she examined it in the natural light from the window, taking her time and angling the canvas in a range of different directions while she studied it. 'Excellent, I will have both. The colours in it are superb and the river detail is perfect. I shall hang this in the lounge as well. It's far too wonderful to hang in the salon where I'd originally intended to display it.'

She placed it carefully on the small table next to the portrait. How much do I owe you?'

'Shall we say sixty pounds each? A small flush crept across Jenny's cheek. 'Is that okay? I started the gallery with most at eighty. But we're almost neighbours and so I've reduced the price.'

Amanda pushed a lock of her long blonde hair back over her shoulder and gave her a dazzling smile. 'Sixty for each is perfect for me. It's generous of you, Jenny, to sell such lovely paintings, at such a bargain price.' Jenny wrapped them and as Amanda carried them across Market Square, a sense of pride settled on her as she stood in the doorway of her gallery.

Bad news arrived from Dan in the mid-afternoon. He would remain in London for another night. Jenny would have been happier if he had returned. If the horrors came tonight, she would busy herself with letter writing rather than going out for a late-night walk.

Her curiosity had increased as the time approached to visit Victoria House, and her mind roamed around a range of different scenarios for the split between Kevin and

Amanda all those years ago. Would she ever know? If Lindy hadn't been able to prise it out of Kevin, then the chances of her finding out were non-existent.

Imagining herself as a modern Miss Marple, she walked down the road to Victoria House with a spring in her step. In her usual style, she arrived on time and entered the front garden for the first time since discovering Kevin's body. A shiver passed through her, but as expected, it looked completely different. The house security lights were on, which lit both the house and the garden in artificial pools of light which bleached out any colour. The scaffolding and the rest of the builder's equipment had gone. The garden had been tidied and renovated to remove all traces of the tragedy.

Amanda opened the door, as soon as Jenny rang the bell, with a radiant smile. Her blonde hair gleamed in the light from the hall chandelier. As always, she appeared immaculate, a smart blue pencil skirt topped with a patterned silky blouse. She ushered Jenny inside with an elaborate wave of her arm. 'We're in the lounge. Your pictures are up!' she spoke with enthusiasm.

A voice from along the passage called out, 'Good evening, Jenny.'

John, in a striped cook's apron, peered out of a door further along the hallway and waved a greeting with a large wooden spoon. The most animated and smiling she had ever seen him. Jenny appreciated the design and decoration of the hall. As soon as she entered the lounge, her eyes were drawn to her paintings, which had been hung in prominent locations, and each had a small spotlight to show them at their best. Her heart swelled with pride as she gazed with a combination of surprise and delight at her handiwork.

With reluctance, she turned away from her pictures as Elizabeth stood to greet her. While she had dressed up for the evening, her clothes were the same dated style she wore in the shop. A thick woollen skirt was topped with a shapeless beige cardigan tightly buttoned up to the neck. Jenny considered her inappropriately dressed for a room with a roaring log fire. She wore a little make-up. A smear of pale lipstick and blue eyeshadow.

'Hello, Jenny, it's good to see you.' A small smile appeared, but her voice lacked warmth. The greeting seemed rehearsed and stilted, but Jenny smiled and accepted a gin and tonic from Amanda. Settling down at one end of a large maroon leather Chesterfield sofa, she placed her drink on the light oak coffee table conveniently placed at the side. Amanda sat elegantly, legs crossed in the armchair next to the fire, on the opposite side to Elizabeth.

John popped his head around the door. 'Elizabeth,' he flashed her a charming smile, 'I could do with a hand. Can you spare a moment?'

The speed of Elizabeth's movement caught Jenny by surprise. In an instant, she leapt from her chair, scurried across the room and took the offered apron. Despite the closed door, Jenny heard their animated chatter as they went towards the kitchen. Relaxing back, she listened to the crackle of the log fire while she sipped her gin and tonic. After a brief silence, Amanda put another log on the fire and then turned her attention to Jenny.

'John, Elizabeth and myself often meet when Nic is away. Elizabeth loves to help John, so it's always great to have another guest.

'She seems most willing to assist him.'

Amanda laughed. 'That's because she's still hoping.'

'Hoping for what?'

'John took Elizabeth out a few times, but nothing came of it. Then he met a woman from Braxton and had a long-term affair. Since his romance broke off, she's hopeful he might renew his interest in her. It's a possibility, as they were close at one time.' Amanda then laughed and her finger twirled around a wispy tendril from her hair and her blue eyes twinkled with merriment. 'However, he has taken a real liking to you.'

Jenny's eyes widened, and she focused on taking a long sip from her gin and tonic to hide her surprise. Taken aback, she was certain that Amanda was mistaken. He was far too young.

Amanda smiled in genuine amusement. 'He doesn't give much away, even to me, but he's my brother so I recognise the symptoms. His normal expression is a frown, but he smiles at you. So, don't be surprised if he asks you out, unless that chap who I noticed yesterday is your man.'

Her words hung in the air. She stared, trying to gauge the level of seriousness behind Amanda's words, but other than a mischievous grin, she gave nothing away. Had John instructed his sister to find out for him? A flush of embarrassment crept across her cheeks. She didn't want John's attention. Her breath caught in her throat as she replied to Amanda's question. 'The man you referred to is a friend called Dan, who I have known for years. He's on holiday for a few weeks so he has come to visit me, although he's returned to London for a few days on urgent business.'

Amanda leaned forward; her eyes narrowed to slits of glimmering blue. 'While we are on our own, Jenny.'

Her voice sounded low and mysterious. 'There is a rumour you were arrested.'

'No, when they took the initial statement, they informed me a more extensive account would be required later. So, they came to fetch me.' The lie tripped effortlessly as nothing would induce her to admit the truth to Amanda. Jenny offered some information. 'The police were particularly interested, as I came past the previous evening on a late-night stroll. You weren't at home, because the security lights didn't come on when I walked along the pavement at the front of the house.'

'No, you're right, I wasn't at home. Nic's trip aboard was cancelled on his way to the airport, so he went to Birmingham and I packed and followed him. She leaned back in her chair and stretched her legs out in front of the roaring fire. 'The security lights need adjusting as they do light up when people walk along the street. It must annoy neighbours. If we're away, then we turn them off. John and Elizabeth decide between them who will check the house each day.'

Jenny's thought slid back to the finding of Kevin's body. Would it be possible to check the house without noticing a dead body on the lawn? Neither John nor Elizabeth would bother to check the house on the day that Nic and Amanda went away. Therefore, they would have discovered the body the next day if she hadn't found it early in the morning. Amanda left Jenny to put the final touches to the dining room.

The laughter that came from the kitchen signalled that John and Elizabeth were enjoying themselves. Vivid impressions had come back to her as she entered the garden this evening about the crumpled, lifeless form lying on the grass. Shaking her head, she pushed the thoughts away. Would the police solve the mystery of Kevin's death? Apprehension settled on her and she wanted Dan to return to give her a feeling of security. Matters with the police, she would leave to Henry.

As she wandered back home full of good food, her mind wandered over the events of the evening. Amanda had been the perfect hostess, full of chatter and amusing stories, but Elizabeth's behaviour had been interesting. She'd only had eyes for John and had giggled like a schoolgirl every time he spoke to her. Why had she been in a passionate embrace with Lionel when it appeared so obvious this evening that John fascinated her? Had she intended stringing father and son along at the same time? Surely not. Revelations about the characters in the village were coming thick and fast. It might be a sleepy quaint village on the surface, but underneath that veneer, passions and hostilities abounded.

30

After another restful night, Jenny rose early to a bright, sunny morning. Her resolve to leave the investigation to the police hadn't changed. Dan would return later today, and she had every intention of being the perfect hostess and showing him the local countryside. Dan liked early morning walks and would be ready before dawn. That would give them nearly four hours to have a walk before opening the gallery.

The small clock in the kitchen chimed seven o'clock. To allow more spare time when he returned, she would complete jobs in the house and gallery for three hours before opening. A dusty blowy day yesterday had covered the gallery windows with a small sheen. They required cleaning so passers-by could see her pictures and be tempted in. Within a few minutes, she had the steps set up in the morning sunshine.

As she neared the end of her hard work, she stopped at the top of the ladder to give her arms a rest. The sight of someone running caught her eye. Coming along the track from the farm shop, a figure in a tight black outfit appeared. The runner's head had been covered in a close fitting black woollen hat. It brought back memories of the break-in at the gallery. Was she being too fanciful? Many people do their early morning jog in black tops and leggings.

When the darkened figures had run away across the field, the one shape gave the impression of a woman. The taller one could have been either sex. She hadn't mentioned the recollection to the police because she couldn't be sure. The runner now approached the Square. It was Jacqui, Tony's wife. Jenny came down the ladder and waved.

Jacqui gave an enthusiastic wave back and changed direction, jogging towards her. As Jacqui pulled off her black woollen hat, she flicked her head to release her hair, which tumbled down over her shoulders. She came to a halt near to Jenny but didn't breathe heavily from her exertions and slid off a small rucksack she had on her back.

Jacqui grinned, 'I'm glad I've met you as there is a question I would like to ask, but it might need a bit of explaining.'

'Okay. Are you ready for a drink? Or have you just started?'

'I've been up past Stanton House already, so I've done enough for today, so a cup of tea would be wonderful.'

'Come in.' Jenny put the ladder, bucket and cloths into the yard, and then led Jacqui into the passage and pointed to the parlour.

'Sit in there. I'll make some tea and then we can chat.'

Within minutes, Jenny walked into the parlour with two steaming mugs of tea. Jacqui zipped up her rucksack. 'What is it you wanted to ask me?'

'It's delicate, but have you had an argument with

Tony?'

The question took Jenny by surprise. 'No. I've hardly seen him for a while. Why do you ask?'

'Well, he talked about you frequently after you moved in and had suggestions about your work, as he liked your paintings. He would let you settle in, and then see if you wanted to paint some local farming pictures, which we could sell in the shop.'

'It's an interesting idea,' Jenny nodded, 'although I don't paint quickly. However, I've hardly seen him recently as he doesn't use the gate.'

Jenny raked through her memory, but couldn't recall the last time that she had spoken to Tony. It seemed strange, as she'd chatted to him on many occasions when she'd first arrived as he negotiated his way through the farm gate. Had she upset him? If so, what had she done?

Jacqui gave a loud sigh, 'Tony becomes stubborn. He argues with people and it can take years before he will speak to them again. Sometimes I can coax him out of a mood, but I need to know what has happened.' Jacqui stood up and picked up her rucksack in readiness to leave.

As they walked across the yard, an idea formed in Jenny's mind. 'You must run regularly as you were hardly puffed when you arrived.'

Jacqui nodded as she adjusted the straps on her rucksack.

'Has Tony ever been into sport?'

'He used to be a keen athlete although he no longer enters races, but he will come with me for a jog, if he's not busy.'

Jenny had assumed the burglars were relatively young because they could run, but Tony had a small, wily frame.

Could her unwanted visitors have been Tony and Jacqui? What a thought!

The roar of a tractor as it entered Market Square from the main road made both Jacqui and Jenny turn their heads. Jacqui waved to her husband, who pulled up near to the track. He turned off the engine, and the Square returned to quiet again, but he didn't dismount from his cab and remained seated. After a long pause, he climbed down and strolled towards them. 'Hello, Jenny.' No smile accompanied the greeting, and his face remained impassive.

Jenny smiled. 'Good morning, Tony. When Jacqui came through the Square about twenty minutes ago, I persuaded her to stop for a mug of tea.'

A feeble grin appeared, but he didn't speak.

Jacqui glanced between them, 'Tony, I've just had a wonderful idea! Why don't we invite Jenny over for dinner tonight as we have other guests?'

Was this a deliberate ploy from Jacqui to gauge the reaction from her husband?

Before he could respond, Jenny interrupted, 'What a kind invitation, but I must refuse, as I've a former colleague staying with me. He's been in London for a few days but is returning this afternoon.'

Jacqui gave a cheeky grin to them both, 'That's perfect, he can come as well.'

Jenny hesitated, as she didn't want to go and would prefer a quiet night with Dan. The idea of them being the burglars still niggled in her thoughts.

'Tanya, Clayton's wife is cooking for us so another two guests won't be a problem. She doesn't worry how many people come to dinner provided she knows in advance. So can you be persuaded?

Tony stared intently and a slight smile appeared at the corners of his mouth. 'If you have made prior arrangements, we would understand. It would be good if you could come.'

Jenny had the strange idea that Tony wanted to speak to her. What was behind his unusual behaviour? Had she upset him?

She gave a beaming smile. 'We would be delighted to come.'

Jacqui scrabbled around in her rucksack then tutted, 'I've left my hat in your parlour.'

As Jenny expected, Tony strode towards the door, calling over his shoulder, 'I'll fetch it!'

After what appeared a long time, he returned, clutching the hat in his hand. 'Couldn't find it. You must have knocked it with your foot, because it was out of sight under the chair. I had to crawl around on the floor before I found it.'

Following dinner, Tony placed his empty coffee cup on the table and stared across at Jenny. 'Would you like to see the paintings in my study?

'Yes, I'd be delighted.' Glancing at Dan, he had become fascinated during dinner with Sandra, Jacqui's sister. She would talk to Tony alone.

As she entered the study, her eyes scanned the watercolours hung on the wall. Tony stood in the middle of the room with his hands shoved into his trouser pockets, shifting from one foot to another, while Jenny took her time examining the pictures. Two local landscapes and an interesting portrait of a black and white sheepdog. The artist had captured the alertness in the dog's eyes. It impressed her, as eyes were difficult to paint.

Tony gave an apologetic cough. 'I wanted to catch you alone to apologise.'

'What for?'

'When you asked me about Kevin's funeral. I snapped at you and drove off. You haven't been in the village long and didn't realise the friction that existed between us. It had been insensitive of me, as you clearly liked him.'

'What gave you the impression that I liked him?'

'One day when I pulled up by the gate, you and Kevin were laughing and he had his arm around your shoulders.'

Had Tony misconstrued a friendly gesture? The conversation was cut short as Jacqui called out, 'Are you there, Tony? Tanya is about to leave, and we need to pay her.'

31

As Dan and Jenny returned to the village, they passed the old railway station and took the path that would pass Victoria House. Dan would be able to see where Kevin's body had been found. Jenny puffed up the incline. 'When we reach the top of the hill, walk slowly. It's only for a few yards that the house and garden come into view. After that most of it is obscured by the fence.'

As they neared the top of the small hillock, distant angry voices filled the air. The noise came from over the hill. They peered through the bushes. Two men stood on a track at the far side of Victoria House from the footpath. Dan and Jenny stood motionless.

Dan pointed, 'I recognise Tony, and I presume that's his tractor outside the field gate.

'Yes, he owns the field.'

'The other man, Nicolas, is the owner of the house. His wife, Amanda, runs the hairdresser's shop across the road. Nicolas wants to divert this path across the field as he finds it intrusive, but Tony has refused.'

The wind blew away the words, but the men gestured towards the field. She pointed. 'The tractor has a plough. Does he intend to plough the field? It will create a mess near Victoria House. The path down the side of the building will become a quagmire as the first part of the footpath from here skirts the edge of Tony's field. They use the path to go in the side gate.'

The men shouted and the gap between them closed. Nicolas raised his fist. Tony took a swing with his fist, but Nicolas ducked. Hitting the top of his head, Tony yelped in pain. Nicolas staggered back bumping into his own car. He rushed Tony, who put his hands up to protect his face. Several blows hit him in the stomach. He collapsed back against his tractor. The power of the man, twenty years younger, became clear. Hit again, Tony buckled and slumped to the ground by the tractor wheels. Nicolas jumped into his car and drove away.

'I will help Tony,' Jenny moved away, 'while I do that, will you ring the police?'

Dan caught her arm. 'Give it a minute.'

Tony pulled himself to his feet and picked up his red tartan flat cap, which had fallen off in the scuffle. He moved gingerly but gained confidence. He opened the gate to the field. Dan grimaced. 'Let's not bother the police.'

'But we witnessed the assaults.'

He grinned at her. 'We've been here before! How many servicemen have you treated for injuries that had been sustained in a fight, but they come up with a reason, such as I shut my hand in a door?'

Jenny nodded.

The tractor roared into life and moved forward into the field. It halted momentarily as the hydraulics from the tractor moved the plough into the correct position.

To avoid meeting Tony, they retraced their steps and

returned to the village. After a coffee at the Manor, they drifted back to the cottage.

Tony's tractor pulled into the Square as they arrived. It no longer had the plough attached. Jenny waved. 'I'll pop over and thank him for the dinner last night.'

Tony waved back, and a broad smile appeared as she approached him. Turning off the loud tractor engine, he climbed down from the cab.' His brown trilby hat sported a large pheasant's feather tucked into the bright green trim. As he reached ground level, Tony grimaced.

'What have you done to your hand? Do you want me to look at it for you?' He raised his eyebrows. 'I used to be a nurse. Come over to the gallery. I'll see if you need to visit hospital.'

Dan waited at the gallery door. 'Tony's badly hurt his hand. I will check it for him.' She guided Tony into the parlour to wait while she fetched the first aid box from the cupboard.

'How did you do it?' Dan's voice sounded friendly and casual.

'I should know better at my age, but I took my eye off an open gate. The wind caught it and the metal bar smacked into my knuckles.'

Jenny busied examining the contents of the first aid box and didn't look until the smile had disappeared. Dan had been right.

Gently, she prodded his outstretched hand, working her way methodically across each of his fingers. 'I spotted you with a plough on the back of the tractor. You don't plough many fields, do you?'

Tony gasped as she applied pressure to his hand. 'Rarely, but I need livestock on Victoria field, but the grass is poor. After I've finished the ploughing, I'll mulch and water, then re-seed.

Would livestock be selected because they were noisy and would further annoy Nicolas?

She pursed her lips, 'You have broken a bone and need to visit the hospital.'

32

A moonlight walk took Jenny and Dan along the old railway track and to the hill overlooking Victoria House which stood in darkness. 'Why have we taken the same walk in the dark?'

Dan pointed, 'I'm convinced Victoria House holds the key to the mystery of Kevin's death.' Each raised their binoculars as they reached the same location, from where they had witnessed the argument earlier in the day.

'The house is on a hill, from the front of the house it has two storeys but only one at the back. So, I could walk onto the scaffold from the back garden and around the house at the level of the bedrooms at the front.' As they chatted in low voices, so the side external lights came on. They lit up the path from the side door of the house to the gate that led on to the footpath.

Jenny whispered, 'That's the main way they go in and out. Tony will be aware that the footpath will become muddy. He is waging a vendetta against Nicolas and Amanda.'

Jenny shuddered and lowered her binoculars, 'His argument is with Nicolas, but he will be happy to include Lionel's daughter as well. A minor disagreement is escalating out of control. Let's hope it results in not speaking, rather than more violence.'

Two people emerged from the side door. As they reached the light Jenny muttered, 'That's Elizabeth and John. I only thought that they went there when Nicolas was away, but his car is on the other side of the house.'

Jenny refocused her binoculars. She doubted what Amanda had hinted at the other night about John and Elizabeth resuming their relationship. It seemed an unlikely combination. Would Elizabeth be attracted to a second man as she already had Lionel?

They stepped on to the narrow public footpath and closed the garden gate behind them. With no hesitation they enveloped each other in a passionate kiss.

'I didn't expect that. This case is becoming complicated. It will take a time for the police to discover the complex relationships in this village.'

A room light came on at the back of the house. With the curtains still open giving a clear view into the room, Amanda entered and crossed to the window.

'Time to go.' Dan lowered his binoculars.

'Shall we retrace our steps, so we do not meet John or Elizabeth?'

Amanda peered out the window. Although certain they couldn't be seen, they didn't move. Jenny waited for the curtains to be drawn. Amanda while looking out of the window took off her dress and underwear. She put her hands to her face as Nicolas came into view and grabbed her. She pushed him away. He punched her in the stomach. With her back against the wall, she slid to the floor with her hand to her mouth. Nicolas turned and walked away.

'What shall we do?' Jenny rubbed her face. 'Whenever together, it appears a good relationship.'

'If we report it, she will deny what has happened. But we can't ignore it. It's not the same as the two men fighting this morning. Try to talk to her. She will wince with bruising for a few days.

'Yes, I will try to persuade her to tell me.'

33

The following morning Jenny wished to discuss the next steps with Dan but he had agreed to go walking in Dovedale with Sandra, who he'd met at the dinner, so she had the whole day to herself. It came as no surprise that Dan would be attracted to the slim and eye-catching young woman, who closely resembled her sister Jacqui.

She banged hard on the back door of the post office without checking if it was unlocked. A few minutes after, bolts scraped, and keys rattled. Elizabeth held open the door and let Jenny enter. 'There is no one else here. After such a busy day yesterday, I'm tidying the store.'

Jenny grinned at the familiar phrase, although the shop and post office rarely bustled. Only a few sacks and a couple of parcels appeared not in their right place on the shelves, 'Do you want to send a parcel?'

'No, I wanted to catch you alone to check you are now fully recovered.'

'That's kind of you. I've settled back to normal now.' She peered around, as though to check whether anyone else could be listening, 'It became too much for my nerves to have an affair with Lionel, so I've ended it. I shouldn't have agreed in the first place.'

'Why not try a man who isn't married?'

'I'm not that desperate. There have been men in my life, but I'm happy being on my own. It's my preference.'

Jenny didn't believe her. 'Amanda told me you and John were together at one time.'

'It didn't last long. He's a good man, but I'm not interested in him.'

The enthusiasm to help John in the kitchen belied her words, as did the kiss outside the gate at Victoria House. Why did she tell lies? What did she want to conceal? John was unmarried and available, so it needn't be a secret.

'Time to open up and start the day.' She busied herself picking up parcels and moved towards the shop.

Elizabeth didn't want to talk, so Jenny would bide her time and wait for another occasion. She ushered Jenny through the shop and out the front door turning the sign to open ten minutes early. Jenny stood on the pavement with a bemused smile on her face. Why would Elizabeth lie about men? There must be a reason, but she couldn't construct a suitable explanation.

What did men see in her? Dressing in a frumpy old-fashioned manner with an outdated hairstyle. she verged on being skinny without a noticeable figure. She must have some attributes that attracted men, but they were not obvious.

34

Since waking this morning she'd mulled over various approaches to meeting Amanda, although she still hadn't decided which one to take. Jenny took a deep breath, as the time approached to engage in what would be a difficult conversation. It was essential to catch Amanda on her own. As she approached the salon, no lights shone, and the closed sign showed. Undaunted, she tried the door handle, but it was locked.

As she hesitated Amanda came from her house and crossed the road. No friendly smile appeared.

'Hello, it's another half an hour before I open.' Her voice lacked its usual bounce, her hair had only quickly been combed and she wore no make-up.

Jenny smiled and edged closer to the locked door. 'Can I have a quick chat before you become involved in your business.'

'You'd better come in,' came a flat toned reply.

While she unlocked the door to the salon, Jenny studied her movements with careful concentration searching for signs of discomfort from the punch. Her movements were slow and precise and had an unnatural stiffness. It would be hard work persuading Amanda to talk. An aura of tension surrounded her this morning. Her eyes were hard and staring, her face pale and her lips pressed together in a thin straight line.

Amanda closed the door behind them, didn't offer a seat and stood waiting with her arms across her chest with no sign of friendliness.

Not a good start to such a difficult topic of conversation. Despite Amanda's unfriendly attitude Jenny couldn't walk away. With strong eye contact she broke the silence. 'I forgot to thank you for the excellent dinner I had at your house. I enjoyed my evening.'

It brought a brief hint of a nod from Amanda, 'You're welcome.' Then she moved towards the door reaching for the door handle to let Jenny out.

Dismayed by the instant dismissal. Jenny didn't want to leave until she'd discussed the injury. The task had become complicated as she hadn't anticipated a dismissive attitude from Amanda.

When she'd mulled over a likely range of scenarios before the visit, she had envisaged them sitting having a friendly chat, but it wouldn't happen.

Taking a deep breath, she forced her voice to remain firm and calm. 'May I book my next appointment, while I'm here?'

Amanda nodded and without smiling turned towards the small reception desk and opened the appointments book. Jenny joined her and together they stared down at the pages. 'Two weeks next Tuesday, at ten o'clock.'

Amanda found the correct page and noted the appointment down without speaking. Jenny would try one last tactic. Not the ideal approach. She didn't want to do it, but there would be no chat without it.

'Thanks, Amanda.' With a cheery wave of her hand, she spun round and deliberately let her shoulder bag swing loose. It cannoned into Amanda's stomach.

Amanda's yelp of pain blocked out Jenny's apology. Her face went white, tears came to her eyes and she doubled over holding onto her stomach.

'What's the matter. Come and sit down. She grasped Amanda around the shoulders and guided her to the stylist's chair away from the window. 'You're in pain and have gone white.'

'It winded me.' She grimaced as she breathed. Sweat beaded her forehead and her hands clutched her abdomen.

Jenny grabbed a small chair and positioned herself facing Amanda. 'I didn't hit you hard did I.'

'No. You didn't hit me that hard but I took a broken chair to the back yard yesterday and I didn't see a large piece of wood sticking out and walked straight into it.'

'That must have hurt. Were you sick?'

Amanda had been looking at the floor as she tried to recover but glanced up at Jenny and frowned.

'Until recently I was a nurse.'

Amanda blinked in astonishment, 'Yes I was sick almost immediately.'

She wriggled in the chair attempting to make herself more comfortable but still had a pained expression on her face. Slowly her colour returned.

Jenny patted her hand in reassurance. After her conversation with Dan, she had anticipated that there would be a plausible excuse about the injury. 'Unexpected blows to the stomach can be dangerous. Pull up your blouse. Let me have a look.'

Terror sped across Amanda's face and she hugged herself tightly. 'It's not necessary.' Her voice trembled and her eyes darted around the room as though searching for a means of escape. 'I'm feeling better.'

Jenny focused her gaze on the attractive woman in front of her. She willed herself to continue. Aggression against a defenceless female was inexcusable. 'It's either let me have a look or I will ring for an ambulance. It may need treatment, especially if you were sick.'

The stern tone of voice made Amanda hesitate. Without another word Amanda grasped the edge of her blouse with trembling fingers and pulled it slowly up.

'Can you stand?'

She struggled from the chair and held up her blouse in front of Jenny who stayed sitting. This isn't necessary.'

Jenny ignored her words and examined the area where the bruises had begun to appear.

She pressed in several places while her eyes searched Amanda's face checking for a reaction. 'You can sit down now.'

Amanda tucked her blouse into her skirt and lowered herself carefully onto the chair. She pushed her hair away from her face and glanced at the gold watch on her wrist. 'I'm busy. Your bag caught me by surprise.' She took in a deep shuddering breath. 'I've recovered now.'

'Stay where you are Amanda and tell me the truth.'

Amanda hesitated.

'The truth or I call the police.'

Tears streamed down her cheeks. She buried her face in her hands and her shoulders shook.

Jenny sat in silence and waited.

Amanda lifted her tear-stained face and sniffed,

'You're hassling me, why would you want to call the police? What have I done wrong?'

Jenny put a restraining hand on her shoulder as she started to stand up, 'For the past twenty years I have been a nurse and examining people was part of my job. A piece of wood didn't cause that bruising.'

Amanda struggled to free herself from Jenny's controlling grip. In an irritated gesture she pushed Jenny away, stood up and took a step back. Standing with her hands on her hips she glared in open defiance, her blue eyes blazing.

Jenny stood and faced her. This conversation hadn't finished yet. Like it or not she remained determined that Amanda should listen. 'Solid objects, like wood, bruise in a particular way. There would be a much deeper bruise where the edge or corner hit you. Often with solid objects you can see the shape of the object in the bruise. In your case it's a widespread bruise.' She paused allowing her words to sink in. Amanda remained silent but her eyes narrowed with resentment.

Jenny experienced a surge of pity for the troubled woman who stood before her. The memory of Nicolas's vicious attack flashed through her mind. His behaviour was unacceptable. Exhaling with exaggerated patience she pushed on with the conversation. 'There are no defined edges on your bruising, so it would have been done with a soft object.'

Amanda turned white again with sadness engraved on her face while her lower lip quivered.

Jenny gave her a long assessing look. Before speaking again, she took a step towards her and rested her hand on Amanda's arm feeling her tremble beneath the touch.

She attempted to keep the question light while inwardly Jenny's body tensed, 'Was it a fist?'

Amanda's eyes glazed over with a layer of tears, which then flowed unchecked across her face once again. Deflated, she sank back down onto a chair and her shoulders shook. Jenny fetched a tissue from the counter, gave it to Amanda, and placed a comforting hand on her shoulder. Then waited without speaking for her to recover.

She needed Amanda to admit the truth. As she calmed, Jenny whispered, 'Nicolas?'

Amanda shivered and moved to a stylist's chair without speaking. Jenny waited in silence as Amanda applied her make-up and brushed her hair. The simple automatic routines seemed to calm her. After she had packed the last of her make up into a pink bag, she swivelled round in her chair.

'He's been under enormous stress at work and that hasn't been helped by a big argument with Tony about the rerouting of the footpath near our house.' She took a deep breath and straightened her blouse with long nervous strokes. 'It's the first time. We had an acrimonious argument last night. My temper got the better of me and I lashed out at him. I slapped him hard across the face leaving a small cut on his cheek from one of my rings. As you can imagine my action helped to stoke his anger. He's never done it before and has been devastated since. Please don't tell anyone, Jenny.'

Amanda pushed herself out of the chair and straightened her skirt. She moved around the room in the pretence of tidying the already immaculate salon. Finally, she stopped and turned to face Jenny. 'It's only bruising.' she gave a dismissive sweep of her hand, which will disappear quickly. Then almost as an afterthought, 'There is nothing else wrong, is there?' Her pale face and piercing blue eyes focused on Jenny with a worried expression.

'No, I can't find any further damage,' Jenny murmured as a deep frown wrinkled her forehead, 'but you should seek advice.'

Amanda forced a smile onto her face, 'It won't be necessary as he promised he'll take a break from work and that it will never happen again.' With a huge exhalation of pent-up breath, Amanda moved across the room, unlocked the door and flipped the sign to open.

Jenny had been dismissed. She had no option but to leave.

As she walked back to the gallery Jenny considered Amanda and Nicolas. They seemed the perfect couple. Appearances could be deceptive. Why had he attacked her in that way? How many times had it happened before? From his exchange with Tony about the footpath, Nicolas had a temper. In one of their discussions, John had mentioned that Nicolas had a hostile attitude and that he'd spoken to him on several occasions, reminding him not to upset Amanda. She couldn't interfere any further, but would regularly check with Amanda, though she doubted whether she would be prepared to admit it again.

35

The banging on the door seemed excessive to Jenny, especially at seven o'clock in the morning. Unusually the noise came from the front door, local people came around the back. Jenny munched on toast and left Dan in the kitchen as she went to investigate the hammering which reverberated in the small cottage.

As she opened the door the Detective Sergeant stood on the pavement waving papers in front of her face. 'This is the re-issue of the arrest warrant for you, in connection with the death of Kevin Cartwright. And this is a search warrant for this house and the premises next door known as Watercolour Gallery.'

Dan appeared and placed a reassuring hand onto her shoulder, 'Do you want me to come with you?'

'No. I shall say nothing until Henry or one of his team are present. Can you let him, and Gerald know please? It's better that you remain here while the police conduct their search of the house and gallery.'

Dan addressed the Sergeant, 'May I examine the warrants?'

The Sergeant scowled and handed him the documents. Having read them, he gave them to Jenny, 'I will ensure Henry joins you at the police station as soon as possible.'

A woman police constable stepped into the hall and searched Jenny before escorting her to the police car waiting at the front of the house. Without a word she joined Jenny in the back of the car. As soon as the seat belts were secured the car pulled rapidly away. Jenny gazed with unseeing eyes out the window. The nightmare hadn't come to an end.

The police focus on her had intensified. Her stomach quivered as she huddled back into the seat. Why did they suspect her? Would she be able to prove her innocence? What would happen if they didn't believe her? Unfortunately, she had been in the wrong place at the wrong time. Why had they obtained a search warrant? If they had asked, she would have granted them permission to search her premises, as she didn't have anything to hide. What would happen to her over the next few hours and days? Coming to live in Peaklow had been a big mistake. It was not a peaceful village.

Shaking with anxiety, she listened again to the police caution being read to her. No amount of searching her thoughts or reconstructing the finding of Kevin's body, could give a clue as to why they had intensified their interest in her. The Custody Sergeant continually scowled at her, because of her refusal to answer the simplest of questions.

She had given her name and address but refused to make further comments. A woman police officer escorted her into the same interview room as before. Two long hours had already passed since her arrival, while all the formalities of her arrest had been processed. What had happened at her cottage since her hurried departure? What had the police been searching for, and what had they expected to find? As she entered the interview room, a rush of relief swept through her that Henry had arrived. Facing yet another police interview would be unmanageable without support.

Lowering herself down onto the chair indicated, a sense of dread engulfed her, twisting her stomach and making her head throb. Before she even had chance to take a steadying breath, the Inspector fixed her with narrowed eyes. 'Do you wish to add to the existing statement you submitted through your solicitor.'

'I do not,' Jenny tensed her shoulders and stared at the Inspector.

'I wish to ask you questions about Kevin Cartwright. Please describe your relationship with him?'

The question took her by surprise.

Taking a deep breath, 'I employed him and had a friendly relationship with him.'

'Did you have sex with him?'

Every muscle in her body went rigid and she drew in a stuttered gasp, 'No, I did not.'

'We have more than one witness who says that he put his arms around you.'

Jenny attempted to remained calm, recalling Tony's comments about seeing Kevin's arm around her. 'He habitually put his arm around women.' Her voice sounded high and tight betraying the strain of keeping her fear under wraps. 'A light-hearted gesture which was meaningless.'

'Would you describe the contact between you as

banter and fooling around?' The Inspector smirked and raised his eyebrows.

'No.' An irritated scowl appeared on her face, 'I would accept myself and Kevin enjoyed banter and some jokes, but there was no fooling around.'

'Did he use innuendo in his banter.'

'Yes, he did, but no different to many men of that age.' Jenny didn't allow the surprise at the line of questioning to show on her face. She had expected the police to focus on Victoria House and her presence nearby at the time he died, and not on her relationship with Kevin.

'Have you ever met Kevin Cartwright away from your gallery, for example on a date, a liaison or any other type of meeting?'

'No, I have not.' Jenny's lips curled with contempt as she enunciated each word with slow precision.

'Apart from when he was working at your premises, did he ever return in the evening or during the night? Let me suggest, after the pubs closed?'

'No, he did not.' She cast a quick glance at the ceiling in ill-concealed exasperation.

His expression darkened, 'Did he ever undress at your premises?'

'Never while I was there, but I cannot say what he did and whether he changed when I went out.'

'Have you ever seen him naked?'

'No, Inspector, I have not.' Jenny struggled to control her temper. She wanted to protest about the Inspector's line of questioning. However, Henry remained silent and had not intervened, so she guessed that he had no objection.

'How much money have you paid him?'

The change of direction surprised Jenny, 'One thousand eight hundred and eighty pounds.'

'What for?'

'Redecorating the house.'

'Did you pay him any other money?'

'No, I did not. I paid by cheque, which cleared my bank account three days later.'

'I can tell you that we have applied to the court for access to your bank accounts.'

Why did the police want to inspect her bank account?

Henry's sudden voice made her jump. 'Inspector, may I ask what you are hoping to achieve by this line of questioning?'

'It will become obvious shortly, Mr Fothering.'

Have you paid any other money into Mr Kevin Cartwright's bank account?'

'No Inspector, I have not.'

'Sergeant, could you produce the exhibit labelled one.' The Sergeant sat at a separate small table and in front of him was a white cardboard box. At the request of the Inspector, he opened the box and removed a large sealed plastic bag that contained brightly coloured material.

'I am showing Ms Maltravers and Mr Fothering, Exhibit One, which is a pair of men's novelty boxer shorts with a Mickey Mouse cartoon pattern in the fabric. Have you ever seen these before Ms Maltravers?'

'No, Inspector.'

'Exhibit Two please sergeant.'

He produced another large plastic bag with a single sheet of paper in it.'

'I am showing the present company a copy of an invoice from Kevin Cartwright Builders. The paper is addressed to Ms Maltravers, and reads For Services Rendered – Three Hundred and Eighty Seven pounds and Twenty Pence. Have you ever seen this before?'

'No,' her breath caught in her throat, 'I have not.'

Henry reached out his hand, 'May I examine it more closely?'

After a few minutes Henry placed the bag back on the table, 'Please carry on, Inspector.'

Without prompting the Sergeant produced a third plastic bag.

'Exhibit Three is a nude photograph of Mr Kevin Cartwright. Have you ever seen this before?'

Jenny shivered, 'No.'

'In executing the warrant to search the premises this morning, these three items were found in a cupboard in the parlour behind the shop.'

36

Tears of exhaustion ran down Jenny's cheeks as she walked from the car to the front door of Stanton House. The shock of being held in custody overnight hadn't left her. Henry had persuaded the police that bail would suit both sides, especially as they had the findings at the parlour to pursue. They refused to let her return home, but with Gerald's intervention she had been released, but would be confined to Stanton House.

She shivered although it wasn't a cold evening. The questioning had lasted for hours. Different detectives had asked her about varying aspects of the case. One had focused on the late night and early morning walks which they treated as suspicious. Jenny had made general points about her previous life in the army and its regime, but had not been prepared, even under intense questioning, to talk about her nightmare horrors.

Jenny had only talked to one person, her commanding officer about the nightmares. Verbalising the nights had brought the horror of guns, explosions, and death back to her. She would not share her experiences with the unsympathetic police.

'My poor woman, you look devastated, come in.'

Gerald ushered her across the hall to the drawing room. Dan crossed to her, put his arms around her and kissed her on the cheek. Even in her shocked and subdued state she could see the difference in Dan. He had never been a tactile person. The only time he had greeted her like that in the past had been when she returned from a war zone. While the police interrogation had been frightening and gruelling it didn't even come close to the terrors of a war zone.

'Gin and tonics all round, then we will eat. After that we need a plan.' Gerald's voice sounded serious. She appreciated being back with people, who were on her side, but could see the evidence had begun to stack up against her. As she hadn't known Gerald for long, she appreciated his faith in her, but she wondered how long it would last.

Gerald banned any talk of the case at the dinner table so she could attempt to relax. The main talking point came from Dan, who had opened the gallery on both days she had been held at the police station and had sold three pictures. 'I've only managed to sell one picture a week.' Jenny laughed. 'And you've sold three in two days.'

Henry gave him a quizzical look, 'Do you know about sales techniques?'

Dan shook his head, 'Nothing at all.'

'What about watercolour paintings?'

'Even less than selling.'

But as the banter passed around the table her mind would not let go of her current circumstances. When she had been in a custody cell last night, she had struggled with the horrors and with the constant and nagging thought of a miscarriage of justice. Although she hadn't killed Kevin, the implicating evidence against her had been building.

The mental agony had made her head throb.

At the end of the meal Gwendoline cleared the table, and Gerald with an implacable look of determination on his serious face turned to Jenny, 'The three men will go through the investigation and work out the best way forward. It has been a stressful two days for you so would you like to join Gwendoline in the drawing room by the fire? I'll find Clayton and ask him to join us. He told me earlier that he would be pleased to help, but he'd prefer to eat in the kitchen.'

'Thank you for the offer, Gerald, but I've recovered, and I want to help with the plan.' Clayton had joined them. Henry would start with an update. Jenny willed herself to listen. The four men although serious had an alertness and purpose about them. Wallowing in self-pity would not release her from this tricky situation. Determination and a positive attitude were needed. Clearing her mind, she focused.

Henry, with the relevant papers spread across the table in front of him, began his appraisal of the situation. 'Up to the discovery of the items in the parlour, the police only had circumstantial evidence. There were good reasons for the connection and frequent meetings between Jenny and Kevin. He had completed work for her. Jenny stated she had moved the flask and paint pot. Even in the short time she has been in the village she is known for her late night and early morning walks.'

Gerald rubbed a hand across his chin. 'It's the three items in the parlour that have convinced the police they have a case?'

'Yes. Although they have been investigating the other circumstantial matters.'

'I cannot understand how those items came to be there. I often use that cupboard. It's not crammed full so I'm sure I would have seen them.'

Dan interrupted, 'I can guess what would have happened as I examined the cupboard. There is a gap between the bottom shelf and the frame. It's about three centimetres wide, so whoever planted the three items could have slipped them in there. Unless on the floor and peering under the shelf they could not be seen. The police would check such spaces.'

Gerald pursed his lips, 'How these items came to be in the cupboard is a key point for us to investigate.' Everyone, including Jenny nodded in agreement. 'While the police will investigate, under these circumstances there is nothing like local knowledge as someone from this village is setting Jenny up for a murder charge.'

Silence followed Gerald's words. Each lost in their own thoughts. The word murder resonated in Jenny's head like a funeral bell tolling. She forced her mind back to the current meeting as Dan spoke.

'I agree with you, Gerald, the villagers will be guarded with the police, but might let a crucial clue slip during a normal conversation.'

Jenny struggled to keep her voice calm. 'Gerald, you've implied that we will investigate.'

'Yes. Do we agree?' His eyes swept across the assembled group. 'Henry, I know you will have reservations.'

'Under normal circumstances I would caution against such action as I mentioned in a private conversation at the police station that the items could have been planted.'

'What reply did you receive?'

'His exact words were, She would say that wouldn't

she. We have no intention of investigating a conspiracy. While I would wish to proceed with caution, I do agree it is a matter for us.'

Dan grimaced. 'The planting of false incriminating evidence gives the obvious conclusion that Kevin's death was not an accident. It's likely, but not provable, that Kevin's death, the break-in and the planting of these three items are linked. The police are not pursuing that line, so I think we should.'

Clayton spoke for the first time. 'This will only be solved by local people. I'm willing to do whatever is necessary as it is crucial that we avoid a miscarriage of justice.'

Dan nodded his agreement, 'Let's start with the assumption Kevin was murdered, otherwise why incriminate Jenny. A second assumption would be that the three items were placed in the parlour cupboard by the murderer. To place them the murderer must have been alone in the room. I tested the doors of the cupboard. They open and close with no noise.'

Jenny gave a long assessing look at the four men, 'I've been thinking as we have been talking. There are a few people I have left in that room. I set it up for that purpose. It is separated from the cottage next door, but I wanted somewhere for people to wait for private viewings. I've made sure there is nothing of value in the room, so I had no concern about leaving people there.'

'Who has been in there on their own.' Dan picked up his pen.

Clayton interrupted, 'I'm one on the list, I've been in that room on my own.' The others laughed which helped to relieve some of the tension that pervaded the room.

Jenny scanned her memory, 'Elizabeth from the post

office, has been in there several times while I made tea. Both Tony and Jacqui have been in there recently but separately. She had come to speak to me. Tony popped back in because she had left her hat behind. The one who has been in several times, is Kevin's widow, Lindy. Then Lionel and his family, both John and Amanda.'

'What about Nicolas?'

'I can't say for certain because he and Amanda came into the gallery and asked if they could have two plastic bags that I use to package pictures. They helped themselves from the parlour cupboard. But I'm not sure whether Nicolas or Amanda went to find them.'

'There were the three lads from the pub, who checked out the place after the break-in.'

Dan shook his head, 'Their action was spontaneous whereas the others could be planned. Women could carry the three items in any bag. Men would need a jacket with large pockets.'

Clayton added, 'With the weather over the past few weeks most would be wearing jackets when they arrived.'

Gerald cleared his throat and raised questioning eyebrows, 'Do you think the nude picture indicates a woman?'

Dan closed his eyes briefly while he pondered the question, 'It is best to keep an open mind on that one.'

Henry's cough brought attention to him. 'Which brings us to the mystery of the invoice. Three hundred and eighty-seven pounds and twenty pence is a strange amount. Most invoices wouldn't bother with twenty pence. It would be either rounded up or down to the nearest pound. However, it appears to be genuine.'

'I paid the main invoice for the work, a much larger

fee, but I've never seen that one.' Jenny shook her head in confusion. 'Why would anyone make out a fictional invoice with my name on it? Any ideas Dan?'

'Fraud has never been my speciality, neither has tax evasion, but fictional invoices are common in such cases. I'll give an old friend a ring as he works in the fraud office and might have some ideas.'

Clayton rubbed a hand across his jaw, 'Given two people broke into the gallery, are we trying to find one person or two.'

'Let's ignore the break-in. It could be a coincidence. If someone were trying to set Jenny up to be the murderer, why would they want to frighten her out of the village? It wouldn't make sense.'

'Let's go about our business in a normal manner. I will meet all the people on our list and tell them Jenny has been questioned about the mysterious death of Kevin. It will become a key topic in village gossip. Any piece of juicy scandal spreads like wildfire. Let's keep our eyes and ears open for strange behaviour or any passing remarks about Kevin.

Henry nodded his approval, 'I'm most willing to help, but I don't live in the village.

Dan smiled, 'I want to talk and explain the news to the people in the village, so as you know about painting, why not come and run the gallery.'

'Good idea. I will do that with pleasure. There isn't likely to be a rapid reaction from the police? They will want to build a strong case before they make a charge.'

'Let's be careful. A murderer is out there. If they feel threatened, then they could strike again.' His jaw clenched as anxiety flitted across his face. 'I think whoever it is will wait to see what actions the police take, but if they are in any doubt, they might choose a different method of retaliation and find other ways to incriminate Jenny.'

The remark sent a pang of worry through Jenny as she hadn't considered that she might be in danger. She'd had enough of difficult and dangerous situations to last her a lifetime and hadn't expected to be worried in a quiet little village. When the case had been solved, she would leave Peaklow. Her mental resolution cheered her, but the immediate problems needed to be dealt with first.

As Gerald stood to indicate the end of the meeting. 'Increasing house security is essential. It's imperative we keep the house secure to protect Jenny.'

Jenny trembled. It was an unsettling note to end the conversation.

37

Jenny found it hard to concentrate. Her mind swirled, searching through past events since arriving in Peaklow, to find some snippet of useful information. So far, she'd had no success. To help her relax, Dan had brought her easel and painting materials to Stanton House. Gerald and Gwendoline had gone out for the evening, so she had set herself up to paint in the old conservatory at the back of the house. The glass and doors had recently been renovated, so she benefitted from good early evening light. Clayton worked outside in the garden preparing the ground for new planting in a side border.

As they didn't want her to be on her own, he'd agreed to work through until Dan arrived. Their presence was a great comfort.

Of the three items found in her parlour, the invoice held the biggest puzzle. The other two were easy insinuations about a relationship with Kevin, although they didn't constitute proof. Henry had promised to discover the police interest, but investigations moved slowly. They would eventually give him the information, but it could be weeks or even months, although he would press them.

Henry had warned Jenny that if the police charged

her with Kevin's death, then it would go to trial, but that would not take place for six months while legal cases were prepared. Even though innocent it would be a long and stressful time to wait. Jenny attempted to focus on her current painting, having chosen something challenging to force her mind away from the investigation.

A photograph, taken high up on the moors of a waterfall cascading over a precipice, sending water plunging down into the valley. Sprays of water on a windy day were blown high into the air would be difficult to paint.

Although absorbed in her painting she clock-watched. A sigh of relief came when Dan shouted a greeting as the front door slammed. He arrived in the conservatory and waved to Clayton. 'You've never seen the gallery so full, and we sold four paintings!'

Jenny settled herself on the large sofa with a gentle smile. 'Were there coaches packed with visitors?'

'No. We sold them to locals.'

'Even more mysterious.' Jenny raised her eyebrows.

'Henry and I couldn't decide whether the locals were buying to show their support for you, or whether they anticipated the value might go up if it turned into a notorious trial.' With a huge grin he settled in a chair.

Jenny could appreciate the funny side of the situation although she didn't want to be an infamous criminal. Tense about the situation she kept reminding herself she hadn't done anything wrong. She was innocent. Just in the wrong place at the wrong time.

The planting of the incriminating evidence in the cupboard at the gallery had shaken her. Somebody disliked her. Why else would anyone be tempted to do such a nasty vindictive act? With a shudder she focused her attention back to Dan. 'How did Henry get on?'

'Some of the interest from customers seemed to be genuine and he had several long conversations about art.'

'Which of the locals came in? Did you recognise any of them?' Jenny blurted out wanting to know all the information. She missed being away from the gallery and the familiarity of her little cottage. 'Tell me every detail. Did any of them seem pleased that I had been arrested?'

'Amanda came early before opening her salon.'

'She is pleasant and runs an efficient business and she is an excellent hostess, and there is no reason to doubt her. Perhaps it's my fanciful imagination under these current circumstances but I'm suspecting everyone.' She was sad that she no longer knew which of the villagers were her true friends.

'Lionel briefly popped in and sent his good wishes. The next visitor was Lindy who had a specific message.'

'What was it?'

'Apparently, something strange about Kevin has turned up and she wanted to find out whether you had any ideas. Although I tried pressing her for more details, she wouldn't tell me. She left rather abruptly saying she would wait until she met you.'

Jenny gave a dismissive gesture with a flick of her hand. 'I don't think there will be much in it. Lindy is going through a difficult period after his death. Kevin, despite outward appearances, wasn't popular and it's rubbed off on her. We have chatted several times and she knows Kevin was promiscuous and had other women.'

'Did she just accept it?' Dan frowned.

'Yes. It started not long after they were married. It appears he chased after women all the time. Everyone in the village knew about his behaviour and Lindy believes they laughed behind her back.' Jenny shook her head in puzzlement. How had Lindy put up with a strange and lonely marriage?

Dan grinned, 'That's the gallery news, do you want an update on village life?'

Jenny smiled back. Dan's presence gave her confidence. 'From the gallery windows you get a good view of all the comings and goings across the square. It's the perfect place to people watch. I'm interested in how different characters respond when they don't know they are being observed. It's just fascinating. Perhaps I should have been a spy.'

'About lunchtime Nicolas came out of the post office. As I had already spoken to Amanda, I walked across the square to update him on the news. We chatted for a few minutes, and he was pleased that you'd been released on bail but was surprised that the police suspected you of being involved in Kevin's death. As he went to walk back across the square on his way home, so Tony came roaring into Market Square on a quadbike. Tony seemed intent on making as much noise as possible as he revved the engine unnecessarily. Added to that the bike was covered in mud which left a messy trail across the road.

Nicolas marched straight over to Tony as he stepped down from the quad. Until that point Tony had been smiling and looking pleased with himself.'

Taking a steadying breath, she leaned forward in her chair anticipating that the exchange wouldn't have been friendly.

'They started arguing again, the same as before edging closer and closer together as the shouting intensified.

I'm not sure what would have happened next, except Jacqui and her sister, Sandra, came out of the post office. Jacqui was brave because she marched across and stood in the middle of them. Tony shouted at her to start with, but she wouldn't move and stood there with her hands on her hips, glaring at him.'

Jenny imagined the acrimonious scene. 'Another man came into the Square and without hesitation marched over, grabbed Nicolas by the arm and yanked him away. Jacqui and Sandra stood on either side of Tony holding onto his arms to stop him following, but his expression remained hard and angry. He continued shouting abuse at Nicholas although he'd already disappeared.

Jacqui shoved Tony towards the quadbike, leapt on the back and they roared out of the Square, in the opposite direction to Nicolas.' Dan shifted in his seat, 'Something did catch my attention. On the back of the quadbike he had a gun box.'

Jenny widened her eyes, 'That doesn't sound good news. A man with a temper like Tony's would be dangerous with a gun in his hand. Who knows what might happen in the heat of the moment?' She shuddered. 'Did you manage to speak to Sandra?'

'Yes.' He twitched a smile 'She told me a piece of news, secret to the family, but it will become public in the next few days.'

'What is it?' Jenny sat forward eager to find out the news.

'Tony has planning permission to use the second field for his caravan site. He can build a shop and cafe at the end of the railway track footpath.'

She gave a small derisive laugh, 'I don't think that

will please everyone.'

'Sandra mentioned that the field had been overrun with rabbits, so he wanted to reduce their numbers. That's probably why he's got the gun carrier on the back of the quadbike.

Jenny looked sceptical, 'I hope he doesn't decide that his Victoria field, behind Nicolas and Amanda's house, has too many rabbits. If Nicolas appeared the situation could be downright dangerous.'

'I came to the same conclusion as well. Sandra didn't think he'd mentioned it, but she would tell Jacqui about my concerns.'

Henry joined them, settling himself in an armchair. 'The police are still investigating matters, but they have given me an update on a couple of issues.'

'The invoice?' Jenny queried.

'Yes, that has been intriguing me, it has been paid!'

'Who paid it?'

'Paid by cash in one of the largest banks in the centre of Chesterfield. The police are following it through, but they are not hopeful the cashier would be able to recognise the person. I've been in that branch before and it is always busy with large queues, especially on market day. The invoice has all of Kevin's banking details so that would be easy to give to a cashier. They would then transfer the money and move on to the next customer.'

Jenny grimaced, 'What about CCTV, the banks always have them.'

He nodded, 'The police have asked for them and will wait for the bank to respond, but the Sergeant didn't seem that interested. She sighed with frustration and ran her hands through her hair, 'Did he say why?'

'Other lines of enquiry were more important.' Jenny could tell by the flat tone of his voice that he hadn't been impressed with the response. Her brain whirred. Why were the police being so narrow minded? They were convinced that she had been involved in Kevin's death. Jenny shoulders slumped.

A frown creased Dan's forehead, 'It is too much of a side issue in a murder case. The police will focus on the crime and on obtaining sufficient proof for a murder conviction. The payment of the invoice is a background issue that they will only clear before the trial. The police turned up early yesterday morning and sealed off the parlour. Their forensic team spent most of the day in there.'

'Do you know the reason for the detailed search?'

'The Inspector had been reluctant to give me the information. I emphasised that we believed our support might be beneficial in uncovering the true culprit quicker. Although reluctant, I kept pushing him and finally he gave me the information. The boxer shorts that were found in the cupboard in the parlour were the ones that his wife confirmed he wore on the day he died. When the pathologist examined the body, he had no underpants although the rest of his clothing appeared normal.'

Jenny was bemused. Somehow this didn't make sense. 'What type of man would go and meet a woman, leave his underpants behind and then go back to work as though nothing had happened?'

Henry focused on Jenny, 'They are seeking other evidence in the parlour. Although judging by the tone of the Inspector, more in hope than expectation.'

38

Weariness descended on her later that evening alone in her room at Stanton House. The events of the past few days had taken their toll, and she found it difficult to remain in a positive frame of mind. She slumped on the edge of the bed and stared down with unseeing eyes, while her hands clenched into fists in her lap. An ache of despair crept through her body.

The police activities had intensified but they were focused on proving the case against her. Today's information from Henry and Dan had given her no solace. Only one more piece of fabricated evidence needed to appear and the police would charge her. There would be no respite from the pressure for a long time. The tension while awaiting trial would be enormous. Willing the day to arrive but at the same time dreading its arrival. She shuddered.

The sudden noise made her dive for the floor. Her military background jumped to the fore and she remained motionless lying face down, waiting and listening. She'd been in enough difficult situations to recognise the sound of gunshot. Without doubt a shot, then the sound of some breaking glass, but not in her room. A slight interval and then another shot. After the third shot her door burst open and Dan dived onto the floor next to her.

'It's not here!' gasped Jenny.

'It could have been an air rifle.' They remained lying on the floor listening. Jenny almost held her breath as she waited for the next shot. No more sounds reached them. Dan propped himself up on one elbow, 'I will find out which window has been broken.'

Jenny lifted her head. 'It sounded as though it was at the back of the house, I'll come with you.' Keeping low they edged their way towards the door.

They crept slowly out onto the dark landing, 'Gerald are you there?'

'Yes, downstairs, I'm armed.'

'Where's Gwendoline?'

'I'm here near our bedroom door, what's happened? Is someone shooting at us?'

'Go back in your room. You'll be safe there but turn the light off and stay away from the windows.'

'Yes, I will. Gerald be careful.'

'We're coming down the stairs, sir!' shouted Dan, as they inched forward keeping low. With slow precision they descended the darkened stairs. The three crept towards the back of the house along the wide corridor. There were no lights, but Jenny's eyes had become accustomed to the dark.

Every few steps they stopped and listened. No further gunfire reached them. Each room on the ground floor was checked. As they'd agreed to use no lights or torches it was a slow process. They kept low as they entered each room and sidled towards the window.

No words were spoken between them. No panes

of glass had been broken in any room. They reached the door to the conservatory. With windows on three sides their movement would be easily detected from anyone outside. A moonlit night bathed the area in a soft light.

Dan whispered, 'I'll check out the conservatory.'

Crouching down below the level of the dwarf wall that supported the window frames, Dan made his way around the edge of the room. Gerald stood in the doorway, his gun at the ready. The seconds ticked and Jenny found that she was holding her breath as she listened to Dan's shuffling movements. Dan's voice broke through the silence, 'It's a side window in here that has been shot out. An air rifle.'

More scrabbling sounds reached them, 'I've found a pellet.' They waited in silence for Dan to return to the safety of the dark hall. Easing himself into a standing position, 'The other two shots have gone through your painting on the easel.' He spoke in a whisper, his voice edged with tension. She shivered and her stomach lurched at the realisation that someone had tried to get at her once again. This time an air rifle, but they could still be out there with a more menacing weapon. 'I'll turn on all the external security lights,' Gerald moved along the corridor.

Jenny slumped down on a chair in the dark kitchen. Fear churned through her.

Dan gave a small squeeze of her shoulder, 'I'll call the police.' In an efficient military manner, he told them his name and the location, and the nature of the shooting. At the end of the call, he strongly suggested the detective team, who were involved in the Jenny Maltravers case be informed.

39

An hour after the shooting the Inspector arrived at Stanton House. Jenny, Dan, Gerald and Gwendoline sat in the drawing room by the re-made fire. There had been little in the way of conversation while they waited. The loud sound of the grandfather clock ticking the time away filled the room. The heavy curtains had been pulled shut across the large window and no lamps burned in the room. The firelight flickered giving both warmth and some comfort. The Inspector joined them, his face grey and serious, and at Gerald's invitation, sat on the couch.

Taking his time, he stared at each one of them in turn. 'Any ideas who would want to do this?'

'No, Inspector,' Gerald responded in a precise and sharp tone, 'we have no idea.'

Nodding in response he turned his gaze to Jenny. His raised eyebrows silently questioned her almost compelling her to voice her opinion. With a calmness she didn't feel she responded, 'The shop and cottage I bought have been empty for the past few years. Since I have been here, I have made no enemies.'

'Any minor disputes or arguments?'

Jenny shook her head. There had been no arguments, but someone was out to make her life difficult. Someone hated her. It had to be one of her friends. A hard knot constricted her throat making it difficult to breathe.

He turned to Gerald, 'Were any lights on at the conservatory end of the house.'

'No, Inspector. There were not. There are external security lights, but they only cover the approaches to the house and not the woodland, because animals constantly set them off.'

After a moment's hesitation Dan enquired, 'It's directed at Jenny, isn't it?'

The Inspector smiled through narrowed eyes, 'Yes, Captain, I have already worked that out. As the curtains are drawn in this room and upstairs in the bedrooms, all of which had room lights, the assailant intended to frighten, otherwise they would shoot out the glass in an occupied room. Before one of you gentlemen suggests it, I'm aware that it is a moonlit night and that the easel could easily be seen in the darkness from the woods.'

Gerald's eyebrows came together in a thoughtful frown, 'Inspector are you thinking about taking Jenny to the safer custody of the police station?' They shared a calculating look, 'But I am sure you are reluctant, because the police have made a decision and you will not be bullied out of it by someone breaking the law.'

'You are exactly right, sir.' The Inspector grimaced as his fingers tapped the notebook in his hand with a series of staccato movements. Gerald eased himself out of the chair and paced across the room. All eyes followed him while they waited for him to continue. Leaning on the back of one of the armchairs his eyes gleamed with defiance. 'Therefore, may I suggest a compromise solution. In the morning I will employ a private security firm to patrol the grounds both during the day and at night.'

The Inspector nodded, 'If you do that, I will raise no objection to continuing the current arrangement.'

After the Inspector's departure, they lingered by the fire with a good measure of brandy, though conversation was sparse. Jenny allowed the warming effects of the brandy to swirl down her throat while she gazed mesmerised by the flickering flames. The Inspector had suggested that tonight's gunfire had been used to frighten them. Well, they had succeeded. Jenny had been shaken by the attack, she feared sleeping as the horrors could easily return so resolved to read the night away.

40

The second day after the air rifle incident brought no respite for Jenny, only more restrictions. While the security team patrolled the grounds, she had been advised to stay away from the windows. She had moved her easel to a ground floor room that gave her light, but she could not be seen from the outside. Clayton hadn't arrived at his normal time, which was unsettling, and so far, no one had received a message from him.

Had something else happened in the village to delay his arrival. There would be a simple explanation for his deviation from his expected routine. It would be another long and boring day which she suspected would result in little progress. With a sigh of frustration, she turned her attention back to her painting.

A fresh start had been made on the waterfall picture and she had applied a blue wash for the sky and a pale grey wash for the limestone ridge. With her brush poised in her hand her mind drifted back to the day when she had taken the photograph. A cool, but sunny spring day, before all this nightmare had begun, and when living in Peaklow had seemed an exciting new venture. How quickly that idea had changed.

A police condition of her being able to stay at Stanton House prevented her talking to anyone from the village. The residents of Stanton House were exempt, and Dan and Clayton because of their military background. A car pulled up on the gravel outside and she assumed another security vehicle.

The front door opened and the sound of soft footsteps advancing down the hall reached her, Dan poked his head into the room. Bleary eyed and unshaven his eyes gazed at Jenny with unblinking anxiety. 'We need to talk. Let's go to the drawing room.' The urgency in his tone was obvious. 'I'll find Gerald.' Within a few minutes the three sat in their usual positions in the drawing room.

Gwendoline had taken one look at Dan's dishevelled appearance and insisted he needed tea and toast. Dan still munching on his toast waited until they were settled before enlightening them. 'The main purpose of my visit is to tell you that Nicolas has been shot dead.' Silence followed this revelation.

Jenny stared in open mouthed astonishment. Even Gerald seemed lost for words. After managing to find her voice she spluttered out, 'How do you know?'

'Last night I took Sandra out for a meal in a nearby village and then later I dropped her back at the farm. I met Jacqui who said Tony must have gone for a drink at the George pub, although she was surprised because his Range Rover and quad bike were not parked in their usual spots.

If he intended having a drink, he parked a tractor or the quadbike by the gate in the Square, and then came home across the fields. Nothing appeared wrong, and Jacqui didn't seem unduly worried. I drove back to Market

Square and as I parked the car, I met Clayton going for a walk with his black Labrador, so I joined him.

'We went on the usual route past the George and came in this direction and then turned back along the old railway track. As we passed the field next to the caravan park, Clayton let his dog off the lead and it disappeared with enthusiasm into the bushes, which line the embankment.

Suddenly the dog let out a loud growl and the movement in the bushes stopped. I shone the torch in that direction. The dog lay still, looking intently in front of him. The torch picked up a body sprawled on the ground. Nicolas lay motionless on his back covered in blood.

We slid down the slope and I checked his neck for a pulse although I already knew he was dead. A few yards away was Tony's quad bike covered in blood. The gun case on the back was open and a shot gun lay half in the box. Nicolas had been shot in the chest at close range. We rang the police and have been with them ever since. To make matters more complicated, Tony has disappeared, and so has his Range Rover.'

Jenny leaned back in the chair and half closed her eyes. Although sad about the death of Nicolas she remained preoccupied with her own difficult situation. Did this mean they would cease the investigation trying to link her to Kevin's death? Had Tony murdered Kevin? Was Tony responsible for the incriminating incidents against her? If so, why did he hate her? What had she done to him that deserved such malice? Questions. Questions. Questions. But no answers. She shook her head in frustration and forced her mind back to the present.

Dan rubbed a hand across his forehead. 'The police

will come here to take statements as they want to interview Jenny as well.'

Jenny shivered and pursed her lips. Why did they want to interview her as she was not involved in Nicolas's death?

'I told the police that we witnessed a fight between Tony and Nicolas.'

Jenny breathed a long slow sigh, 'I'd forgotten about that confrontation, it seems light years ago.'

41

When the Inspector, Sergeant and Clayton arrived they adjourned to the dining room and settled around the large table. To Jenny it seemed a strange setting to be talking about a murder, especially as the large portraits of Gerald's ancestors seemed to be listening with expressions of evident disapproval.

Gwendoline appeared carrying a large tray, 'Tea and coffee on the sideboard.' Without another word she left. Gerald surveyed the assembled group with a grim expression, 'The floor is yours, Inspector.'

'Thank you sir, for the use of your room. I must also thank the Captain and Clayton,' he nodded in their direction, 'for the excellent help they gave my men at the scene of the crime.'

The Detective Sergeant frowned in an irritated manner, 'Would you like me to take them one at a time to make a statement sir?'

'Not yet, Sergeant, I believe there may be benefits in having everyone together.'

'It's unusual sir,' he sounded surprised and his movement indicated he was a little put out by the decision.

'Yes, I realise that, but the Captain is a police officer. The Colonel is the head of the magistrates, which leaves Clayton, who has a spotless record as a brave army Sergeant. While the Major is currently held on bail, her record is also totally unsullied.'

The Police Sergeant opened his notebook and stared down at it with a small frown.

'May I remind the Colonel and Major that you promised full cooperation.'

Gerald spoke in a direct and resonating voice, 'Chief Inspector, that is what we said, and that is what we meant.'

The Inspector nodded, 'I do not wish to discuss the shooting last night. Let's start with the argument between Nicolas and Tony, witnessed by the Captain and the Major, behind Victoria House.'

Dan went to speak, but the Inspector held up his hand, 'I would like to hear the Major's version.'

Jenny had to choose her words carefully. With her army training she was used to giving detailed reports. Before beginning, she visualised the scene in her head. The Inspector would have listened to Dan's version, either directly or via one of his officers.

'We walked along the old railway track and then took the path back to the village that comes down the side of Victoria House.'

'A general walk or a specific one?'

Temptation surfaced to dismiss his question and not tell the whole truth, but it was important to be truthful if they were ever going to solve the problems. With a sharp intake of breath, 'As I had become involved with the police about the death of Kevin, a specific walk so Dan could understand the layout of the house and garden. It's difficult to visualise because the house is built on a slope making the back garden level with the upstairs rooms. I intended pointing out how the scaffolding had been positioned.'

The Inspector interrupted with a slight head shake, 'I've come from Victoria House. The garden has a high fence with thick bushes down the side.'

Jenny shifted in her seat, 'There is one vantage point at the top of the hill, near to the trees and bushes which allows anyone to see the full back view of the house, the path at the side and the back garden.'

The Inspector's eyebrows rose in surprise at this snippet of information and he scribbled a note on the paper in front of him.

'What did you see?'

'We approached the brow of the hill when shouting reached us. As we breached the summit Nicolas and Tony stood close to each other near a car and tractor. By the way they pointed, although we couldn't hear the specific words, they were arguing about the route of the path. Tony swung at Nicolas and hit him on the top of his head. Nicolas returned several blows to Tony's stomach causing him to fall back against his tractor. Then he jumped in his car and roared away.

It took Tony a few minutes to recover and then he climbed up onto his tractor. The engine started, Tony set the machinery and began to plough Victoria field. At that point we turned and headed home via a different route.

'Is the proposed change of route of the path well known in the village?'

'Yes, everyone is willing to offer their view on the matter. The whole field has been ploughed. Tony started that after he had recovered from the fight and probably came back later to finish the job. Though why the proposed rerouting fuelled an argument is beyond me. He owns the field and the footpath already skirts through his field so it's only a minor change.'

Gerald drummed his fingers on the table and fixed his gaze on the Inspector. 'Practically all the fields around the village are left to grass. It's not an area given over to arable farming, traditionally it's always been sheep farming, which is better suited to the hilly terrain. Victoria field is a steep slope and will result in run-off whenever it rains.'

Jenny added, 'Nicolas and Amanda use the far end of the footpath as the main route into the house. Whenever it rains it will now become a quagmire as the water along with the soil runs from the field.'

The Inspector frowned, 'Done deliberately to annoy Nicolas?'

Gerald nodded, his expression grim, 'A fair conclusion, Inspector.'

The Sergeant tapped his pencil to bring the meeting's attention to him. 'Are there any other examples in the village of disputes with Tony?'

Jenny frowned, 'A long running argument between Lionel and Tony about the empty shop next to the butcher's shop'

'Any others? Or were two arguments at the same time enough for him?'

Jenny hesitated. All the faces around the table focused on her. 'You will need to interview Tony's wife, Jacqui.'

'About what?' asked the Chief Inspector.

Clayton interrupted, 'Perhaps I can explain better,

given that the Major is new to the village. There were two long running disputes between Tony and Kevin Cartwright, the deceased builder.' Clayton had captured the Inspector's attention. 'When on speaking terms, Kevin built the caravan site's shower and toilet block some years ago. Tony believed that Kevin ripped him off on the price of the blocks and they had a huge disagreement about it.'

'Seems trivial,' the Chief Inspector spoke dismissively. 'The other one?'

Clayton stared at the Inspector and his eyes narrowed, 'Kevin was a ladies' man. He took a liking to Tony's wife when the three attended a village committee. A fight between Tony and Kevin took place afterwards which a villager witnessed from his window. The witness is reliable and not a village gossip. The following day all three had injuries to their faces. Tony hit Kevin first and as they fought so Jacqui intervened, and Tony accidentally hit her.'

Jenny considered that Clayton had made a clear summary of the events as they tied in exactly to the version that Jacqui had recounted.

'Seems doubtful to me, sir.' The Sergeant stared at his Inspector, 'Women are too sensible to stand between two men, who are about to fight.'

Dan shook his head, 'Tony and Nicolas were arguing again in the Market Square the day before yesterday. Jacqui attempted to intervene and calm the situation by standing between them. There were plenty of witnesses.'

The Chief inspector answered a call on his mobile phone. From his side of the conversation no one could guess the details as he only uttered three words, 'Yes, when and Okay.'

After closing the call, he allowed his eyes to rove around the assembled group.

'Tony has been picked up trying to board the ferry at Holyhead.' Everyone stared at him in silence while his words hung in the air. 'Sergeant, take a statement from Clayton and get from him a list of witnesses to these various incidents.'

The death of Nicolas had frightened Jenny. The village had a murderer, but she found it hard to believe it would be Tony despite his temper. But there could be no other explanation. His quad bike and gun had been found next to Nicolas's dead body and he had been apprehended running away. Did this mean he had killed Kevin as well?

42

After three days of boredom when Jenny had occupied her time with painting, unanswered questions swirled around her mind. Henry arrived at Stanton House to give an update. Gerald, Jenny and Henry congregated in the small drawing room.

Henry beamed, 'It's good news, the police are halting investigations concerning you. The police have given me the papers that release you from bail, so you are free to go wherever you like.'

His words flowed through Jenny lifting a great weight from her shoulders. As her tension released, a huge smile crept across her face. For some unknown reason her eyes filled with tears as she gazed across at Henry and Gerald. Throughout the investigation they had never lost faith in her. She briefly closed her eyes and drew in a deep breath, as she tried to organise her jumbled thoughts.

'Do they want to see me again?'

'No, as they are concentrating their efforts on Tony.'

The news gave Jenny the strangest of feelings. No longer a suspect. She sat up straighter in her chair, as there were a lot of questions now circling around in her chaotic mind. Gripping the wooden arms of the chair, her heart pounded from a combination of relief and elation. With difficulty she focused on Henry's cool and calm voice, 'They will charge Tony with the murder of Nicolas which will allow them to investigate his possible links with Kevin's death, the break-in at your gallery and the air rifle attack here. However, you must understand the latter are minor and they might not pursue them, especially if they opt for two murder convictions.'

Gerald pursed his lips in disapproval, 'That is unsatisfactory. We do not know whether the break-in and shooting are linked to Tony. If they are not, then someone else is trying to get at Jenny.' His words made Jenny gasp, bringing her back down to earth with a thud.

She hadn't considered that scenario. Tension once again began to creep back through her body, replacing the elation of a few moments ago. The muscles in her throat tightened.

Henry nodded, 'I agree with you Gerald, but there is little we can do about it.

Jenny's tumbled thoughts suddenly managed to focus. Could there be a connection? 'Not so long ago I went to Tony's farm for dinner with Dan. Tony's brother mentioned that he had been after my shop.'

Henry nodded, 'We did have a low bid from him.'

'Tony is ambitious. Consider the growth of his farm and coffee shop as well as the extended caravan park. A much bigger park will bring in more tourists. My gallery is the first shop they come to if they are walking into the village. Did he position himself to get the planning position for my gallery at the same time? He could then open a shop or bistro. When I took the gallery at the full asking price, he decided to hassle me out thereby leaving it empty when he could offer a low price once again.'

Henry interrupted, 'You indicated that after the break-in the two characters ran away across the field, which implies they are relatively young.'

Jenny nodded, 'Appearances can be deceptive especially at night, added to the complication they were wearing dark clothing. However, Jacqui told me that both her and Tony have always been keen runners.'

Gerald acknowledged her comment with a thoughtful expression, 'Perhaps you are right my dear, but there is still an element of doubt.'

'I've had some good chats with Jacqui. We get on well.' She gazed across at the two men with a determined look. 'Perhaps she might own up if I agreed not to inform the police.'

'But they would have broken the law twice,' Henry interrupted with a pinched expression and the merest shake of his head. Jenny wouldn't be deterred and had already made up her mind to visit Jacqui as soon as possible. 'Tony would have instigated it. He would not be able to do it again and it would confirm the danger had passed.'

Gerald gave her a probing glance, 'Yes, I can see your reasoning, why not give it a go.'

43

It had taken several days for Jenny to calm and to appreciate she would no longer be required by the police. She had returned to her cottage and her usual routine of opening the gallery. Life had returned to normal. Dan remained in Peaklow, though spent an increasing amount of time with Sandra, walking and exploring the surrounding countryside. Many of the villagers had popped in to offer their support and perhaps in the hope of picking up more gossip. No longer being the centre of attention came as a relief.

Jenny rolled her shoulders to relieve the stiffness as she finished painting as the end of the day beckoned. She had never painted so much as in recent times. As she aimlessly tidied the gallery, thoughts about the future filled her mind. Dan had urged her not to make any hasty decisions, but her mind often mulled over the possibilities open to her.

Had it been a mistake to take the shop in an isolated village where she knew no one. Over the past few days, a plan had formed in her mind. She missed some of her old friends. One solution would be to sell up in Peaklow and buy a shop near the Colchester garrison.

She could enjoy village life in Essex or Suffolk and be able to meet her friends. Life had started so well in Peaklow, but then had gone horribly wrong. The terror of being arrested remained fresh in her mind. If she stayed, would the shadow of her involvement always hang over her? Indecision gripped her and she gave an impatient huff.

With closing time imminent, she went to pull the blinds down, when the front door opening caught her attention. She turned ready to greet a customer, but her eyes widened, and she did a double take. The last person she expected now stood in the doorway. A moments' silence followed when they both stared, unable to move as though frozen to the spot. Jacqui walked slowly into the gallery, her face pale and unsmiling, 'Can we talk?'

Jenny's enthusiasm at Stanton house to discover who had broken into her gallery had waned. At the time she'd been intent on challenging Jacqui to discover whether her and Tony were the guilty pair. Since then, the enjoyment of leading a normal life, free from the police investigations had pushed the idea aside. Obviously, it might have been Tony and the woman now standing in front of her.

Rolling her shoulders, she took a long silent breath to quell the pounding of her heart. Jacqui's usual vibrancy had vanished. Her eyes were puffed from crying, she wore no makeup and her brown hair had been scrunched back in an untidy manner. Jacqui's large brown eyes focused on her with a frightening intensity. Jenny's mind raced. Why had she come here? What did she want to talk about? Her mind swamped with questions. In a slow and unhurried manner Jenny moved across the room.

'I'll lock the door. Come through to the parlour.'

The phrase resonated in Jenny's head. So much of the case against her had been based on what had happened in that room. She would leave Peaklow. Jacqui hovered uncertainly, shifting from one foot to another, clasping her handbag under one arm as though frightened it would be snatched away.

Jenny didn't offer a drink, as she had no intention of leaving anyone on their own in the room. 'Sit down, please.'

Jacqui hesitated, sighed deeply, and slumped down. She took a tissue from her bag as though she expected to cry. 'I need your help.'

'Help with what?' Jenny's voice sounded far brusquer than she intended.

'To prove that Tony didn't commit the two murders.'

Even before she had finished the sentence, Jenny shook her head, 'I don't know anything about the deaths, Jacqui. I'm not a lawyer. Even if I wanted to help, I'm not sure there is anything I could do.'

Jacqui groaned and dabbed at her eyes with a crumpled tissue, 'He will be put in jail for something he didn't do.'

An edge of hysteria had crept into her voice, which now wavered with emotion.

Jenny closed her eyes and summoned a deep breath, holding it for a long moment before puffing out her cheeks as she exhaled. This would be a tricky conversation.

'Jacqui, I can appreciate the support for your husband and it's praiseworthy of you to stick by him. It will be the courts who will decide, not the police or anyone else.'

‘You don’t understand.’ Her voice trembled and she studied her hands in her lap where her fingers twisted the wedding ring. ‘If he is kept on remand for six months before a trial, he’ll go crazy. The evidence against him is damming, but he told me he didn’t murder anyone, and I believe him.’

Jenny lifted her shoulders in a half shrug before replying.

‘Jacqui, he is a man with a temper. When he loses it, he hits out without warning. The gun and the quadbike belonged to him, but you already know that information.’

Jacqui drew in a stuttered moan as she rubbed a hand across her face, ‘He had a fight with Nicolas and got knocked out. When he came back to his senses, Nicolas lay at his feet and had been shot.’

The quiver in Jacqui’s voice brought out the sympathy in Jenny, who knelt in front of her and caught her hands. ‘Jacqui, you need to face reality.’ She attempted to keep her tone gentle while she explained the situation from her past medical experience. ‘A blow to the head can invoke temporary amnesia. When people recover, it can seem as though they have been knocked out, but they haven’t. Anyone around them would notice no difference. So, Tony hadn’t necessarily been unconscious, but had temporary amnesia.’

‘But he woke up on the ground,’ spluttered Jacqui.

‘With many blows especially to the head there can be a delayed reaction. The shock of the impact comes to the body later and a collapse is a common symptom.’

‘Do you think he did it?’ Jacqui glowered and her voice had a hard edge.

‘It’s not for me to decide. I don’t have an opinion on

the matter. I daresay the most crucial bit of information would be the fingerprints on the gun.'

Jacqui sobbed. 'There were only Tony's.'

Jenny let go of Jacqui's hands and resumed her seat.

'Jenny why do the police keep asking him, what items he hid in your parlour. What's that all about?'

The question caused Jenny surprise and consternation in equal measure.

She took a deep breath, 'Jacqui, did you know that the police arrested me on suspicion of causing the death of Kevin.'

Jacqui nodded.

'Someone planted some objects in this room to try to incriminate me.'

The look of surprise on Jacqui's face seemed genuine and a frown crinkled her forehead, 'Why would anyone want to get you charged with murder?'

'The police are linking the events here together with the murders.'

A look of disbelief spread across Jacqui's face, 'Do they think Tony is responsible?'

Jenny replied, 'When the gallery was broken into there were two of them, both could run, and were dressed in black.' She waited almost holding her breath wondering how Jacqui would react. Silence filled the room.

Gradually the realisation dawned across Jacqui's face. Her eyes widened and she winced in evident displeasure at the implication.

'Do you think I'm responsible?' her voice screeched as she leapt up from the chair, 'I came to you for help! Then you tell me that my husband's a murderer and that I'm a burglar! The sooner you leave this village the better!'

She stormed over to the door, yanked it open and slammed it as she left the parlour. Then the back door slammed.

With a sense of regret Jenny stood up and moved to the window. Her shoulders slumped and she heaved a loud dramatic groan. The truth remained elusive. If she'd been more understanding of Jacqui's difficult situation, she might have found out something useful. Instead, she had succeeded in alienating and annoying her. Jacqui stormed away across the back yard but suddenly she stopped.

Clutching the gate, she stood motionless, apart from her shoulders heaving as the sobbing racked her body. Jenny's reaction didn't extend to sympathy, but she did pity her. But had she been one of the burglars?

Jacqui twisted around and wiping the tears from her eyes squinted in dull eyed disbelief at the door, which she had slammed. With her head lowered she stumbled back across the yard. Jenny remained at the window. A light knock sounded on the parlour door and it opened wide.

Jacqui stood sobbing in the doorway. The uncertainty of the whole situation left Jenny rooted to the spot, while her heart hammered in her chest. Jacqui stood in the doorway weeping with great shuddering sighs. With a smothered sob, 'I promise you Tony and I did not break into your gallery.'

Mixed feelings swept through Jenny. Opting for a direct approach, 'At the dinner party Tony admitted he had shown an interest in my shop. The extension to the caravan site increases the need for a restaurant or wine bar in the village.' Her words lingered in the space between them adding to the crackling tension in the room.

Jacqui remained in the doorway, 'I'm sure you have

made up your mind about me.' Her chilling voice spat the words out through gritted teeth while she glared with animosity. 'Long nails, smart clothes and probably never does any work.'

Jenny didn't comment, but a tinge of heat spread across her cheeks, as such an image had crossed her mind. 'Tony does business by gut feel and intuition. Before I married, I worked in an accountant's and had been taking my professional exams. I stay in the background and he does the deals. I worked out a practical business case. A bistro is a good guess. We planned for an Italian restaurant. My calculations showed that even if we had used the gallery, this room and converted the outhouses, it wouldn't take enough money in the busy season to make it a viable business for the whole year.'

Jacqui's analysis surprised Jenny, but she remained silent, unsure how to react. Jacqui stepped into the room and with quiet precision closed the door. She wiped away the tears with a flourish of her handkerchief. 'I know I can trust you with a secret. Before you had put a bid in for this shop, we had transferred our attention elsewhere and we are near a final deal with the owner of the George. It's a local's pub that serves food and only just makes ends meet. It has the space to transform it into a better class pub with an Italian restaurant. The local trade will keep it ticking over and we will make money on the restaurant.' A self-satisfied smile slowly appeared.

They stood looking at each other with neither prepared to break the silence that enveloped them. Jacqui brushed the remains of the tears away, 'Now will you help me?'

Jenny plonked herself down into the armchair and

waved a hand at the other empty seat, 'Tell me why you think I might be able to help?'

Jacqui settled herself. Her skin had become blotched and red from crying and her hair dishevelled, but a grim determination set the line of her jaw. She took a deep steadying breath before beginning, 'You and Dan relate to the military. I've seen both of you with Clayton. When you were on police bail you stayed at Stanton House with the Colonel. You move in different circles to the rest of us in the village.'

'What difference does that make?' snapped Jenny with a grimace.

'You have the intellect and the background to examine matters and propose alternative solutions. The murders appear open and shut cases to the police. They are collecting the details and are convinced Tony killed both men.'

Jenny exhaled slowly, 'I can see the shooting of Nicolas is certain, but not Kevin's death.'

'Jenny, I'm open and honest with you and the police. They are convinced he killed Kevin.'

'Have they told you any of the details?' Jenny waited, unsure whether she wanted to continue this conversation.

'On the morning that Kevin died he came to the farm shop, after Tony had left. As usual with Kevin he was up to his tricks to get me into his bed.'

Jenny glanced away as she thought of the implications. 'Don't look so surprised, he was a sex maniac. He tried bribery, veiled threats and blackmail.'

Jenny hooked onto the word blackmail. It had been used before in connection with Kevin. Did Jacqui have important information? Tilting her head in a questioning manner she waited for Jacqui to continue.

'He threatened to tell Tony that I'd been sleeping with John at the pub, but if I had sex with him, he wouldn't expose my other liaisons. All of which were a total fabrication.'

'Why did you put up with him?'

'It's a small village, most of the time I ignored him, but that morning he came to the shop with every intention of seducing me. Tony had forgotten something and came back. The usual scene between them ensued, which only became interrupted by customers arriving in the shop and me stepping in between them. Tony issued his usual threats.'

'Did Tony know that Kevin had been trying to seduce you.'

'No, of course not.'

She gave a dismissive flap of her hand, 'He thought him a general womaniser and wanted to keep him away from me. That is why the night of the carnival committee meeting he followed him and hit him. When alone with Kevin even for a few minutes he would be explicit in what he wanted.'

'Why didn't you tell, Tony?'

She fixed Jenny with an intense stare, 'Be sensible, Jenny. I couldn't tell Tony. I could not have anything that Tony did to Kevin on my conscience. I don't know what he would have done, but he would have pursued him. So I stayed quiet. It didn't become a big deal as I didn't see Kevin often.'

From recent revelations about Kevin, it had become obvious that he would try a variety of tricks to get women to go to bed with him. Could his behaviour have meant that someone had gone after him with the intention of murder.

Jacqui's shoulders slumped and she stared down at her lap.

'While his temper doesn't help his cause, it doesn't place him at the scene of Kevin's death which is why the police pursued me.'

She gulped and her hand flew to her throat, 'But the other piece of evidence does.'

'What?' Jenny's curiosity surfaced.

'Nicolas and Amanda park their cars on the other side of the house to the footpath. There is a garden gate which gives access to their cars. Inside the gate is an outdoor power socket which Kevin used to power the lights on the scaffolding when he was working there.'

Jenny guessed, 'Did the police find Tony's fingerprints on the plug or socket?'

Jacqui nodded, 'He admits he put his hand over the gate and pulled the plug out, but on the night before Kevin was killed.'

'Why did he do it?'

'Jenny you must understand Tony and Kevin have been at loggerheads for years. He would do any little thing that would annoy him.'

'Did he steal his paint pot and flask?'

'I don't know. He used to tell me about the little tricks he played on people, especially Kevin and Lionel. One day I told him he behaved like a nasty little kid and I didn't want to know. Why didn't he just grow up! After that he never told me about any of his tricks, but I suspect they still went on. Stealing a paint pot and flask is exactly the type of thing he would do unfortunately.'

'Okay, I can see that both cases look conclusive, but his own solicitor is in the best position to question matters.'

Jacqui's voice lost its whimpering and turned vehement. 'He will be little help. I met him yesterday and his whole approach is to sit back and wait for the police to prove the cases. He kept saying 'burden of proof,' but with what I've told you a jury would convict him.'

'We've come full circle, Jacqui. I do admire your loyal support for him, but you might have to face the reality that he did do it.'

'He's always been truthful to me, but if you were on a jury, you would return a guilty verdict.' Jenny didn't answer. 'I need you and your friends to help me.'

'I don't see what we could do even if we wanted to.'

'Don't concern yourself about anything becoming public. All the help I need from you can be done in this room.' Jenny raised her eyebrows. 'I would like some idea of how the killings could have taken place assuming Tony didn't commit them. It's mainly the method of how it could be achieved. I'm far less interested in who could have done them.'

Jenny hesitated, about to shake her head but didn't.

Jacqui paused and her expression darkened, 'Let's take Nic's death. Tony and Nic are fighting. The gun is on the quadbike. If Tony didn't shoot him, how could someone else? Also, how could someone surprise Kevin enough to shove him off the scaffolding?'

The last remark from Jacqui had troubled Jenny's mind for a long time, while she had been held on bail. 'Please Jenny, with your friends, give me a couple of hours thought in this room. Nothing more. It's not much to ask when I might lose my husband to a life in prison.'

Jenny battled with her conscience. 'No promises Jacqui, I won't dismiss what you say, but I might not come up with anything.'

'That's good enough for me,' Jacqui stood signalling an end to the conversation. Jenny thought back through the conversation as Jacqui walked across the yard. Had she been too abrupt and unhelpful? Indecision swept through her, should she help or not.

Jenny sat in her parlour for a long time after Jacqui's departure. Her initial reaction had been to dismiss Jacqui's request and leave it entirely to the police, but she began to waver.

While Tony might have been arrested for two killings, three matters hadn't been cleared up. The break-in, the air pellet shooting and the planting of the three objects in this room. Did she believe that Jacqui and Tony hadn't been responsible for the break in? If it was the truth from Jacqui, it was not them, then who had entered the gallery that night?

The recollection prompted Jenny to open the cupboard and look to see where the objects had been found. Dan had described it perfectly and she could understand how the items could be slipped under the bottom shelf. Opening the cupboard, a hundred times would not reveal what had been concealed.

Someone wanted her out of the village. If not Tony and Jacqui, then who? More importantly, if Jacqui had told the truth about the George, then Tony would have no reason to want her out of her cottage. Could she check out whether Tony and Jacqui were buying The George?

Jacqui's business acumen had surprised her, but she could see the logic. Tony's temper might have got the better of him and he had killed two people, but that would still leave the attacks on her presence in the village unanswered.

Alternatively, Jacqui had stood in this room and lied convincingly.

Jenny's phone rang interrupting her twirling thoughts. 'Hi Jenny, it's Lindy. Welcome back.'

'Hi, Lindy.' Jenny had been surprised she hadn't dropped in.

'My mum had to be taken to a specialist hospital in Derby, so I've been staying down there. She's out of hospital now and on the mend, so I'm home. I'm desperate to talk to you. Did Dan give you the message?'

'Yes, but as time has moved on, and you weren't around, I anticipated that the problem might have gone away.'

'No, it definitely hasn't. When something unexpected came up the police took no notice, but I did. Can we talk soon? What about a meal tonight but can we make it later than usual?'

The request appealed to Jenny. The landlord of The George didn't come into the bar, until after nine o'clock, when he took over from John. With luck she might be able to glean the information which would substantiate Jacqui's view, about Tony not being interested in her shop.

'Fine by me, let's make it eight o'clock.'

44

Lindy and Jenny had chosen a small table near the window. Once the drinks and food had been ordered Lindy chatted about her mum and the problems she'd had to deal with. Jenny had begun to tuck into her steak and kidney pie.

'Can I ask your opinion?'

'Is it the problem you mentioned about Kevin?'

'Yes, I couldn't tell Dan in the gallery. I had to speak to you personally.'

She was curious about what Lindy wanted to tell her.

'The police came to the house and asked for my permission to look through and print out the bank accounts. As I have nothing to hide, I signed the relevant papers. They wanted more than I had in the house and so they made the request to the bank. A bank official rang me to query the extent of the information. As I was concerned about my mother at the time, I told him to give the police what they asked for, and to send me a copy. I didn't suspect anything unusual.'

Jenny's mind flashed back to the invoice found in her

parlour cupboard and her interest surfaced.

'What caught your attention?'

'An extra account that I didn't know about.'

'Perhaps Kevin opened it and then forgot about it.'

'No, you don't understand. It has a lot of money in it.' Her voice rose and her agitation was palpable.

'What do you call a lot?'

Jenny guessed at a few hundred pounds. 'More than twenty thousand pounds.' Her voice fell to a whisper as she uttered the final word and lowered her gaze.

'That is a lot?' Jenny frowned, 'where did it come from?'

'I've no idea.' Her voice sounded uneasy almost fear-ful.

Jenny responded with an obvious explanation though she suspected Lindy would have already checked. 'Perhaps Kevin had transferred profits from the business account.'

'The main business one appeared fine. It has a reg-ular transfer to our savings account. He'd been doing a lot of work over the last two years and there were several thousands worth of savings. But the other account is a mystery.' Worry tinged her voice and she gave Jenny a long assessing look. 'Can you think of any explanation?'

'Perhaps he had been working hard and the money had flowed. He might have decided to open a business savings account to help you with the shop.'

'Yes, that's my guess as well but the amount sur-prised me. I went through the accounts, but I could find no transfers from the business account. All the money came from payments.'

'What size of payments?'

'As far as I remember they were between one and four hundred pounds.'

Jenny's thoughts returned to the invoice found in the parlour.

'The more I have thought about this account, the amounts seem unusual. They must have come from small jobs, but Kevin mainly did larger tasks, which were often around two thousand pounds or more.

'Could you find any indication in his paperwork to show the jobs for which he could have been paid those amounts? The stirring of an idea began to form in Jenny's mind, but she kept it to herself, and waited for Lindy to continue.

'Only its title, FSR. It meant nothing to me, but at the front of one of his workbooks that he used for estimating the heading read, For Services Rendered.'

Jenny guessed but what could she tell Lindy? Furthermore, she had no way of proving it. Would the police work it out? At one time, they were interested in the invoice they'd found in the parlour cupboard, but mainly to implicate Jenny in Kevin's murder. With Tony in custody, and a good case against him for both killings, would they bother about an extra business account. She guessed not.

'Does the business money come to you?'

'Yes,' Lindy nodded in acknowledgement, 'either of us could sign for the joint accounts. All the main transactions were in a joint account, and the bank told me that the FSR account had been set up the same. I must have signed,' she gave a small laugh, 'but I don't remember it.'

Jenny absorbed this information with a satisfied smile. Lindy could use the money immediately which would be good for her. 'I'm sorry Lindy, but I can't come up with any explanation.' Jenny forced her voice to sound calm and flat as she couldn't voice her ideas. 'I will have a think and come back to you if anything springs to mind and perhaps come around one time to look at the details.' Jenny suddenly had an idea, but she would need to lie. Her throat muscles tightened. 'When Kevin worked at my gallery, he had a small camera with him. Did you check whether it had been stolen?'

'To be truthful I wouldn't know.' A brief laugh escaped her lips. 'He loved little gadgets, but never bought anything expensive. There is a drawer full of them. If you come round to look at the accounts, I'll show them to you.' Lindy's friends came into the pub, which pleased Jenny as it enabled her to end the conversation. Lindy joined her friends and Jenny went to the bar where she stood pretending to read the local newspaper. John smiled as he wandered down to that end of the bar, 'Same again?'

'Yes, please, John.'

As he placed the drink on the bar, he gave a small frown, 'I can't come for a walk, as I'm going to spend some time with Amanda.'

Jenny gave an understanding nod. 'I haven't been to see her to offer my condolences. I've been worried that the sight of me might upset her even more.'

'Nonsense,' John slowly shook his head and smiled, 'she would be pleased to see you. Neither Amanda or I could work out why the police would suspect you for killing Kevin. She has taken a liking to you since you've come to the village.'

'In that case will you tell her I will come and see her soon.'

'She'd like that.'

The pub clock struck nine.

The landlord appeared behind the bar and served a couple, who had just come in. John put on his coat and with a small wave of his hand in her direction, he left.

Jenny stayed at the bar to finish her drink. The landlord, an overweight bald man, prowled around the bar area checking everything appeared in order. He didn't start conversations. Jenny chose the most obvious route to engage him in a discussion. Everybody loved a bit of praise.

'I enjoyed your steak and kidney pie, that's why I keep coming in here.'

'My wife makes them.' Came the gruff reply. 'No shop bought ones here.'

'I can understand that by the taste. She must have to work hard running a kitchen for a pub.'

'Not much longer, I hope.'

'Why is that?' Jenny raised her eyebrows in enquiry. 'Are you leaving? That would be such a disappointment for me.'

A smile touched his lips but soon disappeared. 'It doesn't pay well and it is hard work. We put it on the market a few years ago, but had no interest. Then a couple of months ago someone approached us.' Once again, a fleeting smile appeared on his lips. 'They made an offer which we accepted but with the trouble in the village recently, I reckon it will fall through, but I can only hope it succeeds.'

He couldn't have only been more specific if he had mentioned names, but the conversation convinced her Jacqui had told the truth. That left her with a serious problem. Why would Tony and Jacqui want her out of the gallery if they were going to take over the pub? It made no sense to her. She shuddered. If it hadn't been Tony and Jacqui, the people who wanted her out of the village were still at large and might try again. The uncertainty troubled her. The prospect of moving to Essex grew more favourable as time passed. Then she could leave the in-fighting of Peaklow to others.

45

By the time Jenny returned home and had settled into an armchair, Dan had arrived. He sat and listened to some odd snippets of her conversations with Jacqui and Lindy, though didn't offer much in the way of any comments. Jenny didn't elaborate the whole conversations; she'd save the important details for later. She briefly told him about her thoughts of moving back to Essex. A frown creased his forehead, and he studied her for a long moment. 'I'm not sure that would be a good move.'

'Why not?'

'Even with the stress of what has happened here, I've never seen you look so contented. When the current problems pass away from your mind, your face lights up with smiles.' Dan's comments took Jenny by surprise. 'Also, it is evident from meeting people in this village that they like you.' Jenny gave a small grin but shook her head. 'Has even one person snubbed or ignored you because of your arrest?'

'No, that's true.' She gave a breathless laugh. 'Most have been kind in welcoming me back.' His fingers tapped a rhythm on the arm of the chair and his eyes gave her a meaningful look, 'So now is the time to get to the bottom of these issues.'

'What do you mean?' She narrowed her eyes and stared at his earnest expression with some confusion.

'There is always a danger in police work that you make too many assumptions. The killing of Nicolas appears certain. It fits with what I observed. A man with a temper, who lashes out. When at the caravan field he had a loaded gun. A temper murder. It makes it more comfortable for me as a police officer if the personality of the people fit their actions.'

A silence followed these observations which allowed Jenny time to mull over his words. It seemed a logical statement that the person fitted the crime. Tilting her head to one side, 'You mentioned assumptions.'

'There is an assumption that the two deaths are connected, but the first shows no sign of temper. Tony and Kevin had a confrontation at the farm shop on the morning of his death. If the killing had taken place as soon as he had left, or at least within a couple of hours, it could be rage and the vengeance that goes with it. But the death occurred much later in the day. Did there appear to you to have been a fight on the scaffolding?'

'No,' Jenny shuddered as the images of Kevin lying at the foot of the ladder leapt into her mind. She pictured herself moving along the scaffolding and remained certain that no fight had occurred.

'You can't sneak up on someone on scaffolding.' Dan smiled in amusement, 'It's too noisy. Tony might have gone searching for Kevin. He would have been around the village the next day. Any signs of facial injury?' Jenny shook her head, 'Not that I remember.'

'We don't know whether Kevin had any marks to

indicate a fight.'

'Not that I could see from the side of his face.' The finding of Kevin's body weeks ago had triggered a whole succession of worry and anxiety. At one time she thought the nightmare would never end and that she would be charged with murder.

'The police suspected you, which indicates to me he suffered no fight damage. The police wouldn't arrest you if he had been bashed and bruised. So, with no sign of a fight, the situation concerns me as to whether both killings relate to Tony.'

He levered himself out of the armchair and selected some logs from the basket which he then placed on the fire. When it roared to his satisfaction, he resumed his seat.

'My conversation with Jacqui left me convinced that Tony and her didn't break in here.'

'That's my point exactly.' He slapped the palm of his hand onto the arm of the chair to emphasise the fact. 'It's another assumption that they are connected to one or both of the deaths. There are far too many guesses for my liking and not enough hard evidence.'

His animated and forceful argument brought a smile to Jenny's lips. Just having him here in Peaklow for the last few weeks had made such a difference. She studied him with bright curious eyes, 'Won't the police doubt it in the same way as you do?'

'That's a difficult question, it's not that simple. To my mind this is a complex case, but my department would always deal with the crime to which you have an obvious culprit, Nicolas's death. We would take that full speed ahead for a conviction.' His eyes flashed with eagerness.

'Little time would be spent on the other death, which could be a genuine accident. The minor crimes of the break-in and the airgun pellets would be ignored.'

Whilst Jenny could understand this argument, she didn't find it acceptable. Several crimes had been committed and they all needed to be resolved. If Tony wasn't responsible for all of them, then who was?

With a frown of dissatisfaction, 'What about the planting of the three pieces of incriminating evidence in the parlour?'

'Not worth investigating.' Dan gave a dismissive wave of his hand, 'I would go for the conviction for the murder of Nicolas. Often when it is obvious that the case is solid, then the person would be advised by their own solicitor to plead guilty, in the hope of receiving a more lenient sentence.'

His words offered her little in the way of comfort. 'What about the other crimes?'

'As part of the bargaining to get a reduced sentence they will often admit other crimes. The police and prosecution would accept the admission. A second death would increase the sentence, but the others would make no difference.'

Silence followed this pronouncement. It remained complicated and her brain whirled. They needed a night-cap. She rose from her chair, crossed to the small side-board and poured a good measure of whiskey into the two cut glass tumblers. Once they were settled and she had taken a few appreciative sips, she readdressed her concerns, 'Following the logic of your argument, if Tony broke in here and planted the incriminating evidence then Jacqui is lying.'

'Do you think she is?'

'No, I don't and that leaves us with a problem. If her and Tony didn't do the break-in at the gallery, then who did, and what about the other incidents. I feel we are going round in circles,' her voice though calm had an edge of weariness.

'Yes, we are. In most cases at the start of an investigation, I get nowhere and become frustrated at the lack of progress. It's a natural part of the process. Then it's a question of sifting through the information trying to find the relevant detail which holds it all together. To find the solution, we must clear the fog. We need a plan!'

'Are you going to stay in Peaklow longer?'

'I vowed I would stay until a resolution was achieved, or do you want me to go?'

She didn't want him to leave, she'd got used to his handsome smiling face being in Peaklow.

'I want you to stay, but will you have the time to help me?'

He laughed, 'I suppose you mean, Sandra? Well, tonight was the last time we were seeing each other.'

'That's a pity. I thought you liked her.'

'She's attractive, but to be frank, a bit boring and doesn't appear interested in anything. Several times we've been back to the farm, and I've spent more time talking to Jacqui, who has much more life about her.'

'There is something I've worked out about Kevin this evening after talking to Lindy.'

Dan smiled, 'He was a blackmailer!'

'How did you know?' she spluttered a laugh.

'The invoice.' His twinkling eyes regarded her with amusement. 'I kept coming to the problem of why someone would place an invoice to incriminate you. A business invoice would make sense in a fraud or tax evasion case, but not a murder. The boxer shorts imply sexual, as does the photograph, so why wouldn't the third item be linked to the same?'

'A gigolo?' Jenny chuckled.

'I might agree with you if we were in London and no one knew where he went in the evenings, but a builder in a remote village. We can rule that out.'

'I asked Lindy about a small camera that I'd seen in his possession one day when he worked here. It had been a good supposition as according to Lindy he liked gadgets.'

'Anything else you found out?'

'Yes, a crucial piece of information,' Jenny's smile widened. There is a separate account, that Lindy didn't know about, called FSR, For Services Rendered, with over twenty thousand pounds in it.'

She leaned forward and grinned with evident enjoyment waiting for Dan's reaction.

Dan eyed her thoughtfully and grimaced, 'Unfortunately he was a successful blackmailer.'

'Why unfortunately?'

'He made a great deal of money out of it. Surely that makes him successful,' she raised her eyebrows in disbelief. 'It meant he had many victims.'

He drew in a deep audible breath and rubbed a hand across his forehead. 'If he'd only had one, then it might be easier to track down.'

'Why the invoice,' her brow wrinkled with confusion, 'I don't understand!'

'He targeted women who could pay. Some might own businesses. It would be easy with an invoice to put it through as a business expense.'

'That's terrible!'

'But clever. How much were the amounts?'

'Between one and four hundred pounds according to Lindy. She said I could examine them and check out his camera gadgets. I assume you will accompany me.'

'Do you think Kevin's death was accidental or deliberate?' Jenny's voice sounded taut with tension.

'The murderer made the mistake of making the scaffolding untidy. If it had been clear, I would go for accidental, but I'm inclined towards murder.'

'Because of the blackmail do you think it would be a female?'

'A woman is being blackmailed. She could be the killer, but if a man in her life found out, he might do it.'

'Jacqui wants us to think of an alternative to Tony. She is adamant that he didn't kill Nicolas and wants us to come up with a different scenario. It's tricky because the bike and gun belonged to him and then afterwards, he scarpered. It makes him the obvious culprit.'

'We need to work out a motive and method for each crime before we decide who had the means and the opportunity. It's going to be difficult to work on the premise that the same people or person did them both.'

'Are we going to do it tonight?'

'No. It's far too late. The warm fire coupled with the whiskey has made me too sleepy for any deep analytical thinking. Let's complete a round of meeting people first to see if anything further of interest turns up. Apart from coming with you to meet Lindy, I shall meet with Henry, to find out if he has more information. Why don't you get yourself out and about in the village? Don't forget about relationships, Lionel's son-in-law has been killed.'

Jenny lapsed into silence as she sipped the last of her whiskey. Where to start? Who should she chat to first? Her mind wandered back over some of the details. Elizabeth mentioned that Kevin had tried to blackmail her. Also, she'd had an affair with Lionel and yet a short time later had been passionately kissing, John, his son. Yes, Elizabeth might be a good place to begin. She might have some useful information without realising it. Jenny would think about how to tackle her.

46

'It's good of you to come,' Amanda had a warm welcoming smile as she opened the front door of Victoria House.

'Let's go into the kitchen, I'll make us a coffee.' Her smart court shoes tapped on the tiled floor as she led the way down the hall. As Jenny entered the kitchen the smell of freshly percolating coffee greeted her. She settled at the breakfast bar and Amanda poured the coffees into mugs. Despite the trauma of Nicolas's murder, she was smartly dressed in tapered black trousers with a silk blue blouse. Her makeup was perfect, but her eyes were puffy

'I couldn't be sure whether you would want to see me, given my involvement with the police.'

Amanda's eyes widened, 'Jenny. I know in my heart that you would never do anything wrong. Since we first met, I had a feeling we would become good friends.'

'That's a kind thought, Amanda. I will help in any way I can.'

Amanda averted her eyes for a moment. 'At such times the only comfort is to be surrounded by friends and family. I have my dear John, who has always taken care of me.'

Jenny patted her gently on the arm in a small gesture

of comfort, 'He's close to you.'

'Apart from John, I have my friend of a long time, Elizabeth and now I have you as well. Can we forget about the injury you examined and never mention it again,' she spluttered, as her grip on Jenny's arm tightened.

Jenny sensed the sadness and shock that lay just beneath the surface of her intensely staring face. 'The poor man had been under stress with his business. Unfortunately, he lost his stability for a while,' her voice trembled with emotion, 'and it cost him his life.'

Jenny's throat contracted with emotion, 'I won't mention it again.'

'He suffered terrible tension and couldn't sleep being fraught with worry. Even I couldn't pull him out of it. Sadly, you became aware of his uncharacteristic behaviour. Never had he retaliated with physical violence after an argument.'

The tears streamed down Amanda's face. Jenny stood and put a comforting arm around her shaking shoulders. As the crying subsided Jenny resumed her seat.

Amanda fished in her pocket for a tissue, dabbed her eyes. 'The stress boiled over in his argument with Tony. Whenever Nic became tense or nervous he would snap at me, but with Tony I had never seen him so livid. Between you and me they had a fight outside here one morning. Nic wouldn't let the argument go. Tony aggravated him even more when he ploughed the field.

When Nic came home the following day, Tony had spread farmyard muck across the whole area. It came so close to the fence, a load of it came into the garden. The smell permeated everywhere. Nic without a moment's hesitation stormed off to confront him. Everyone in the village knew Tony would be shooting rabbits at the caravan site. I begged him not to go, but he wouldn't listen.'

'That's enough sadness for one morning. Time for a change of discussion. No matter how many times I retell the events it's never going to change the outcome.' Her voice wavered with emotion, but she managed to keep the smile in place. Now let's cheer ourselves up with a bit of gossip. While the police kept you away from the village, two men minded the gallery. We don't get many new faces around the village and two good looking men came as a surprise to many of the villagers. Are they friends of yours?'

'Henry, the older man is a keen watercolour painter so his expertise was useful as I couldn't be there myself. The other is Dan, a former colleague and friend of mine who is staying for a while.'

Amanda twirled her hair through her fingers, 'Both are fine and handsome men.'

'Yes, I suppose they are. Henry is a new acquaintance, but I've known Dan for many years, he's such an old friend that I tend to take his looks for granted.' A faint flush tinged Jenny's cheeks and she busied herself by taking several slow sips of her coffee hoping that Amanda wouldn't notice. Why had she blushed?

'I saw him a couple of times with Sandra, Jacqui's sister.'

'He took her out to dinner, and they went out walking on several occasions. Although he's on holiday, I'm tied up most days with the gallery, so it made sense for him to have some company while I opened.'

Amanda seemed more composed since they'd moved the discussion away from the death of her husband. Despite her expression remaining serious an aura of calmness seemed to have enveloped her. Jenny wanted to move the conversation away from Dan, 'As I approached your house this morning, I couldn't fail to notice the For-Sale board outside.'

Amanda nodded and tears threatened, but she brushed them away in an impatient gesture with the back of her hand. 'There are too many memories here. It takes an age to sell a property, so I thought I would make a start. John gave me the idea, but it seems the best way forward.'

'Will you stay in the village?'

'I'm not sure. There are so many decisions to make. I have my own business but have been a sleeping partner in Nic's, so now I will take over the running of his company and as it is much bigger than mine which means staying in Birmingham more often. Nic built up the firm from nothing.'

Jenny walked slowly back to the gallery. It had been a difficult and emotional conversation. At times she could have wept as well. Amanda seemed able to talk about the terrible event, which was so much better than bottling everything up inside. She also appeared to be bearing up well under the circumstances, and she vowed to visit her regularly.

As the time approached to open the gallery, she considered rearranging the pictures as she now had several of the local area. The paintings of local scenes near Peaklow would be much more popular than a scene from Afghanistan.

47

Dan and Jenny strolled down the High Street to chat with Lindy about the FSR account and the gadgets that Kevin had collected.

'You like Lindy, don't you?' Dan enquired as they headed towards her house.

'Yes, I do, she has a positiveness about her that I appreciate. Despite the terrible shock of Kevin's death, she is determined to get on with her life, and is anxious to set up her own business.'

Jenny nodded a greeting to many people that passed, having become acquainted with a growing circle of villagers both young and old. Dan had been right about the local people, many had expressed positive views about her return. The attempts to intimidate her out of the village had stopped, and with no contact from the police she had relaxed again but had lost heart for Dan's investigation. She wanted peace and quiet in her country retreat.

A buoyant Lindy answered the door and led them through to the front room of the cottage. Bright and breezy, with an extra smile for Dan, they chatted about village news for a while, touching briefly on the murder of Nicolas. Then Lindy with a serious expression took out the bank statements and passed them to Jenny. As she and Dan sat on the settee, they examined them together. Neither commented and finally Jenny handed them back with a smile of thanks. Needing to make a comment about them she racked her brains for something bland, as she didn't want to reveal her thoughts on the matter.

'The small payments certainly mounted up didn't they, and the money will be so useful in setting up your own business.'

Lindy nodded and without answering replaced the statements in a large drawer of the sideboard. 'Are you still interested in seeing his gadgets?'

'Yes, but that's more Dan's expertise as he understands technology.'

'They are upstairs in Kevin's office, I'll take Dan up and then let's have a girl's chat.'

Lindy giggled as she spoke to Dan in the upstairs room. Within moments she had returned. As she sat down opposite Jenny, her expression changed. The smile slipped away, and her eyes appeared haunted by an inner anxiety.

'Jenny, I'm worried. The more I have thought about this FSR account the more I'm convinced that it is illegal deposits.'

Jenny tensed at her words as this could be a tricky conversation. Had Lindy arrived at the conclusion that Kevin had been a blackmailer?

Keeping her voice bland, 'Why do you think that way?'

'I've only ever been involved in the periphery of Kevin's business, but in the evenings, he would tell me about his current job and I've often helped with ordering building materials. This morning I examined his old workbooks, and checked through the invoices drawer in the filing cabinet. Everything appeared normal. There were a few invoices outstanding, but nothing unusual but his business notebook clinched it for me.'

'Go on.' Jenny braced herself.

'Kevin used his book for materials and estimates. From memory the jobs seemed right and the invoices followed. There were no gaps. When did he have the time to do any extra jobs? He would often mention a little extra work, but nothing on the scale of the FSR. Do you think it could be illegal?'

Jenny shuffled in her chair as she considered the best way to reply to the direct question, 'Let's give him the benefit of the doubt. There might be some simple explanation.'

'That's what I hope. Can you help me find a logical explanation?'

'I can't think of an immediate answer, but we can ask Dan.'

As though on cue Dan thumped down the stairs. 'There is something else, Lindy whispered, but I'd rather tell you on your own.'

'Okay, leave it to me.'

Dan came into the room, 'Interesting collection of cameras.' He stared at Lindy, 'I took the batteries out so that they don't leak. There is one that is jammed, he spread out his hand revealing the small camera, shall I take it and see if I can repair it?'

'Thanks a lot, Dan, I'm not good with technology.' She laughed, 'But if you want to talk about bricks and building sand, I'm the girl for you.' He grinned and popped the camera in his jacket pocket.

'Lindy is worried that the FSR account results from Kevin's illegal activities. There must be many explanations, which could be interpreted legally.'

'How did he get on with the tax man?' Dan sat down in one of the armchairs with a smile.

Lindy laughed, 'Like most self-employed I expect. He reckoned they wanted more than their fair share, but generally okay. Why do you ask?'

'It would make sense in his business to separate his labour costs from the materials that he purchased for the customers. The tax man might well accept that he could charge some expenses for the work in handling them but might want it separated.'

'Now, why didn't I think of that. There are a couple of firms that always want the materials separated from any other business we do with them.'

'Are you happier about that account, now?'

'Yes, much clearer.' A relieved expression washed over her face.

'Do you think I ought to go through the accounts and cross check them?'

'No, I wouldn't worry. I'm sure under the circumstances the tax man will take a generous view.' Dan stood ready to leave.

'I want a quick word with Lindy, so I'll see you back at the cottage.' Dan took the hint and closed the front door as he left.

Lindy grinned as soon as the door clicked shut, 'He's a good looking guy.'

'Yes, he is handsome. A long-time friend who has come for a holiday.'

Lindy moved herself around in her chair so she could lean closer as though sharing a secret. 'I couldn't tell you this in the pub when we met, as someone might have overheard us, but I've a little bit of gossip that will amuse you. I hope to buy the shop between Lionel's and the post office so I asked the estate agent if I could view the property again and take some measurements. As it is empty, they let me have the key for a day. The shop has a small flat above it. When I'd first viewed it, Kevin and I were living here so I assumed we would either rent the flat out or use it for storage. Because of my change in circumstances, I went there early one evening to see whether I could move into the flat, now I'm on my own.'

'Makes a lot of sense providing you would be happy living in a much smaller area. It's much bigger than I remembered so I took various measurements to assure myself I could live there.' A smile came across her lips.

'What is it?'

'As I moved into one of the rooms some strange noises caught my attention. I stopped and listened. They became louder and came from Elizabeth's flat.' The smile turned to a laugh, 'Elizabeth makes a hell of a noise when she's having sex!'

Both burst out laughing. Still giggling with amusement Jenny took her leave promising to meet up for tea in the George one night soon. As she strolled back to her cottage, she allowed her thoughts to wander to Elizabeth's behaviour. The outward appearance she presented was of an old fashioned, dowdy woman. However, she seemed to be man mad behind her frumpy exterior. What a strange woman.

48

Jenny and Dan settled themselves in the armchairs of the small sitting room either side of the log fire, to mull over the visit to Lindy's.

Dan opened his hand. 'Let's start with the FSR account. The amounts were for round numbers. One hundred or two hundred. The only different one is the invoice found in the parlour. Three hundred and eighty-seven pounds and twenty pence. The strange amount doesn't tie in with the others in the FSR account. Therefore, I think we can conclude that Kevin had nothing to do with that invoice. Your invoice has been paid, so it must have been the murderer, who had been trying to set you up.'

'Do you think the police would have noticed?'

'Even with a cursory examination of the account, that payment stands out. The police might have noticed it, but then they dropped all investigations concerning you. It then follows that the murderer must be one of Kevin's blackmail victims. Otherwise, how would they know that Kevin issued such invoices or have the details of the account.'

'Assuming it is Tony, how did he find out about Kevin's blackmailing activities?'

'The obvious way would be through Jacqui, as he is possessive of her. Perhaps he found something suspicious, and she had to admit to a little dalliance.'

Even before he finished speaking, she gave a dismissive shake of her head, 'Seems weak to me. Jacqui is independent minded and would deal with the issue. But what about the gadgets?

'Without doubt they were spy cameras. It underlies our idea of sexual blackmail. The cameras are hidden in simple everyday objects such as a large tape measure which could be left anywhere without arousing suspicion.

A small mirthless laugh broke through her lips, 'That suggests he could have sex with a woman and take pictures at the same time? Could the cameras be programmed to take pictures at set intervals?'

'Yes, as they were spy cameras, they would also be silent.'

With a hopeful look in her eyes, 'I don't suppose there is any evidence on them?'

'No, but that is suspicious. Most people leave photos on their camera until they download them or scrap them for the next use.' He delved into his pocket and extracted a small spirit level attached to a key ring. He held it up to the light and examined it closely pointing at one end of the spirit level. 'This is one of the spy cameras I took from Kevin's haul. It's jammed and doesn't work, but it might have pictures on it that Kevin couldn't erase. I'll send it back to base and ask a technical guy to look at it but having sex and photographing it only partially explains the blackmailing issue.'

Jenny shook her head.

'Let me explain first. The account had been started

three years ago, and contained about twenty thousand pounds. Each transaction averaged two hundred pounds, which would work out to be one woman every two or three weeks to blackmail. That's too high to be credible, involving a lot of time on illicit affairs with a wide range of victims. Therefore, some of it came from blackmail but not all of it. There must be some other way he had money paid into that account.'

Jenny eased herself out of the chair. 'Time for a nightcap. It might help us think.' She poured two generous measures of malt whiskey, then returned to her seat by the fire.

Dan waited for her to settle, 'Another problem to think about. Lindy is the most likely suspect for Kevin's death. After all it's often a spouse. It's easy to create the scenario as he had been unfaithful for a while. Becoming the laughingstock of the village has hurt Lindy more than him going with another woman. Perhaps she found out about the FSR bank account. She works at a builder's merchants and comes from a building family so she would be at ease climbing a ladder.'

She nodded, 'I understand. She'd had enough of him. He's working late, she arrives at Victoria House and climbs the ladder. Kevin would think nothing suspicious. She leaves the gate open and when the opportunity appears pushes him through the gap.'

Dan sipped his whiskey before continuing, 'She's small, but because of her background she is probably quite strong.' He leaned back in his chair and gave a self-satisfied smirk, 'Kevin wouldn't be expecting it and he would fall.'

'No, I'm not buying it. If she did it, why would she

make it untidy and remove the gate or just left the gate open. She had been adamant with me and the coroner's office that he didn't suffer an accident.'

'We'll make a detective out of you yet.' He smiled

49

Jenny turned up the track that led to the back of the shops which fronted onto Market Square. Lindy had invited her to see the shop she wished to buy. She waited in the sunshine outside of the big barn on the far side of the track and gave an enthusiastic wave. She looked an outdoor country woman in her smart waxed jacket and two-tone knee length leather boots.

She jingled the keys excitedly and unlocked the huge double wooden door. As the doors swung back on their creaking hinges Jenny followed her into the barn, which Lindy planned to use as the main storage location of the building materials. After the warm sunshine the interior had a chilly air, exacerbated by the concrete floor and the long period it had stood empty. Through the single window in the roof a shaft of sunlight lit up the rafters and the dust motes which danced in the air. The two-storey building had extensive floor space and easy access for lorries. Built from local limestone the barn had weathered the centuries and remained in good condition.

Jenny stood in the middle of the floor space gazing out through the double doors towards the back of the intended shop. Although only a short distance the barn was not connected to the shop. Since the break in at her gallery, Jenny had a heightened awareness of keeping things protected.

A frown creased her forehead, 'How will you deal with security? When you are in the shop, there will be a lot of goods in this barn.'

'A woman I work with will join me. As she often works in the yard at work, she would be ideal. Also, I'll put cameras up.' She sighed and her shoulders sagged. 'Kevin would have loved installing cameras.

Jenny moved away from the barn towards the flat hoping to distract Lindy from her thoughts of Kevin and cameras. They climbed the exterior concrete steps and stepped into the empty space. The spacious flat had a large lounge, a small galley kitchen, plus two bedrooms and a bathroom. Essentially it was in good condition and would only require decorating and cleaning.

After half an hour or so of measuring and chatting through some ideas they had finished what Lindy wanted to achieve. As they left and locked up, so Jenny glanced down the track. Lionel walked backwards and forwards moving crates around outside the back of his shop.

In a cheerier voice than normal he shouted, 'Good morning, Jenny. Hello, Lindy.'

'That's a surprise,' Lindy whispered to Jenny, as she acknowledged with a smile and a small wave of her hand. Jenny waved her arm in his direction. Turning to Lindy, she touched her lightly on the arm and inclined her head, 'I want to speak to Lionel, so I'll let you leave.'

With a happy smile Lindy strolled off down the track singing to herself. Jenny wandered in Lionel's direction as this seemed the perfect moment to speak to him on his own. Although she had spoken to him on several occasions when buying meat in his shop, it didn't lend itself for a serious discussion. There were always too many people around and she needed a private conversation.

Leaning against the fence and appearing relaxed, he waited for her with a smile. She joined him and rested her arm on the fence, 'We haven't had much chance to speak, Lionel. I wanted a quiet moment to say how sorry I am about the death of your son-in-law. It must have been a great shock to your family and especially Amanda.'

For a long moment silence hung in the air between them. Tilting his head, he treated her to a searching gaze through his pale blue eyes. 'Thank you, you are thoughtful. You are right, his death came as a shock.' As he spoke, he moved from the shade and came to a halt further along the fence to stand in the sun. 'It could have happened at any time. I hoped there would be no reason for Tony and Nic to encounter apart from a nod of recognition in the street.

'Because of their tempers?'

'Yes. Tony has always flown off the handle and hit out, but Nic was a slow burner who then exploded. I tried my best to persuade Nic not to approach Tony over the footpath. But he wouldn't listen to me, and in the end, it cost him his life.'

Jenny experienced a surge of pity for Lionel. 'You sound as though you had a good relationship with Nic.'

'Yes, although he was too domineering over Amanda. But I suppose all father's say that about their daughters. Amanda is more confident these days so she could deal with him, and they were good for each other.'

Jenny's mind drifted as images of Nicolas and Amanda swirled through her thoughts. They had been a striking couple. Amanda blonde and beautiful and Nicolas dark haired and handsome. What a shame their relationship ended tragically.

Lionel leaned back against the fence, closed his eyes and tilted his face to the sun. A small smile played across his lips. 'After the years in a cold wasteland of a butcher's shop, the sun is so wonderful.' She had never seen or heard him like this before.

Keeping her voice light-hearted, 'Are you planning to retire to a plush villa in Spain?'

He chuckled, 'It's strange you raise the topic.'

Opening his eyes he grinned, 'The other day my wife suggested it would be good to retire to Spain. It came out of the blue as she's never mentioned the idea before. Also, Amanda keeps suggesting I hand over the shop to John and retire. Although she then wants me to buy next door.' Indicating the empty shop and barn with an inclination of his head, 'Then she would move her hairdressing business in there. Though perhaps her ideas have changed with Nic's death. Lindy is a good lass. She's lost her husband and has set her heart on the shop. It would be a despicable action to take it from her.'

The change in Lionel continued to take Jenny by surprise. He closed his eyes and turned his face to the sun once again. Without opening them, 'I don't know what is happening in this village, but I don't like it. I've lived here all my life. The biggest crimes I can remember are minor break-ins or traffic offences. Two deaths and the break-in at your gallery are not right. Something's happening and I don't know what and neither do the police if they are going around arresting people like you.'

'It is unsettling.' She shivered. It had been so scary.

Lionel suddenly opened his eyes, 'You're not thinking of leaving, are you?'

'I would like to see it out here. It's a lovely spot, but my patience is wearing thin.'

'I can understand but give us at least one more chance.'

The words of reassurance from him meant a great deal to her. His eyes closed again as he turned his face upwards to the sun. This time without opening them, 'Elizabeth won't talk to me.' His voice had a hint of lightness. 'I've told her it's all over. I'm too old to start having elicit affairs. It's a mystery to me why she wanted to start one.'

Suddenly he shook himself out of his lethargy, 'I must get these crates sorted, otherwise I shall be here all day.' He levered himself away from the fence and pushed up his sleeves. With a nod of farewell and a warm smile she left him to continue his work.

As Jenny wandered back down the track, she became convinced Lionel had hidden depths. On an impulse she decided that an informal chat with a certain woman would be a good idea. Turning towards Elizabeth's flat above the post office she climbed the steps and hammered with determination on the door. It opened quickly and an apprehensive Elizabeth led her through to the lounge. There had been no smile of welcome and she'd peered at Jenny through narrowed eyes.

Wearing her usual old-fashioned clothes, she eased herself into a sagging armchair with a sigh. Jenny didn't wait to be invited to take a seat but perched herself on a nearby chair and swept her eyes around the drab uninteresting room of beige and brown.

Jenny couldn't be sure why, but she had no intention of putting her at ease. 'Elizabeth, we have got to know each other well since I've come to this village.'

Elizabeth nodded and squirmed uncomfortably in her seat. Jenny let out an exasperated breath, 'I do not know what you are up to!'

'I don't know what you mean.' Her eyes shifted nervously, and she gazed towards the window.

'I've been speaking with Lionel. Why aren't you talking to him?'

'You know,' she fidgeted in her seat and gave an uneasy laugh that disappeared in an instant.

'No, I don't!' Jenny huffed in annoyance, 'that's why I have asked the question.'

'He wanted to end the affair.'

'That's what happens if you take up with married men. Why couldn't you do it with good grace?' she gave a dismissive wave of her hand, 'after all you started it.'

Elizabeth's head jerked up, her jaw dropped, and a small gasp escaped her lips, 'How do you know? Did Lionel tell you?'

'No, he is far too discreet for that,' lied Jenny with aplomb. 'It must have been you. He is a man of habit, who follows the same routine every day. He would never dream of starting an affair with someone down the road, who he'd known for years.' She stared at Elizabeth intently with narrowed eyes, 'Why did you start it anyway?'

Tears filled Elizabeth's eyes and her lower lip trembled. Jenny offered no sympathy and no smile while she waited for an answer. 'He is much older than me, but I've always liked him.' She gave a pathetic sniff as her eyes overflowed and tears trickled across her cheeks. 'Over the years we often have ten minutes together before business starts. It came from those sessions.' Jenny's doubtful face must have registered with Elizabeth, 'I'm on my own and sometimes cannot move or lift some of the boxes. Lionel comes to give me a hand. Although recently he has sent John.' Folding her arms across her skinny body, a look of defiance spread across her face. 'Lionel is snubbing me, that's why I'm not talking to him.'

'For goodness' sake, Elizabeth, he is not snubbing you.' A flash of annoyance swept through Jenny. Why did she behave like a sulky teenager? 'He has taken a sensible approach to avoid embarrassment. Can't you see that?' her voice rose in frustration.

'Yes, I suppose that could be the reason.' Although Jenny could sense no commitment in her voice.

Jenny gritted her teeth. It seemed an ideal opportunity to delve a little deeper into the men in Elizabeth's life. 'I'm glad you mentioned, John.' Elizabeth had a worried frown as she straightened her brown wool skirt and avoided Jenny's eyes. 'I'm not sure what you are up to Elizabeth. First you have an affair with Lionel and then I see you passionately kissing his son, John.'

Elizabeth drew in a stuttered gasp as tears once again streaked down her reddening cheeks, 'I don't know what you mean.'

'I often walk at night. On one occasion I came over the hill from the old station. In the moonlight I do not need a torch. You came out of Amanda's...'

Elizabeth buried her head in her hands, and groaned, 'I can kiss who I like.'

Jenny leaned forward and caught hold of her hands.

'Look at me.' She spoke slowly emphasising each of

the three words. Her grip remained firm, while she waited until Elizabeth lifted her head, although she averted her face and avoided eye contact. 'You can have sex with whoever you please. You are a grown woman, but I'm your friend and I am just offering you the advice to be careful with whom you become involved.' Jenny released her hands and leaned back in the chair allowing the silence to stretch between them.

The blood had drained from Elizabeth's face and she huddled back in the armchair. 'Yes, I understand. Thanks for trying to help me.' Jenny studied her face expecting to see doleful eyes, but her eyes sparkled with a distinct look of defiance. She stood up indicating that the conversation had ended and led Jenny towards the door.

Pausing with her hand resting on the doorknob, 'After all that has happened to you in the village, I expect you will be leaving, but it will be sad to see you go.'

For some reason no real conviction seemed attached to her words. Why say them if she didn't mean them? A lot of people in the village seemed interested in her plans to leave.

'I'm staying.' She allowed her words to stretch out giving them a certain emphasis to show her determination. As she wandered back towards the gallery, she removed thoughts of Elizabeth from her mind. Dan had gone out all day to meet an old friend. As she had painted a great deal lately and hadn't intended opening the gallery, she decided to clear the outbuildings. A job she'd been itching to complete.

Several hours of hard work showed with piles of rotten wood and numerous rubbish bags carefully stacked in the yard. She had managed to completely clear the old buildings and to sweep them out. With a sense of achievement at a good job done, she picked her way to the back door between the rubbish and the piles of old wood. The next day she intended to order a skip so she could empty the yard. The clear out would now allow her to start on the renovation work for the outbuildings. With a variety of ideas spiralling through her head she rubbed a weary hand across her forehead. Dog tired from the manual labour she went to bed early and fell asleep as soon as her head touched the pillow.

50

'Jenny! Jenny! Wake up!' shouted Dan, 'Quick get up! The house is on fire!' He shook her roughly on the shoulder forcing her to open her eyes. Jenny struggled to come to reality from her deep sleep, but the urgency in his voice soon penetrated her drowsiness. Suddenly, the impact of his words hit her. In one swift movement she grabbed her dressing gown as Dan hurried her towards the door.

The darkness and danger enveloped her as he shouted, 'We'll go downstairs and out the front door, it's the shortest route.' The smell of burning and smoke reached her nostrils and throat. Panic gripped her. The house was on fire. Dan grabbed her arm and together they groped their way down the darkened stairs. With each step the smoke became thicker. Her eyes watered and she choked and spluttered with every breath. The dark grey smoke swirled around them like a dense fog. Halfway down they stopped both doubled over with coughing. They were choking and needed to reach the front door and fresh air soon. He spluttered, 'We must get out. Hold your breath and we'll go for it!'

'I'm right behind you!' she gasped.

Dan's footsteps thundered down the stairs. Jenny

held her breath and willed herself to follow him. She stumbled, and half fell down the remaining stairs to the short hallway. The streetlights illuminated the smoke billowing through the door that joined the shop and cottage together. Dan put his foot out and kicked the door. It slammed shut, but enough smoke had already entered the cottage.

Jenny coughed and spluttered as she tried to breathe. Her eyes stung and streamed with tears. She staggered and blundered her way to the front door. Her mind screamed at her. Get out. A few more steps. Dan fumbled with the locks and finally the front door swung open.

A wave of relief swept through her as the rush of fresh air hit her. She stumbled into the street and Dan caught her. Pulling the front door closed he then half lifted Jenny away from the building. Jenny coughed and spluttered as they sat together on a low stone wall.

She struggled to open her sore eyes and couldn't stop shaking while her teeth chattered. Dan's commanding voice reached her as he contacted the fire brigade from his mobile. If Dan hadn't woken her, she could still be trapped inside. Putting her head in her hands she sobbed.

'Are you alright, Jenny!'

'Yes, yes!' she spluttered through her tears as he put his arm around her in a gesture of reassurance. 'It's just shock. I'm not hurt.'

'Stay where you are. I'll look around the back,' Dan left her sitting on the wall. Through her watering eyes she peered across at the gallery but couldn't see in because the blinds were down.

With a jolt Jenny suddenly thought of the people in the next door cottage and rushed to bang on the door.

She kept hammering and shouting and after a few minutes the door opened. They had already been awakened by noise out the back and had smelled the smoke. They had closed their windows, quickly dressed and came out peering around with anxious expressions.

They joined Dan, who helplessly stared at the fire in the back yard. The man shouted above the crackling noise of the fire, 'There's a hose connected to the tap in my back yard if you can get over the end wall of the garden.'

Dan scaled the wall with ease and a stream of water soon poured on the flames near to the cottage. It had minimal impact as the remainder of the rubbish in the yard burnt fiercely.

Within ten minutes the intensity of the fire had increased but then blue flashing lights lit up the night sky. The fire brigade pulled into the Square at speed. The leading fireman assessed the situation and shouted commands. One hose and two firefighters with extinguishers tackled the fire and within minutes a smouldering black mess remained in the yard.

Jenny retreated to the safety of the small wall, hugging her thick dressing gown around her. She still trembled but her eyes had stopped stinging and her throat seemed easier. By this time many had been roused in the village and had congregated in small groups at the edge of the square. Some had dressed and others were well wrapped in their night clothes. The police arrived and spoke with the firemen standing on the periphery. The team wouldn't leave until certain that the fire would not reignite.

A fireman approached and asked for the house keys. Neither Dan nor Jenny had thought to pick them up.

They broke into the front door of the cottage with minimal damage and two firemen entered the house and then the windows started opening.

Dan and Jenny waited, sat side by side on the wall in silence as the police and fire service busied themselves. Many people had lost interest and gradually drifted away. Jenny had recognised Elizabeth and Amanda. No doubt, Elizabeth had rung her, as the noise and shouting would have woken her.

The leading fireman came up to them. 'The house is safe. Your habit of closing most doors restricted the flow of the smoke. The worst affected room is the parlour at the back. The heat of the fire broke the glass so there has been a large influx of smoke, but it has been put out before the fire could cross into the gallery.'

Jenny and Dan returned to the cottage to dress and open more windows as the noxious smell of the smoke had filled all the rooms. She couldn't go down the passage to the back door as the fire fighters were there. The fire had not reached the gallery, but the porous canvas of her paintings would be permeated, and she would not be able to sell them.

Jenny made coffee. Firefighters who weren't busy accepted. The leading fireman and a police officer held a long conversation near the front of the gallery. Dan tugged Jenny by the arm, 'Let's join them. I want to hear the cause of the fire.'

Dan addressed them with a solemn tone of voice, 'Gentleman, I am staying here at present.' They nodded, look confused but didn't speak. There have been several suspicious incidents involving this gallery. I am here in a personal capacity as a friend of Jenny.' He put a reassuring hand on her arm and gave her an encouraging smile. Delving into his jacket he produced his warrant card, 'I am a Captain in the Royal Military Police, investigation branch.'

The fire officer glanced at the card, his face serious, 'Come with me.' They walked into the back yard and picked there way round the debris and approached the back door. Temporary barriers had been put on the outside near the door and in the passage. The door had been half closed. Jenny stood back so that Dan could get a thorough look.

The fire officer pointed, 'My guess is that the seat of the fire is there by the back door. If you look at the letter box, you can see the remains of wood put there to wedge it open. Jenny stared, took a step back and put a hand across her mouth to stop the scream that reverberated around her head. Her whole body shook. The fire had been started deliberately. Someone had tried to kill her. 'I have informed my police control room the fire is suspicious.'

Dan nodded his agreement, 'I would think there is little doubt about it. I presume the forensic teams will come. Could you also inform Inspector Robinson.'

'I believe that has already happened as he has asked to be contacted about any incidents in this village. May I take a statement from both of you.'

Jenny who had been leaning against the wall for support managed to find her voice and muttered, 'Yes, of course. I'll come first and Dan can stay here to examine the situation.'

51

'Here we are again, Chief Inspector,' Gerald waved his arm to indicate the assembled. Jenny and the others sat in the dining room at Stanton House. The mood remained serious, as the police had already confirmed the attack to be arson. 'We have another serious crime, but this time I would call it attempted murder,' Gerald turned his cold and appraising eyes towards the Inspector.

The Inspector interrupted, 'I am aware of the severity of the offence, and that it is the third major crime incident in this village within the last few weeks.'

Dan gave a slight cough to draw the Inspector's attention, 'Are you treating Kevin's death as murder?'

The Inspector sighed and his face crinkled with annoyance. He appeared tired as his eyes were weary and blood shot, his face grey and grim. 'Let's not worry what the crime is called. There are two suspicious deaths and arson.'

The last word sent a strange shiver through Jenny. Arson couldn't be an accidental occurrence, it was deliberate. Someone was out to get her. Gerald had mentioned attempted murder. Someone hated her. But who? She shook her head with confusion. Over the last week she'd relaxed, assuming all the incidents were over. But she had been wrong. A ball of fear formed in her stomach as the images of her smoke-filled house flicked through her mind. She gulped and fixed her eyes on the Inspector's troubled face.

Flipping open his notebook, he gazed around the table at the assembled group. 'The focus of my attention going forward will be the arson. Murder charges have been brought for the killing of Nicolas, but the death of Kevin is still under investigation.'

'What have you done about the break-in at the gallery and the shooting at this house?' Gerald's stern voice filled the room.

The Inspector would be under pressure here, but she gave him credit for coming to the meeting. 'In both cases there is little evidence to follow up.' Gerald glared at him. Dissatisfaction emanated from him. His jaw clenched, he narrowed his eyes and fixed his cold gaze on the Inspector's face.

The Inspector contemplated his audience with an indecipherable look in his eyes, 'There is a twofold approach.' His words caught everyone's attention. 'As we speak, officers are being deployed in the village. By now a mobile police unit will be set up in Market Square. It has the full facilities for a major incident.' He paused and checked his audience allowing his words to have full effect before continuing.

'The village and surrounding area will be targeted with a poster campaign listing the incidents and asking for witnesses or anyone who has further information to contact the police.' His manner conveyed a sense of satisfaction that he had made a positive commitment to solving the crimes. 'All posters have mentioned the substantial reward that is available for information leading to a successful prosecution.'

Dan interrupted with a frown wrinkling his forehead, 'Have the police put up the reward?'

'No, an anonymous benefactor.' Jenny glanced at Gerald, but he studied the notepad in front of him with intense concentration. 'There will be house to house enquiries throughout the whole village.'

Gerald's face relaxed and he appeared mollified by the Inspector's words, 'You mentioned a two-fold approach,' his voice still sounded cool although less severe than previously. 'What is the second part of your approach?'

'This meeting sir.' He lifted his chin defiantly and fierce determination deepened the lines on his face. 'Previously you volunteered and provided help. I am hoping you know something which you have forgotten that may provide a vital clue.' All around the table had expressions of extreme concentration. Jenny read a mixture of resolve, worry, commitment and eagerness on their faces. It signalled their collective concern to help in any way possible.

Clayton's voice broke the silence, 'You have arrested Tony. Is there anyone else who is helping with your enquiries?'

'Not currently, but we are visiting the farm that Tony owned and interviewing his wife. First indications are that she remained at home with her sister.'

The Chief Inspector turned to face Dan with a challenging stare, 'I believe you know her sister, Sandra.'

'Yes, I've met with her on several occasions.'

'Would you say she would be reliable as a witness and tell the truth.'

'There is nothing about her character, in the meetings I have had with her, that would indicate anything untoward. I believe she would tell the truth.'

He nodded, 'All key people in the village will be interviewed.'

Gwendoline entered the room, apologising for the interruption. She whispered in Dan's ear.

'Excuse me, Chief Inspector, I have a surprising visitor.' With his eyebrows furrowed in confusion he left the room. The Chief Inspector glanced at his notes and his mouth formed a grim line, 'I believe it is essential to arrange for the security of Jenny.'

Jenny's stomach clenched as she thought about her safety from the unknown person, who hated her enough, to attempt to burn her to death. Keeping her voice calm and her fears well-hidden, 'Gerald has kindly allowed me to stay here again, while my cottage and gallery are being cleaned and repaired. He has also been good enough to re-employ the security firm, so I shall be safe here. Dan will also be staying as the cottage is not habitable.'

The Chief Inspector nodded and gave an understanding smile, 'Shall we move on?'

Dan returned and resumed his seat. 'Inspector, my visitor was Sandra, Jacqui's sister, who popped in to give me information.'

The Inspector's eyes widened in obvious surprise. 'Did she have something to say that might have any interest on the current investigations?'

'It's difficult to say, but certainly something that I would follow up.'

'Go on,' his tone piqued with curiosity.

'She visits her sister Jacqui about every six months

and usually stays a fortnight. This time because of the trouble she has stayed longer.' His low unhurried voice echoed around the silent room. 'One reason she has stayed has been to work in the farm shop, as several staff decided to leave as they didn't want to be associated with a murderer. As she packed away crates in an outbuilding, she caught sight of a newspaper article that had been put out for re-cycling. The front page had a picture of the murdered man, Nicolas. Sandra mentioned that during her last visit he often came to the farm and regularly talked to Jacqui. As she hadn't known his name, she therefore hadn't associated him with the murdered man.'

Head shaking and confusion greeted this information. Jenny remained undecided about its relevance. Did it mean that Jacqui had been having an affair with Nicolas? Had that been the real reason Tony had murdered him?

'Okay,' the Inspector broke the silence, 'but perhaps he had a week off work and wanted to buy some vegetables.'

'No.' Dan brushed his rather flippant remark aside with a flap of his hand. 'I don't think that's the correct explanation. If they had met in the shop, she wouldn't have paid any attention. But she explained that their meetings always seemed to be out of the way. One time she went into a storage shed and found them talking earnestly together. She never saw them together in the public spaces.'

The Inspector wrote some notes, 'I'm sure you appreciate many enquiries result in legitimate reasons for visits and confidentiality, but we will pursue all leads.'

Gerald who had remained quiet for quite some time interrupted, 'Have your enquiries given you any indication that the attacks on Jenny could come from outside the village?'

The Inspector pursed his lips, 'I am convinced that the crimes come from within the village, but the attempt to set up Jenny as responsible for the suspicious death of Kevin has defeated me. I can think of no motive. She has only just moved in so why would she be a target? Unless, of course, Jenny you have any idea?'

All eyes turned towards her. With exaggerated care she scanned her memory. Her face tightened. 'My only thought has been the shop that I bought. It appears that Tony had an interest in it at one time, but then his and Jacqui's thoughts moved on. Although how wanting a shop could link to murder is beyond me.' She lifted her shoulders in a half shrug and gazed around the faces.

Dan narrowed his eyes, 'Chief inspector, did you proceed with the invoice? Lindy told us that you had taken copies of the bank statement.'

The Inspector frowned in concentration, 'Let me look at my notes.' He flicked back through the book that lay on the table in front of him. Finally, finding the correct page, he tapped his finger on the information written there. 'All the amounts paid in were round numbers apart from the one found in the parlour. A forgery, the specific amount stood out.'

'Were there any leads?' persisted Dan.

'None. The crucial camera at the bank had malfunctioned and the cashier didn't remember the payment.' He gave a weary shake of his head. 'It is a busy branch and with the bad weather that day people wore anoraks and hats. The resulting description is too vague to define whether male or female. We are revisiting evidence and will speak to Kevin's wife to find the reasons for the account as she is one of the signatories.'

Dan gave a wry smile in response to the information, 'Jenny and I checked the account and spoke to Lindy, but she could shed no light on its purpose.

Jenny added, 'Did you know that Kevin had been fascinated by gadgets especially cameras. A drawer in Kevin's office contained a number of spy style cameras, which were hidden in everyday objects.'

'Blackmail?' He tapped a finger against his lip and his expression morphed into a frown. 'Anything interesting on the cameras?'

'All wiped clean.'

'That's suspicious, but hardly criminal.'

'One had jammed so I sent it to a technical guy in Colchester to investigate the contents.'

'Will you keep me informed?'

'Yes, of course.'

Clayton had been silent up to that point. 'So, there's the possibility of Kevin taking pictures and then using them for blackmail.'

Dan nodded 'That's one line of thinking. It would give a good motive.'

Clayton gave a small cough and took a surreptitious look at the faces around the table. 'Tanya, my wife, has noticed a change in behaviour in a woman she knows well. She is jittery. Kevin painted her house. I wonder whether the two events might coincide.'

'If we could positively identify at least one victim,' Dan's voice sounded clipped and cool, 'we would know whether our guesswork is true.'

The Inspector nodded his agreement. 'Now we come to the main reason why I have asked you here today. The most difficult crimes that land on my desk are invariably based in villages. Everyone knows everyone else's business, but no one will explain what's going on to the police. The door-to-door might reveal information, but I'm not holding my breath. Even if a woman police officer interviewed this woman the chance of a positive outcome is slight. Can I hand this one back to you Clayton and Jenny? Between you, can you find out whether it is true?'

Jenny and Clayton both nodded. Jenny's mind whirled as she thought through a variety of approaches. It gave her something positive to think about. It was good to be involved.

The Inspector continued, 'My officers will focus on the fire and the break-in. Most people will give information if they know anything, but even then, they think through who might be implicated first.'

52

The following morning Jenny walked down the high street with Tanya who explained, 'Mary is shy, but normally calm although recently she has become jittery. She won't go out unless necessary and refuses invitations for coffee which she would normally accept. Clayton explained to me about Kevin and the possibility of blackmail. It seems so farfetched for such a quiet village as Peaklow.'

'When we meet Mary, your gallery and painting might be a good ice breaker. Mary wants to come to your gallery as she does a little painting herself, but she wouldn't want to buy anything, so she won't come in to look around.'

Jenny gave a small laugh, 'Talking about painting is never a problem for me. Tell me more about Mary? Is she married?'

'Separated a few years ago. Every Friday, early in the morning, she does the flowers in the church, and finishes at ten o'clock. Look!' She nodded her head in the direction of the churchyard. 'She is coming out of the church.'

As predicted, at first Mary had refused the invitation with all the usual excuses. The clinching fact had been her enjoyment of painting and meeting a real artist. Within ten minutes the introductions had been completed and they sat in Tanya's front room. As they discussed how Jenny approached her watercolour painting, so Mary relaxed.

With an effort Jenny attempted to move the conversation away from painting and onto more village matters. Keeping her voice light and friendly, 'It's hard to believe we've had so many crimes in the village. You've lived here much longer than me, Mary. I'm just a newcomer. Have you ever known a time like it before?'

'No, definitely not.' spluttered Mary, wringing her hands in her lap.

Tanya leaned forward in her chair in a conspiratorial manner, 'Poor Jenny here has been at the centre of those attacks.'

'It must be so difficult for you,' Mary put a hand up to her throat and played with the pretty glass necklace around her neck. With a worried frown she stared across at Jenny.

Tanya fixed her eyes on Mary's face, 'Did you know Mary, Kevin's death could be deliberate and not an accident?'

'Yes,' she mumbled, 'I had heard that rumour, but why would someone want to kill him.' Mary shuffled in her seat and her eyes took on a haunted look, 'It's unpleasant to talk about these events, they upset me.'

Tanya ignored her friend's plea, 'No sensitivities Mary. These matters need to be aired if they are ever going to be solved.' She leant across and patted her reassuringly on the hand. 'For a while poor Jenny was implicated in

Kevin's death and they arrested her. They even kept her in one of the cells at the police station overnight.' Tanya focused on racking up the tension. Jenny concentrated on keeping her face calm and her expression friendly.

Tanya pressed on with determination. 'She's completely innocent so anything we know that could help the police; we must tell them. I've answered all their questions.' Pausing she raised her eyebrows questioningly, 'It's strange but they lost interest when I told them Kevin hadn't completed any work on my house.'

Mary's face turned pale and she drew in a stuttered gasp.

'I'm sure you must have got it wrong Tanya,' she straightened her skirt with long nervous strokes, 'why would the police be interested in what work Kevin did?' Her strained voice was laden with emotion.

Tanya took no notice of her friend's discomfort. 'We all know that he was a womaniser.'

'I don't listen to such gossip,' Mary's frantic eyes stumbled around the room as though searching for a means of escape.

'Even I became embarrassed by the questions they asked me, and I don't blush easily,' Jenny added for effect.

'They started with me because my gallery had been Kevin's last job before his death at Victoria House.'

Tanya gave a rueful scowl, 'It's becoming obvious they think a woman pushed him off the scaffolding.' She raised her hands in a pushing motion and smiled, 'Death by revenge.'

'That's horrible, Tanya!' Mary's hand flew to her mouth and her eyes bulged with horror. I don't want anything more to do with it, and why do we have to talk about it?'

Jenny pressed on with determination, her voice steady and low pitched, 'There's a killer loose in the village. Doesn't that worry you?'

Tanya spoke through gritted teeth to keep up the tension. 'I'd much rather he or she was caught, but I'm guessing the police want to know whether Kevin had another life apart from his building and decorating work.'

Jenny's eyes narrowed, 'I spoke with Lindy yesterday. The police must suspect Kevin had ulterior motives because they have taken his bank account details and his cameras.'

Mary gasped and slumped back in the chair, her face a ghastly white. She emitted a groan.

Tanya leapt up, 'What's the matter, Mary? Are you ill? You've gone as white as a sheet. Mary, talk to us.'

After fetching her a glass of water, they made her put her feet up.

Jenny intent on keeping up the pressure, 'You might need to be checked over by your doctor. A fainting fit for no reason could require further investigation. I used to be a nurse. It has the classic symptoms of a sudden shock, but we were only talking about the village.'

Tanya intent on having the final word, 'We only mentioned Kevin's cameras and his bank accounts.'

Mary burst out crying.

In a gentle manner, Tanya grasped hold of Mary's hand, 'Come on, Mary. Let's hear what's troubling you.' She shook her head and her lips quivered. 'It's to do with Kevin isn't it? Why don't you tell us, we might be able to help. We could then tell the police, but not mention your name. It's better to tell us.'

Mary regarded them with a resigned look, 'Will you promise not to tell them my name?'

'If we don't Mary, the police will come to you anyway. They are doing a door-to-door.'

'They might not worry you if they get the details they want,' Jenny smiled encouragingly.

'Come on, Mary.' Tanya patted her hand, 'We've known each other for years. There is nothing to be ashamed about, you are a single woman without attachments.'

Mary lowered her head and slumped into silence. They waited patiently for her to choose her words. Jenny almost held her breath as this could be the breakthrough that the investigation needed.

Mary lifted her head and gave a tight smile, 'I liked him, and we spent time chatting to each other. He made me laugh and I found him utterly charming. As he had been painting the outside, I'd given him a back door key so he could turn the electricity on.'

Early one morning he came into the kitchen when I had only half dressed. You can guess the rest.' Tears streamed down her face. 'It left me feeling embarrassed and I made sure it never happened again. Every day he worked on the house I made sure I went out.'

Tanya smiled encouragingly, 'I noticed you became nervous; it must have been the same time.'

Mary grimaced, 'No, not then. Although I felt upset, I managed to go on as normal. Every time I got home, after checking he had left, I would burst out crying. As you say I'm an independent woman, but I've never done anything like that before and I didn't like it.'

'Is that all, Mary?'

'I wish it had been. About a fortnight after Kevin had finished the job, he came to the house. It had reached the end of the month and I hadn't received a bill. He handed me the bill, for the agreed amount. As I went to write a cheque, he put another invoice on the table, 'You'll probably want to pay this in cash. I read it, For Services Rendered - £200.'

She gulped in air and composed herself again. 'He then laid down photographs. I couldn't believe them. They were me and him, I had no doubt.' She took another deep breath. 'No amount of pleading worked with him. He remained hard and ruthless. The easy banter and charm had vanished. Pay by the end of the week or they go on the internet.' Worry tinged her voice and tears streamed down the unhappy woman's cheeks.

Tanya put her arm around her friend, 'You have been completely duped, haven't you?'

She nodded.

'Stop worrying. We will do our best to protect you, but the police will want to know where you were on the night that he died.'

Jenny hoped Mary hadn't been at home alone, but the first hint of a smile creased her lips. She took a deep breath as she recovered her composure. 'I went to a birthday party in Derby for the whole day and into the evening. It's my old school friend, so she will be able to vouch for me.' A broad smile appeared on Mary's face, 'And she is a police officer.'

53

Jenny and Tanya had reported their findings to the police and everyone at Stanton House. Dan walked into the drawing room at Stanton House, gave Jenny one of his dazzling smiles, and dropped into an armchair, 'At least we can be certain Kevin blackmailed women. But I'm sure it's more than the sex photos of women as there is too much money in his account.'

'What else could he have been up to?'

Dan didn't reply immediately and appeared deep in thought. Then he gave a smirk of quiet satisfaction, 'He's in people's houses and offices. Once he started a job no one would take any notice of him being around. Perhaps he kept his eyes and ears open for confidential documents. For example, how would Tony have reacted if Kevin threatened to tell everyone about his proposal to buy The George?'

Jenny narrowed her eyes and gave him a condescending smile, 'No, I'm not convinced. I think he propositioned women like Mary.'

'He could never compromise the number of women necessary in the timescale,' interrupted Dan.

Jenny arched her eyebrow. 'Mary explained that he

caught her early one morning and hadn't expected him at that time. What if he did the same with other jobs. He could be on scaffolding, ladders or other vantage points and get photographs through windows. The threat could be the same. He would publish names and pictures on the web.'

'Yes.' Dan leaned forward and nodded his head with enthusiasm, 'I'd go along with that idea.'

'Does it help us?' Jenny shrugged, 'It doesn't seem to get us any closer to who murdered him.'

With no sign of a struggle, it must be a woman and someone he knew, otherwise he would be on his guard.'

Dan tilted his head to one side, 'I'm assuming from what I have learned about him that he had been fit, which makes it strange he couldn't defend himself.'

Jenny acknowledged with a brief nod, 'While he drank a lot of beer it didn't show. He nipped up and down ladders with no problems. Something happened to put him completely off his guard.'

Jenny needed a coffee so she went to the kitchen, while they mulled over what they had been discussing. She added chocolate cake to the tray and returned to the drawing room and joined Dan.

Once settled she reapplied herself to the problem. 'Jacqui asked us to come up with a scenario for both deaths, that didn't involve Tony. It's worth it for Kevin's, but not for Nicolas's killing as that seems straightforward.'

They lapsed into silence, while Jenny devoured her chocolate cake. 'What are you thinking, Dan?'

'I would like to have a detailed look around the whole of Victoria House.

It's the top floor that holds most interest but even

if we drop in to speak to Amanda that won't achieve my aim.' Jenny mouth moved into a slow smile.

'You've thought of something,' Dan's face split into a wide grin, 'what is it?'

'Amanda's house is for sale, why don't you become a prospective buyer?'

Dan gave a rumbling laugh and his eyes twinkled in a mischievous manner, 'Will you call her?'

Half an hour later they approached the front door of Victoria House. Dan rang the bell. Amanda opened the door and shook hands with Dan. Amanda looked immaculate in a black pencil skirt and grey cashmere jumper. Her hair shone and her makeup was perfect. Jenny tugged self-consciously at her shapeless anorak and straightened her shoulders. Amanda focused her attention on Dan.

'We haven't met but I know you are a friend of dear Jenny, although it came as a surprise that you were considering living in Peaklow. I had the impression that you were here on holiday.'

Dan smiled, 'I'm in the Army, but expect to leave soon. Jenny surprised me when she settled here, but I've fallen in love with the place. It would be good to settle down after many years of uncertainty when I have always been on the move. I like the double fronted house as it's like the one my parents owned, although that had been built on flat ground.'

'I love the place, but it holds too many memories of Nicolas.' Her eyes glazed over with tears. 'I need to move to our other house in Birmingham. The business needs me, and will give me a positive focus, so I'm looking for a quick sale. For the time scales, does it depend on you leaving the army?'

'No. If it's the right place I'd be prepared to buy it before leaving.' Amanda led them through the immaculate rooms downstairs. The lounge, dining room and kitchen were all decorated and fitted out to the highest standard. It appeared to Jenny that she moved around a show house. Everything coordinated. Nothing out of place. It appeared incredible that someone lived there. No magazines or newspapers were visible.

Amanda led them upstairs, 'I've made this the main bedroom because it's quieter at the back of the house and has such a lovely view onto the terrace and then the garden. A large ornate brass bed dominated the room, and once again the furnishings coordinated, with cream and plum being the colour theme giving it a luxurious impression. Even a small ensuite shower room had been cleverly fitted into the far corner.

The night they'd watched Nicolas hitting Amanda, as she stood in the window, came back to Jenny as she glanced around the room. 'The other bedroom at the back looks onto the terrace as well, Nic would use it as an office when he worked from home. There are two bedrooms at the front.'

'Are these just spare rooms?'

'Yes, we sometimes have guests, so both are suitable for them.' Amanda crossed to the window. 'Both overlook the front garden, and each has a side window.' The viewing soon ended and with appreciative murmurs of thanks they took their leave.

Jenny stared wistfully across at her cottage and gallery as they walked back to the car. Although habitable after the cleaning, the security issues kept them at Stanton

House.

'What did you make of Victoria house? Is it clearer in your mind?'

'Delightful and in immaculate condition.'

'Aside from the estate agent bit, did it help with Kevin's death?'

'I must admit, no.'

'What about Amanda?'

'Beautiful, focused and self-assured.'

'Could she be one of Kevin's victims?'

'No way. She can handle men.' He gave a small laugh while keeping his eyes fixed on the road ahead. 'While there is a history between her and Kevin when they were young, she is not a victim.'

Progress became slow as they were stuck behind a tractor, with no hope of passing on the twisty narrow road. Dan keeping a light hold on the steering wheel allowed the car to chug along. 'My guess is that the coroner will return a narrative verdict on Kevin's death. The police and coroner cannot be sure and will describe what happened as best it can be understood. They will pursue the murder charge for Tony. I would also guess the arson and break-in will be left on record as open files, until new evidence materialises.'

A sigh caught in Jenny's throat, 'That's a pretty depressing conclusion.' If the arson attack and the break-in weren't solved, she would sell up and leave. The arson attack troubled her. Someone had wanted to kill her, and that person would be able to try again if the case remained unsolved. A shudder ran through her body.

'You're going to have to live with it, I'm afraid. The mobile police unit has been there for several days. The house to house in the village has finished. They will go through the statements, but that's a lengthy task to be carried out by the rump of the team.'

'Won't they keep trying?' Jenny cleared her throat and fiddled with the zip of her anorak.

'Yes, until the next major incident occurs elsewhere in the county, the Inspector will move on and the team will gradually reduce.' They drifted into silence. Jenny's thoughts about the arson attack left her in an anxious frame of mind.

'If they don't solve the crimes, then I shall leave here.'

'That's what I would recommend.'

54

Early the following morning the gallery had been made ready to open, but Jenny didn't have the heart or the enthusiasm to make a new start. She straightened the last few pictures but didn't pull up the blinds or turn the sign on the door that announced the opening of the shop. Standing in the middle of the gallery, apathy washed over her.

Dan had gone for a long solitary walk, which would no doubt be a prelude to him announcing his return to Colchester. A pity as she had enjoyed having him around. She rolled her shoulders and decided to leave the gallery closed.

As she stepped out of the front door of the cottage, her eyes drifted across Market Square as it basked in the warm spring sunshine. What an idyllic setting. The sun lifted the colours of the limestone in the picturesque cottages from drab grey to silver. With surprising suddenness her mood lifted and with a spring in her step she walked across the Square to the post office.

A few weeks ago, she had attempted to become a detective and find out a little about Kevin's death. The recollection made her grin, as she'd assumed the persona of a modern-day Miss Marple. What a long time ago! So much had happened. Hesitatingly she came to an abrupt halt, as an idea formed in her mind.

As she weighed up the pros and cons of the situation, being proactive appeared the best option. With a deep steadying breath, she turned away from the Post Office to the edge of the Square. A good walk in the fresh air would allow her time to think and refine the initial idea into a more purposeful plan. With long determined strides, she set off along the track to the farm shop, though she didn't intend visiting there this morning.

As she strode along her mind wandered back to her first taste of village scandal imparted by Jacqui, on her visit to the farm shop. How events had changed!

Negative thoughts swarmed into her mind, but she refused to accept and allowed herself to revel in the stunning landscape through which she walked. The sun warmed her back.

Speaking out loud, 'Dan you are right the case will drift. Other more important crimes will happen, and it will be pushed aside. Not knowing who is behind these attacks will leave me unsettled. But only one piece of information would be needed.'

With a grin of determination, she wanted to have one more attempt. This village was a perfect place to live and she wanted to stay, but the crimes had to be solved. She would give it her best shot to find out relevant information to help the police.

Where should she start? Even this first question perplexed her. She paused by one of the farm gates, leaning against it, allowing the sun to warm her face as she stared across the field to the distant hills. No obvious starting point occurred to her. Her mind raced in circles achieving nothing. In frustration she closed her eyes and willed herself to approach the problem more logically.

Of the people she knew, many were closely connected with Kevin. A good place might be to work out whether anyone of them had both the means and motive. The walk had helped to lift her spirits and instil a more positive approach. With Dan's help she would make a list of all the people and try to assess their involvement with Kevin. Not an easy task but it might shed some light on the problem. However, time to retrace her steps and visit the post office.

She joined the queue at the counter with Lindy, who gave her a warm smile. 'Hi, Jenny. You haven't met my mother before, have you?'

Lindy turned towards the woman beside her, who leaned heavily on a stick. Her salt and pepper grey hair was neatly styled though her face appeared frail and weary. A smile flicked at her lips and she nodded at Jenny. Lindy decided to nip down to the butcher's while her mother waited. A stern woman, the initial half-smile had gone. Tutting to herself she glanced at her watch. Waiting in queues was obviously not one of her strengths.

Attempting to distract her from the tedium of having to wait Jenny began to chat, 'Lindy mentioned you were on your own, so you must be pleased that she finds the time to visit you so often.'

She received a curt reply, 'She comes two or three times a week, but only stays about an hour.'

A puzzled frown creased Jenny's forehead as Lindy had told her that she spent several evenings with her mother. Strange but perhaps her mother had become confused, as Lindy had told Jenny she'd been in hospital. Attempting to make further conversation, 'I was sorry to hear about Kevin.'

A frown of indignation appeared on her face, 'I told Lindy she shouldn't marry him, and I have been proved right. He chased women. Mind you, even though she's my daughter, Lindy is no better.' She gave an exaggerated roll of her eyes and her mouth tightened in disapproval. 'She is always after the men.'

The observation took Jenny by surprise. Perhaps her mother had mistaken her interpretation as no rumours circulated about Lindy chasing men.

Jenny went for a short stroll around the village after leaving the post office. Could this piece of information about Lindy be a starting point? Might it turn out to be the crucial piece that solved the whole investigation? Murderers often came from within a family. Kevin's unfaithful behaviour gave Lindy a motive. The embarrassment in the village hurt. Jenny gulped, as she liked Lindy and didn't want to think of her as a murderer. However, she did have a good motive.

Until the revelation from Lindy's mum, Jenny believed that Lindy had spent whole evenings keeping her company. Had the police checked it out? Even if they had, would a mother cover for her daughter? She wouldn't expect her daughter to be capable of murder.

Jenny's mind buzzed. How would Lindy go about murdering her husband? Lindy knew where he worked that night, so to pop over and see him wouldn't have been difficult. A possible scenario formed. She came from a building family and the quickest way to meet him would be up the ladder. She visualized Lindy stealthily creeping up the ladder and prowling along the scaffolding boards. If she had deliberately left the gate open, the opportunity could have come. Kevin wouldn't expect his wife to shove him off the scaffolding. Of course, they might have argued and she'd pushed him. But then why make such a fuss about safety? If she had killed him then she would keep quiet unless it had been a double bluff.

With her mind swirling she walked back home. As she went in, Dan called out from the gallery. He sat at the corner table staring with intense concentration at the screen of his laptop. He beckoned her over with an impatient flap of his hand.

'Look at this!' he pulled up a chair next to him. Jenny eased herself down. 'My mate at Colchester managed to retrieve the photos on the camera that we borrowed from Lindy.' Pressing one of the keys the screen filled with a picture. Jenny raised her eyebrows. 'That's Lindy and she's naked. She has come from the bathroom and is walking along the landing. Do you think Kevin had been trying out one of his spy cameras?'

Dan nodded, 'There are several others of her, either partially or completely undressed. None of them are posed and several of the pictures are hit and miss. Some have been chopped off and others only have an arm or a leg. Kevin had been trying out a new toy.'

'What do we do now?' Jenny stared at the pictures with a frown of disapproval.

'Lindy would be cross if she'd known what he'd been doing. Do we destroy the pictures and tell her it is broken and irreparable, then we can throw it away?'

He gave a small shake of his head and flicked onto another picture. Jenny leaned forward, 'That's not Lindy.

Although it's only a back view of below the shoulders, it's too slim for her.'

Dan frowned still staring at the picture, 'We are going to have to give it to the police.' He rubbed the back of his neck and gave a deep sigh, 'This is evidence. It could be one of his blackmail victims.'

Jenny frowned and studied the image, 'Do we show Lindy first? It could be a friend or relative of Lindy's. Kevin might have been practising with his cameras when they had a visitor. I think we ought to talk to her first.'

'It's a dangerous way forward.' His forehead creased with disapproval, 'What happens if she murdered her husband?'

'It's the right thing to do, Dan. If she murdered her husband, it would be reasonable to suppose she knew about the blackmail, so she would have disposed of his cameras. Why would she risk keeping them?'

Concern grew on his face as he listened. He hesitated. 'Okay, let's go and see her.'

'No, that will never work,' she put a restraining hand on his shoulder.

'Even if she knows something, she will keep it to herself with you there. I'll do it on my own. It can look more casual which means she might be more forthcoming.'

Early in the evening Jenny knocked on the front door of Lindy's house. It would be a difficult conversation, and she nervously shuffled from one foot to the other, as unease rolled through her while she waited on the doorstep.

As she had been walking down the road, so she mulled over the idea that his death was an accident. She had conjured up a different chain of events. A dramatic incident had made him drop his guard on safety, and that's why the scaffolding had become a mess. It appeared the most plausible solution.

As the door opened Jenny expected a normal lovely smile from Lindy, However, a stern face and eyes that flashed with anger, were the greeting she received, followed by a choked almost venomous comment, 'Oh, it's you.' She strutted away from the front door and left it open. Jenny took the invite to go in. She followed Lindy into the lounge. Lindy spun round with her hands on her hips. 'I thought you were my friend!'

Jenny drew in a stuttered gasp. 'I am, Lindy. What's wrong? What's happened?'

Lindy snorted with derision, 'You were interrogating my mother this morning!'

Jenny's eyes narrowed. Such petty accusations were a futile waste of time. 'I did not!'

'Mum said you asked her questions about me.'

'That's untrue. I asked if she felt better.'

'I was still there at that point.' She tapped her foot with impatience.

Jenny would not back down. 'I offered condolences about Kevin. After that I didn't ask any questions. Your mother did the talking.'

'What did she talk about?'

'Lindy, why are you questioning me? I had a general conversation in a post office queue.'

'Mum maintained that she could tell by your face that you didn't believe her.'

'Lindy, listen to me carefully!'

In those few brief moments Jenny devised an approach to elicit the information she wanted from Lindy. 'I became confused because you told me one version and your mother something different.'

'About what?'

'You've told me on several occasions you spend several evenings a week with your mother, but she told me you only popped in for an hour or so. It's not important as far as I'm concerned and there will be a hundred reasons why the lines between the three of us have become crossed.'

Jenny expected a fierce denial from Lindy, but instead her eyes filled with tears.

'Oh my god!' she drew in a stuttered gasp as tears streamed unchecked down her face. Groping for the arm of the nearby chair, she lowered herself down. With her head in her hands, she rocked herself slowly backwards and forwards. The sound of Lindy's desolate sobs filled the room.

Jenny eased herself into the adjacent armchair and waited in silence. Gradually the intensity of her sobs reduced. 'What else did she say?'

'Nothing of importance. General chit-chat.' Jenny gave a small dismissive flap of her hand.

'No doubt she mentioned what a bad husband Kevin had been, and what a bad daughter I am. Didn't she?'

'No man is ever good enough for a daughter. Your mother has been ill and people then see the world in negative terms.'

Lindy stared. 'The police were here the other day. They told me they would re-visit the statements and would cross check the information with other witnesses.'

'They explained that to me as well,' Jenny kept her

voice calm.

'If my mother tells you, a perfect stranger, the truth, then she will tell the police.' Her voice cracked. Jenny was unable to offer any words of comfort, as she needed to hear the truth.

'One hour visits?'

The sobs had subsided a little, but the tears streamed. She made no attempt to wipe them away. 'My mother thinks I'm man mad. I'm not, but I've found someone who is kind and considerate.' A flush deepened her cheeks. 'I spend the first part of the evening with him. He works in this area and goes home to his wife and kids at the weekend, although not the weekend Kevin was killed as he had overtime to do.'

'Lindy, you are in a mess.' She knelt in front of Lindy and wrapped her arms around her trembling body.

'He won't support me, he'll do nothing to harm his wife and kids.'

'Why do you go on seeing him?'

'I don't know,' Lindy sniffed, 'except he is the first man who has been kind and helpful to me. He has given me the confidence to go for the shop. We don't have sex every time.'

Finally, Lindy let out a long sigh, 'I know you've already worked out what it means. My mum will tell the police I didn't come until after nine-thirty.' She stared down at her hands resting in her lap and shook her head in dismay.

'The man I met will not say I'd been with him at the time Kevin died. Added to that the police always suspect the wife.' The words lingered in the space between them. After a long pause, she lifted her head and stared at Jenny, her face scrunched up with anxiety. 'I had a motive,' she whispered, 'because of his infidelity and now they will be able to show that I had the opportunity.'

'If you didn't kill him, you have nothing to fear?'

Lindy's almost hysterical voice broke through the turmoil in her mind. 'But what can I do?' she howled.

Jenny leant forward and grabbed Lindy's hand.

'Listen. I'm desperately trying to help the police find the people who are guilty. The person who killed Kevin also set fire to my gallery and cottage with me inside it.'

The revelation made Lindy look and fix a stare directly at Jenny, 'Was the fire deliberate? I assumed it had been an accident.'

'No, it was arson. That's why I'm closely involved in helping the police. But I could do with your help.' She released Lindy's hand and leaned back in the chair.

'Of course. I'll help. It will assist me, if the real killer is found. What do I have to do?' She raised her eyebrows intrigued.

'It will not be pleasant for you.'

'Okay. Kevin gave me pain when he was alive. I guess he won't stop even though he's dead.' She gave a wry smile.

Jenny moved across to a small table near the window and opened her laptop. 'Come and sit next to me, but I'm warning you this will be a shock. Dan took the jammed camera and asked a friend to fix it. This is what he found on it when he repaired the camera.'

Jenny flicked a key and the first nude photo came on to the screen.

Lindy gasped. 'That's me. The bastard! I didn't know that he had taken it.' Jenny flicked through the next few pictures of Lindy.

'None of them look posed to me. Were they taken with his spy cameras?'

'They must have been. I wouldn't have posed for him. If I'd known about this, I would have left him.' A mixture of anger and nerves shook her voice.

'There's another shock.'

Jenny flicked to the last picture.

'That's not me! It must have been one of his conquests.'

'Are you sure Lindy? Please study it carefully. It might be the strange angle as it has been taken from near the floor.'

'No, it's definitely not me.'

She peered carefully at the photo. 'Can you magnify the bottom of the legs in the shadow there?' Lindy touched the screen with her finger and peered through narrowed eyes as Jenny enlarged the area.

'Look there! A dark mark on the inside of the leg near the top of the calf. 'That's a birth mark.' With a sudden movement Lindy stood up and turned her back on Jenny and pulled up her right trouser leg. 'Look! No mark!' She flopped back down, 'So he took photos of his other women as well!'

55

By the following morning, after a restless night, uncertainty gripped Jenny. Dan had received a call from the garrison the previous afternoon, instructing him to lead a major investigation into the deaths of two soldiers. Within an hour he had gone. Jenny's evening after she had returned from Lindy's house had been lonely. It had been the first night alone, and she missed his cheerful presence.

The conversation with Lindy had convinced her not to play the grand detective. She had no intention of re-opening the gallery. Before the end of the week, she would put it on the market. The grand idea from the previous day of finding that last vital piece of information had vanished. She would leave it to the police.

Having decided she would have no further involvement in any form of investigation she felt obliged to see Jacqui. When they'd had a previous meeting, Jenny had given a tacit agreement to try to find some solutions that excluded Tony, but she had made no progress. Although her mind had ranged through a variety of scenarios, she had failed to find a suitable explanation that exonerated Tony from committing the murder.

That fateful night he'd been at the scene of the

crime, he'd argued with Nicolas and his fingerprints were all over the murder weapon. From Jenny's viewpoint, he was guilty.

A slow and ponderous walk took her along the track to the farm shop. While she appreciated the scenery, she no longer revelled in its beauty. This short chapter of her life had finished, and she would leave. The person who hated her remained at large. It was far too unsettling and foolhardy to remain in Peaklow.

As she arrived at the farm shop, she noted that business thrived with a generous number of cars parked outside. Pushing in through the entrance doors her eyes focused on Jacqui who looked busy refilling some of the fresh vegetable baskets. Hesitating in the doorway, she absorbed the transformation. The elaborate hairstyle had gone to be replaced by a bun. The elegant clothes had been swapped for dirty jeans and a thick scruffy tee-shirt. She had no manicured nails. Jacqui's hands had been working hard.

As the doors swished to a close behind her, Jacqui straightened up from her crouched position, and a broad welcoming smile appeared, 'Hi, Jenny. It's good to see you. Come on, I'm due a break and I'm dying for a cup of coffee.' Jenny had expected a frosty reception, but a cheerful Jacqui led her upstairs to the coffee shop.

Jacqui waited for their coffees at the elaborate machine, 'I owe it to Tony to keep the business going until he gets back.' Her positive words filled Jenny with admiration. Carrying their mugs of cappuccinos, they selected a quiet corner, where large leather sofas bordered a low coffee table. Once they were settled, Jenny with a directness that surprised her, 'Do you believe that he will be found not guilty?'

Jacqui didn't reply straight away but sipped her coffee and stared across the table with a flicker of defiance in the twitch of her lips. 'You think I'm a rose-tinted dedicated wife, don't you?' She tilted her head to one side and her steely blue eyes focused themselves on Jenny's face, 'I do believe him when he maintains he had been knocked out.' Her tone of voice had a savage edge to it and brooked no comment or negotiation.

The silence between them lengthened. Jenny examined her coffee as she mulled over Jacqui's words. Her unswerving support and loyalty to Tony was breath-taking. On many occasions Jenny had attempted to imagine a different sequence of events at the scene of the murder but had failed miserably. No matter which way she approached it Tony was guilty.

Jenny glanced across with a mingled flush of anxiety and frustration, 'I didn't get anywhere about others committing the crimes rather than Tony.'

Jacqui groaned in acknowledgement and rubbed a hand across her forehead. Just for a fleeting moment, weariness clouded her features, but in an instant, it had vanished without trace. 'No, I guessed you hadn't, otherwise you would have come back to me.' Her face had a distant look as she resumed the conversation. 'The police have been round several times to question me.'

'First about my relationship with Kevin.' A bitter smile curved her lips. 'I'd been reluctant to tell anyone the whole truth, but I'm an innocent party and while it's embarrassing, I didn't want Tony to find out. But if the police are ever going to unravel what has been happening in this village, then it's important for them to have the whole facts at their fingertips. I should have told you the truth as well.'

'It doesn't matter.' Jenny gave a dismissive flap of her hand.

'I've told Tony the whole story now and the police also have all the details. I didn't want to lie to you.' A smile quivered on her mouth as she fixed her eyes on Jenny. 'Let's finish our coffees and then I'll show you what happened.'

Jenny became intrigued and curiosity bubbled to the surface. As she opened her mouth to ask a question, Jacqui continued before she had time to utter a single word. 'My association with Nicolas came as the second line of questioning from the police. Their line of investigation was why had he come here so often? I don't know who told them, a frown creased her forehead, but it required explaining.'

In an uncertain tone Jenny asked, 'Were you close friends with Nicolas?'

'Yes,' she nodded, 'I couldn't be bothered with the village politics, between Tony and Lionel's family. I found it childish and narrowminded. Life's too short for such petty-minded behaviour. Anyway, we chatted and continued to meet, as we discussed ideas to banish these long running feuds. The meetings were innocent, nothing flirtatious about them. I'm happily married to Tony, and Amanda and Nicolas were a handsome couple. We both wanted to find a way forward.'

She placed her empty coffee cup on the table, and in one fluid movement from the low slung sofa, she sprang to her feet.

'Come on, I'll show you the problem I had with

Kevin.' Jenny shuffled herself into standing with none of the grace of Jacqui. With purposeful strides Jacqui strode down the stairs and out of the farm shop. Once outside she led Jenny towards the farmhouse where she lived, but instead of taking the route to the front door, she took a detour towards the back garden.

'This way.' She called over her shoulder. At the end of the garden, she opened a wooden gate and followed a short path through the trees. It led to a small side door of a barn. Much to Jenny's surprise, the strong wooden door appeared to be locked. Jacqui pressed several numbers into the keypad fixed next to the door. Jacqui stood aside with a look of mischievous excitement on her face, as she ushered Jenny inside.

Jenny came to an abrupt halt just inside the entrance. Her eyes opened wide with astonishment. 'Oh, my! What a surprise!'

'It's our swimming pool. Tony wanted to keep it a low profile, because he thinks people would treat us differently, so it's only for family and close friends. But I know I can trust you not to gossip about it.' Jenny nodded as the vapour from the chlorine reached her. 'There are no side windows only roof lights, so it's private.'

The pool with underwater lighting was surrounded by a wide deck with sun loungers. Complete with pool side showers, a jacuzzi area was attached to the main pool, and a wooden structure in the far corner was probably a sauna. Everything about it oozed luxury. It was as though she'd been transported to a posh spa retreat.

Jacqui moved along the edge of the pool beckoning Jenny to follow her. They seated themselves on soft cushioned rattan chairs. Jenny remained silent. For once words failed her. She hadn't expected to find anything like this at the end of the farmhouse garden. Once they were settled and Jacqui had finished pointing out the wide range of facilities it offered, her expression darkened. 'How Kevin got the number to the door I do not know, but he must have come in and set up a hidden camera. Of course, it is private, so I don't wear a swimming costume.' A faint flush tinged her cheeks.

Jenny's mind immediately honed into the perceived problem, 'Did he blackmail you?'

'He tried, but it didn't work. The week before he died, he sent me an email with some pictures attached, and an invoice.' She gave a throaty little laugh. 'The pictures of me were rather flattering much to my amazement. Anyway, the gist of the communication was, if I didn't pay, he would post them on a widely used website.'

An expression of unmitigated fury sliced across her face. 'I replied and told him to go to hell. All went quiet, but then about a week later, he turned up at the farm shop on the morning he died, to persuade me to pay. Once again, I refused and told him exactly what I thought of him.'

She gave a smug smile, 'I swore at him and my language was colourful. Later that day he sent me a link to the website which had the pictures on. His last email informed me I had a week and then he would send the link to Tony.'

'Did Tony find out?'

'No, not until I told him, and by that time he was in custody.'

56

Jenny walked slowly back to her cottage with Jacqui's revelations bouncing around her mind. When she had first met her, she appeared to be a woman who spent time on her looks and not much else. Then she revealed her business acumen, when she'd explained why they'd lost interest in purchasing her shop and cottage. Now, a hard worker, keeping the shop and farm going while her husband stayed in jail. An actress kept flitting through Jenny's mind.

Why did she go through the elaborate description of the hidden camera with Jenny? What could the reason be? A big house plus the swimming pool barn would be easy for her to slip away on the night Kevin had been killed. She could have been there when Nicolas had been murdered. Tony would never give her away. Perhaps she had an involvement with Nicolas more than she would admit. It would hold with Tony's version of the events that night. Nicolas had knocked him out. Jacqui had been there and picked up the gun and shot Nicolas. Then she left the scene before Tony came back to consciousness.

Jenny stopped and leaned on a gate. She stared with unseeing eyes across the landscape as her mind filled with the perceived events. After several minutes she sighed with frustration. No that wouldn't work. Tony would be aware of her presence and would probably admit to murder to protect her.

Jenny pondered her thoughts on the way back to the cottage, as she plodded her way along the stony track. They circled in her head and instead of clarifying the situation, she became confused. When she reached her cottage, she stored the vegetables she had bought.

She missed Dan's company and didn't want to spend the afternoon sitting at home alone, so she set off to the caravan site. She wanted to build a picture of what had happened that night, so needed to be familiar with the layout of the land. The new field had been brought partially into use and a few caravans were already parked at the edge of the area. The building of the new cafe neared completion. Dan and Clayton had explained that Nicolas's body had been found in the corner near to the bank.

The open field had only one corner thick with bushes, so that must be where the murder had taken place. Perhaps Jacqui had followed Tony that evening. If she'd hidden in the bushes with the intention of hearing the argument, Tony wouldn't have known of her presence. After he'd been knocked out, she scrambled through the bushes, picked up the gun and shot Nicolas.

The scenario that played through her mind appeared perfectly feasible and she nodded in a satisfied manner. The motive for killing Nicolas remained elusive, but they'd had many clandestine meetings. Had Jacqui deliberately left out an important snippet of information. As she strolled back home her mind ran through the perceived sequence of events. It all fitted together well. As she walked into Market Square, she met Sandra.

Not wanting to miss the opportunity, she stopped for a chat. They talked a little about the weather, and as the conversation faltered, Jenny grasped the opportunity and blatantly lied, 'I had another load of questions from the police about Kevin's death.' She gave a theatrical sigh for good measure before continuing with her deception. 'I suppose you are not involved as you weren't in the village at the time.'

Sandra hesitated while a frown of concentration crept across her forehead. 'No, you're wrong, I'd arrived a few days before and informed the police that on the evening of Kevin's death, I stayed at home with Jacqui.'

'Catching up with your sister, I suppose?' Her lips moved into a momentary smile hoping this encouragement would keep Sandra talking.

'No. I needed the time to deal with emails and Jacqui worked on the business. Paperwork and projections.'

Jenny leaned forward in a conspiratorial way and whispered, 'What a wonderful pool. Jacqui showed me earlier today when I visited the farm shop.'

'I've been asked not to mention it to people. But that night I spent most of the evening at the poolside. It's such a wonderful place to have right on your doorstep. Jacqui joined me for a while, but then had work to do.'

As they took their leave of each other Jenny's mind spiralled around the single thought that Jacqui did not have a watertight alibi for that evening. She could easily have nipped out undetected, pushed Kevin off the scaffolding and returned before anybody missed her. Jenny suspicions of Jacqui had intensified but what should she do about it?

57

Jenny hadn't been home long and had just settled herself in the sitting room with a magazine when Tanya, Clayton's wife, unexpectedly arrived. They hadn't spoken together since the morning they'd tackled Mary about her liaison with Kevin. Jenny organised tea and a plate of biscuits, and then settled down to enjoy Tanya's company and find out the purpose for her visit.

For some reason Jenny detected a sense of urgency about Tanya. Her usual calmness had vanished. After a few sips of tea and an absentminded nibble at a biscuit, Tanya fixed her gaze on Jenny. 'You and Dan have been helping the police, but there is one piece of information that has come to light. I've been working all morning, including the lunch time shift at the Manor and wanted to pop in on my way home. The police came to check on my statement today and Clayton sent them up to the Manor. I find it confusing when they talk about dates, but the night Kevin died I worked on the tables, so when they came to re-interview me today, I checked who I served to jog my memory.'

This sounded interesting. Jenny munched on another biscuit and concentrated on Tanya. It wouldn't be trivial if Tanya had made the effort to come and see her. 'Lionel came to dinner that night.'

'Was that unusual?'

'He comes in a few times a year, but it is always with friends or visitors he has staying. But that night he ate on his own which is unusual.' She pursed her lips. 'He had little to say but that's typical of Lionel.'

'What time did he leave?' 'Nine-thirty two, I checked it on the computer, he paid the bill, said good night and left.'

The time interested Jenny, 'It could have been close to the time of Kevin's death, so I wonder whether he noticed anything?'

'The other minor point is on the night of your break-in. When Clayton met Elizabeth and Amanda, they mentioned they'd been to the Manor. Once again it had been an evening when I worked. We had no record of them for that night and I don't remember seeing them together. Of course, if they popped in and had a drink and paid cash there wouldn't be any record.'

They finished their tea soon afterwards, as Tanya was anxious to get home and neither made any further comments. As Jenny thanked Tanya for the information and showed her out the back door, so a police car arrived in Market Square.

Jenny walked to the back gate with Tanya with mounting apprehension. Surely, they hadn't come to arrest her again. With her heart thudding, it stopped outside the butcher's shop. Tanya and Jenny stood chatting for a few minutes both wanting to find out what was happening.

After a few minutes Lionel strode around the side of the shop accompanied by two policemen. They got into the car without a word being spoken and it drove off at high speed. Shock and amazement filled their faces as the police car roared away.

Jenny returned to her sitting room and realised the plate of biscuits was empty. While she'd been focused on Tanya's news, she'd nibbled her way through the whole plateful. She remained certain that Tanya had only eaten one. With an exasperated sigh she settled back down in the armchair to mull things over. She was convinced that Jacqui had been the culprit. It would have been easy for her to slip away from the farm without being missed. Jenny wished that Dan was still here so she could talk through her ideas.

Her mind went back to Lionel's swift departure in the back of the police car. Perhaps the police wanted Lionel's help, as he appeared to be a key witness they had missed. He must have returned from the Manor restaurant at around the time that Kevin had been killed. No, she shook her head slowly from side to side. Lionel wouldn't be involved, Jacqui was the real villain.

Jenny didn't think it wise to be on her own in the cottage. People would find out Dan had left. Would there be another attack on her?

The idea made her tremble and she rang Stanton House. Gwendoline said she would be most welcome to stay there, but they were out of the house until about nine o'clock. She gave a sigh of relief as she put down the phone. It would be safer to stay there, and nine o'clock suited her.

58

Late afternoon and too early to cook a meal, she busied herself with housework to pass the time. As she tidied away, she came across her laptop which prompted her to sit down with the intention of sending an email to Dan. She wanted to thank him for coming to stay and remaining for support during the police investigation when they were convinced, she'd been involved in Kevin's death.

As she opened it up so the naked photo of the woman with the birthmark came up on her screen. She hadn't cleared it off after the meeting with Lindy. With nothing else to do, apart from more housework which came low on her priority list, she sat down and with eyes narrowed and her head close to the screen she scrutinised the photo inch by inch. Neither her nor Dan had picked out the birthmark. Systematically she moved around the photo magnifying each bit in turn. It revealed little extra detail. A white line down the edge looked like a chair leg, but the photo contained no more information.

Pack up and leave came to the forefront of her mind. The estate agent could sell the shop and cottage while she returned to the south. Imposing on Gerald for many more nights wasn't feasible. She composed an email to

Dan, thanking him and bringing him up to date with any extra information, including the plush pool complex at the farm. As she closed the lid on her laptop, another ploy sprang to her mind that might give her a more secure feeling for a few days. Why didn't she make it known in the village she intended leaving? Whoever had attacked her wanted her out of the village, so they would get their way, without further intimidation of her.

Once the decision had been made, she sat for a few minutes working out the best approach. Jacqui must be told immediately. Jenny's visit to the farm shop and chat with Jacqui that morning might have given her ideas for another attack. This time she decided against walking, so jumped into her little white Ford Ka, and gripping the steering wheel with determination sped off to the farm. The shop had already closed so Jenny knocked on the door of the farmhouse.

'Twice in one day.' Jacqui with raised eyebrows and an astonished smile ushered her inside. Jacqui led the way to the kitchen, where Sandra seated in a rocker next to the bright red Aga, gave her a welcoming smile and a wave. She had intended to impart her news and leave, but it might seem a bit false. Why would she drive all the way out here just to tell them she intended leaving?

No, she'd have to come up with a better reason, and then casually drop her news into the conversation. As her mind desperately sought for a feasible excuse so Jacqui's voice jerked her out of her reverie. 'I'm glad you've come, only I intended to come and see you tomorrow as there's some hush-hush news about The George. The deal is still going ahead and the date for completion has been set.'

Sandra didn't look interested in the impending conversation, 'Shall we put off the swim until later, Jacqui?'

'No,' she paused and a smile tugged at her lips, 'let's go now as we planned and Jenny can join us.'

Jenny gave an immediate reply, 'I haven't got a costume.'

'Neither have we,' laughed Sandra.

Jenny self-conscious about her body had no wish to go swimming with nothing on, but then a thought crossed her mind. The photograph and the birthmark. It would be a good way to check out Jacqui and Sandra, as she'd be able to clearly see the backs of their lower legs.

Jacqui chatted away as they walked to the pool barn. As soon as the door closed Sandra peeled off her clothes. Jenny hesitated, but kept a careful eye on Sandra as she went to the pool side and dived in. No birthmark.

'Come on, don't be shy,' Jacqui called as she removed the last of her clothes.

As she walked across to the pool, Jenny focused on her lower legs, but she had no birth mark on her calf either. Jenny took a deep breath and as quickly as she could undressed and dived in.

59

Jenny had a peaceful night at Stanton House and spend a large part of the morning talking to Gerald about possible decisions. He expressed his sadness at the thought of her leaving. Part of her wanted to stay, but the crimes had to be solved first. As she had been lying in bed the previous night so her mind kept drifting back to Jacqui. She had the means and opportunities and possibly the motives to kill both Kevin and Nicolas.

In one way, Jenny admired her poise as she appeared so cool and calm. Was she a good actress? Was it just a veneer to confuse the police and her friends? But it could only be supposition on her behalf. Yesterday while they were swimming, she'd told Jacqui and Sandra about her intended departure.

They had both expressed their surprise and disappointment at her decision. But could she believe it? Leave the cases to the police. She intended telling others in the village she would leave, the news would spread quickly then everyone would know, it might help her tension.

With some trepidation she opened the front door of her cottage. Gingerly she walked through the rooms with all her senses on high alert. Since the break in and the arson attack, she always checked through the house and gallery when she arrived home. She didn't know what to expect, but after finally checking the gallery, nothing appeared amiss. As she had spare cardboard boxes from moving in, she packed away her painting gear.

After being satisfied with her morning's efforts, she decided to have a pub lunch, then a call on Amanda as it was a day the salon didn't open. After that she would wait for closing time at the post office, and would tell Elizabeth her news about leaving.

John, at the George, appeared busy stocking the bar and so she read a magazine and ate her lunch. The brie and salad sandwich in a huge cob roll tasted delicious, and the bowl of chips that she'd ordered as a side dish vanished at an alarming rate. As she left the pub, she waved her hand goodbye to John and went towards Amanda's house, along the High Street. A brisk walk later in the day might be needed as the waistband of her trousers had tightened considerably after such an indulgent lunch. She met Mary and stopped for a few minutes to speak with her. Since talking with Jenny, she'd taken up painting again with renewed enthusiasm, and wanted to tell Jenny what she had achieved and to ask her advice. The jittery woman that Jenny had first met had vanished.

As she stood on the doorstep after ringing the bell at Victoria House, so her mind returned to the discovery of Kevin's body. Although she'd found him a pleasant and likable man the revelations of the past few weeks had changed her opinion. A womaniser and a blackmailer. Would he have tried to blackmail her at some point in the future if he hadn't been murdered? Although she didn't want to believe it, she expected that would have happened.

59

She shuddered and returned to the present moment as the door opened. The surprise registered on her face immediately, as John stood smiling in the doorway.

'John,' she chuckled, 'how did you get here before me? I only stopped for a quick chat.'

He laughed, 'Come in.'

'I came along the road straight here and I know you didn't come past. Did you fly?'

John smiled with good humour and his eyes danced with mischief. 'I have a few hours off in the afternoon. I'd stacked the last of the crates in the pub car park, so I've popped over to see Amanda. As kids we used to go over the fields at the back regularly.'

Jenny wrinkled her forehead in confusion, 'The walls are high and there is a large ditch from the back of the properties to the railway embankment.'

'Tony has only recently bought the fields, but when Amanda and I were young they belonged to an old farmer called Tom. He was happy for us to play in his fields and taught us how to build a stile in a dry stone wall, so we built our own routes across the fields. Also, we put in a secret bridge over the ditch. Kid's ideas, but I still use the route to get to Amanda's from the pub.'

They went into the kitchen and met Amanda wearing a housecoat. 'Hi, Jenny. Please excuse my appearance, I intended changing but then John arrived. He has only popped in for a few minutes.' John kissed her on the cheek and said goodbye to them.

'I've planned to go out in half an hour,' Amanda stacked some dishes in the dishwasher, 'Come and talk to me while I get changed.'

Jenny followed her up the stairs to the main bedroom. The housecoat came above Amanda's knees. As she followed her up the stairs, she had a clear view of the back of her legs. No birthmark. Jenny seated herself on a chair by the window while Amanda opened a large wardrobe. As she dressed herself in smart tailored grey slacks and a pale pink cashmere jumper, Jenny explained about leaving the village.

As an afterthought she added that Dan had been summoned back to Colchester and hadn't decided about the house. She found it difficult to concentrate on the conversation with Amanda.

Out of the window, the hill and trees where Dan and her, had hidden to get the views of the house, were visible. From there they'd witnessed the aggressive argument between Nicolas and Tony, and Nicolas's vicious attack on Amanda. The crimes came back to her mind with some force. It had been the view of the back of Amanda's legs that recalled the photograph, but it couldn't have been her. The close-up of the white leg of a chair came to mind, and her thoughts jumped back to her last visit to the house with Dan. The room Nicolas used as an office had white furniture. Both the bed and cabinet were white. An idea formed in her mind. It was clutching at straws, but it had to be worth a try.

Jenny took a deep breath, which Amanda didn't notice because she concentrated on her make-up. Pressing her hand to her chin as though deep in thought, 'Have you found a small medallion by any chance?' Jenny avoided eye contact keeping her gaze towards an unremarkable picture on the wall of a rose garden, as she lied.

'It had been attached to Dan's key ring and he thought it might have come off in the bedroom when he took his handkerchief out.' She scraped a hand through her hair and risked a glance towards Amanda's face. Did she believe her, or did she suspect that she hadn't told the truth?

'Why don't you go and check while I finish getting ready? It might have rolled under the bed.' Jenny moved swiftly across the landing. The perfect opportunity to inspect the room unaccompanied. She hesitated in the doorway scanning the white furniture which included a dressing table stool with white legs. The camera could have easily been placed in the knee hole of the dressing table and would pick up the dressing stool and anyone walking across the bedroom.

She peered under the bed in case Amanda came in, but she didn't. Returning to join Amanda, she shook her head.

Amanda surveyed herself in the full-length mirror, turning this way and that until satisfied with her appearance. She glanced at her watch and apologised for the rush as she escorted Jenny down the stairs. As Jenny stood by the front door, Amanda touched her lightly on the arm, 'Before you leave, we must have an evening out together, I've enjoyed having you around and I am so disappointed you don't want to stay.'

Jenny's mind raced as she went back to her cottage and settled with a cup of tea and her thoughts. Jacqui didn't have a birth mark and so couldn't be the mysterious woman in the photograph. Neither did her sister, Sandra. And after the visit to Victoria House she now knew that Amanda also had no birthmark. Perhaps the photo had no link to the killing.

Jenny took out her computer and loaded the picture again. While white furniture was common, for some reason Jenny had convinced herself, the picture had been taken in that room. This presented a new mystery to her. Kevin only had access to Victoria House for a short time. As he painted the windows, he would need to be able to open them.

Nicolas and Amanda didn't want to stay there as the scaffolding and tarpaulins made the house too dark. It appeared unlikely that they would have a guest when they were away. Therefore, the photo didn't make sense. If the house had been empty, why would Kevin leave his camera set up? The birthmark woman remained a mystery, and there appeared no connection with Jenny's prime suspect Jacqui.

60

Jenny shutdown her laptop with a snap of frustration. She had made no progress with her speculation. But her mind had been made up by the attacks on her and she would leave Peaklow. The temptation to relocate near the garrison in Colchester, where she could see her old friends would be easy, but her life had moved on. Should she do the same again as when she had found Peaklow. It would be good to paint in the Lake District.

Why not stay there for a while and try out a new village. This time she would rent in the village for six months before buying. It would be a safer option. A glance at her watch confirmed the post office would be closed. She had spent too much time in idle speculation. Dan had disappointed her because he hadn't responded to her email or been in contact since he had left. She missed him, but once back in his normal role he would have total concentration and would only remember her later.

She trudged up the steps to Elizabeth's flat who smiled as she opened the door. Jenny gave her a friendly smile in return, 'Are you busy this evening, Elizabeth? I wanted to have a chat with you and I'm going to the Manor for a meal, will you join me?'

After Elizabeth had changed, they walked up to the Manor and chatted about usual matters such as the weather, and some of the paintings that Elizabeth had particularly liked. Jenny explained where she had painted them and gave Elizabeth more information about her army life. Tanya served them as they settled down to an evening meal, with a shared bottle of the house red wine.

At the end of the indulgent sweets, Elizabeth excused herself to go to the ladies. Jenny's mind drifted as she sipped her coffee and gazed around the restaurant at the other diners. A trip to the Lake District for location painting appealed. She'd find a picturesque village as her temporary base and install herself there for a few months of painting and relaxation.

The decision brought a calmness to both her mind and body and she smiled to herself in anticipation. Elizabeth came back, but as she went to sit down so she jumped up again. 'Oh no, I've snagged my tights on the chair.'

She turned around and slightly pulled up the hem of her skirt. 'Look!'

Her tights were torn, but Jenny's attention went to Elizabeth's leg.

'You've also got a mark on your tights above the snag.'

Elizabeth held up her skirt and gave a little laugh, 'It's not a mark on my tights it's a birthmark.'

Jenny's mind raced. Determination gripped her. The perfect opportunity now presented itself to find out the truth.

She let Elizabeth sit down, 'It's been a good evening and I think we could become good friends, but there is one issue.'

Elizabeth seemed surprised but remained silent. Jenny wiped her lips on the crisp white napkin and allowed the silence to develop before continuing. 'Sometimes you lie to me, and I don't like it.'

'What do you mean?' Elizabeth had a mutinous look on her face.

'I know you've been to bed with Kevin. There is evidence.' Jenny hesitated. Why had she blurted out the words in such an abrupt and aggressive manner? In retrospect a little subtlety would have been a better approach. But the realisation came too late, so she pressed on with her accusations. 'I am right aren't I, Elizabeth?'

'It's not true! It's not true!' hissed Elizabeth. 'I'm not listening to anything else. I didn't kill him!'

Jenny leaned across and grabbed her hands to stop them waving around, 'You must go to the police and explain. You must!' Anger and nerves shook her voice, 'Will you go?'

'How could you say such a thing.' Her voice sounded almost savage and a flash of temper lighted her eyes. Elizabeth wrenched her hands away from Jenny's grasp, stood up and strode towards the door. Jenny followed her hoping to stop her leaving but became blocked by a waitress and couldn't get across the busy restaurant.

By the time Jenny had reached the main door, Elizabeth ran at full tilt across the car park. Jenny couldn't run that fast so would have no hope of catching her.

'Is everything alright?' asked Tanya as Jenny returned and stood next to her table. Her hands grasped the back of the chair as her legs turned to jelly and threatened to give way. 'Tanya,' she spluttered as a sob caught in her throat, 'I have done the most stupid thing in my whole life.' A cold tremor ran through her body, 'I'm going to need Clayton's help. I...'

'You've gone white. Sit down, don't say anymore I'll ring him straightaway.'

61

Within minutes Clayton arrived. Jenny went to explain but he shook his head, 'Not now, let's get you home first. This isn't the best place to hold a private conversation.' Once they were back at the cottage, Jenny quickly explained about the photograph taken with the spy camera, the birthmark and her suspicion that it had been taken at Victoria House. Clayton listened with intense concentration only interrupting when he needed clarification.

Where had Elizabeth gone? Had she returned to her flat above the post office? Not wanting to be left alone they nipped across the square together and climbed the steps to Elizabeth's flat. Fear clenched like a tight fist around her chest and her breath quickened. Clayton hammered on the door. They waited, straining their ears in the ensuing silence but no reply came. Clayton nipped to the back lane and confirmed her car had gone. Had she gone to the police?

They re-crossed Market Square when a silver-grey Vauxhall pulled up outside the gallery. Jenny recognised it immediately and her heart thudded with a mixture of excitement and relief.

What perfect timing. She desperately needed his

support this evening. As he got out, she flung her arms around him, 'Dan,' she spluttered, 'I'm so pleased to see you. I've been so stupid.' Tears filled her eyes as she clung onto him, feeling his strong arms wrapped around her. Clayton interrupted, 'Probably better not to park there and be too obvious.'

Dan didn't question Clayton or ask Jenny for an explanation, but gave her a reassuring squeeze on her shoulder, and clambered back into his car and drove away. Jenny and Clayton waited in silence, standing in the dark doorway to her cottage. A few minutes later he came trotting back, 'I parked at the back of the George car park. It can't be seen from the road.'

Clayton nodded, 'Let's keep our wits about us as we go in.' Again, there was no questioning from Dan. The men checked methodically through each room to make sure the cottage was secure. They ensured that the only light in the cottage came from the front room. From the outside a normal household late in the evening. Jenny explained the story once again, admitting how foolish she had been. Tears of tension filled her eyes as she completed her explanation, but the presence of the two men gave her confidence.

Dan weighed up the information, 'She might have gone to the police. People give themselves up or decide to tell the truth for a variety of reasons. The deciding factor is often that someone else knows for certain.'

Jenny clutched at his words hoping that he was correct, but a shadow of doubt still niggled her. Somehow, she didn't think that would be Elizabeth's course of action.

Jenny shivered, 'I don't know that she killed Kevin,

but I'm certain that she must have been with him. She has often looked after the house for Amanda, so the photograph could have been taken on another occasion before that night.

If they were together in the room at Victoria House, 'Perhaps a noise made him go out the window to investigate,' Dan frowned in concentration.

'Elizabeth knows you have a clear idea of her involvement. My guess is that she has either gone to the police or somewhere quiet to think it through.' His soothing reassurance helped to relieve some of her anxiety but not quite all of it.

'Do we ring the police?' She asked with a slight tremor to her voice.

Dan gave a mirthless chuckle, 'We would have difficulty in convincing the local constable. The police would be reluctant to get the Inspector out of bed for an ambiguous conversation. We'll stay on our guard tonight.'

He glanced across at Clayton, who gave an almost imperceptible nod to show his agreement.

'If Elizabeth comes back and is in her flat in the morning, we could persuade her to accompany us to the police station. It would look better from her point of view.'

Jenny gulped, and a cold sweat filmed her body, 'There is one thing that could be critical.'

'Elizabeth has a key to this cottage, I gave her one to the back door, in case of an emergency.'

Whatever happens Clayton and I will be here.' Dan squeezed her shoulder in a gesture of reassurance.

'Thanks, guys,' Jenny attempted a smile, but her lips didn't cooperate. The words seemed inadequate as she wouldn't have been able to cope with this situation on her own.

Clayton's forehead creased in concern, 'The first few hours will be crucial. Shall we position ourselves fearing the worse, then we can stand down if there is no problem. Later in the night we could do a rota.'

Dan nodded his agreement, 'Sounds good to me, better to be safe than sorry. Jenny your best position will be at the top of the stairs. If Elizabeth arrives, she will use her key, and no doubt call out to you as she comes in. You can answer which will mean she'll come through to the cottage. I'll be behind the door in the front room, I can turn the light on in the hall. From there we can see her before she sees us.' Jenny familiar with precision planning listened carefully.

Clayton added, 'I'll be in the parlour behind the open door. I can follow her into the cottage. She will probably want a chat, but we'll make sure.'

She took up her position on the upstairs landing, Dan wanted no one in Elizabeth's sight when he turned on the light. Jenny still cross with herself for her foolish approach with Elizabeth, slumped on the landing out of sight with her back resting against the wall and her knees drawn up to her chin. As she sat there in the darkness, she kept her breathing light and listened. At times she almost held her breath as she strained to hear the slightest sound. Dan and Clayton would invoke their army training, as they watched and waited. There would be no communication between them. It wouldn't be needed. They'd discussed their plan in detail attempting to cover a range of possibilities.

The small clock in the front room chimed two

o'clock. Jenny let out a long slow breath as she stared around her in the darkness convinced Elizabeth would have come before now. The smallest of noises reached her. She tilted her head to one side and held her breath. A metallic scrape reached her ears. It sounded like a key being slipped into the lock of the back door.

Fully alert she waited, hoping to hear Elizabeth call her name. Silence, apart from a slight draught of cooler air. The back door had been opened. Perhaps a slight creak of the floorboards, but she couldn't be sure. She stiffened. Every muscle in her body tensed on high alert. Her mouth was bone dry. Her heart rapped against her ribs and rang in her ears. Unease rolled through her like a chill dark wave, as she waited and listened, huddled on the dark landing.

Dan had carefully set up the front room. A high wing backed armchair had it's back to the door so anyone coming in would not see the person in the chair. An open book on the arm, and a reading light over the chair was turned on. He wanted to give the impression of Jenny falling asleep in the chair while reading. The doors through the cottage had been left open. Jenny's eyes focused on a weak moving beam of light which flickered in the darkness of the downstairs passage. A torch?

Why would Elizabeth use a torch? Shadows shifted. Her eyes were glued to the wavering shapes that danced along the walls. A sensation of dread crept up from the pit of her stomach.

Her army training had never covered hidden surveillance, so she followed the men's instructions and stayed out of sight on the upstairs landing, but ready to respond with her voice if needed. Time ceased to exist as she crouched on the floor. Waiting. Listening. Hardly daring to breathe.

Whoever had entered the house had done so with quiet stealth. They didn't want anyone to know. The knot in her stomach tightened. Elizabeth must be coming to get her. Did she have a knife? How did she intend to kill her? She shivered but did not move. Her stomach lurched and she visibly jumped as Dan's voice rang out loud and clear, 'Now!'

Two piercing screams sliced the air sending a chill of horror through Jenny. Gun fire echoed through the cottage. Jenny instinctively flattened herself onto the floor with her hands shielding her head, her ears straining for more sounds. A loud bang. Then more loud hysterical screams and the sound of furniture crashing to the floor. Loud groans vibrated through the darkness.

What was happening, wailed a voice inside Jenny's head. She lifted her head half expecting to see Elizabeth advancing up the stairs towards her. Then Clayton's voice shouted, 'Safe and secured!'

Dan responded, 'Safe and secured!'

His voice again pierced the darkness as he shouted, 'Jenny, lights!'

Jenny summoned all her strength and staggered towards the light switch.

She flicked on the hall and landing lights. 'Jenny. Come down and pick up the gun!' Dan's commanding voice echoed through the cottage. Jenny hurtled down the stairs. In the doorway between the gallery and the cottage. Clayton knelt on the back of a hooded black figure, pressing the face hard into the floor. The figure under him didn't move but groaned in pain, their hands secured behind their back. Clayton's hand clenched tightly over the mouth.

In the entrance to the front room the same pattern. A hooded black figure sprawled under Dan. The moans were loud, but a strong hand over the mouth prevented words. The person's hands were also wrenched behind their back. 'The gun is there,' Dan gave a flick of his head towards the armchair. As Jenny went to step past, she hesitated.

'Don't worry,' Dan had a grim but reassuring smile, 'these two aren't going anywhere.'

Jenny picked up the gun and put her training to use by removing the bullets.

'Mine's female,' Dan's voice sounded serious.

'And mine,' added Clayton.

Jenny's mind worked fast. Perhaps a link existed between Jacqui and Elizabeth. Unusual as she didn't know they were friends.

Dan interrupted her thoughts, 'Come and search them Jenny, we don't want any more surprises and then call the police.' As she searched the woman under Clayton, she could feel the fight had left her. She remained motionless but sobbed. Clayton held her firmly with a knee resting on her back, so she couldn't move.

Jenny scanned the two hooded figures to reassure herself that they were fully secured then dialled 999. The two men had a relentless hold of the two women preventing them from speaking, moving, or doing any more damage. The one under Dan still struggled, but only groans came as the energy of fighting back drained from her.

Dan again issued the orders, 'Jenny, come and take

the hoods off. Let's see who we have.' 'I know this is Elizabeth,' Jenny pulled off the hood of the woman under Clayton. He released his hand from covering her mouth.

'Yes I'm right, her hair is unmistakable.'

Elizabeth buried her head in the carpet, 'I haven't killed anyone,' she sobbed noisily.

Sirens filled the night. That was quick. The shot must have been heard by a neighbour. Suddenly it all made sense, Jenny shook her head slowly from side to side. The last piece of the puzzle fell into place, making her shudder, as she moved towards the woman under Dan.

'I know who it is. It's Amanda.'

At the sound of her own name she resumed her fierce struggles, but Dan had a firm grip. Jenny tugged the dark hood back with trembling fingers, and Amanda's glossy blonde hair fell across the floor on either side of her head. Jenny grimaced, 'Keep a firm grip on her, Dan. Whatever you do don't let her go.' She pointed towards the writhing form. 'You've got a double murderer underneath you.' As she uttered the words her legs turned to jelly, and she sank down onto a nearby chair.

Jenny's accusation produced an invective from Amanda, 'You should have bloody perished in that fire. That was the plan!' Her voice held an icy coldness that made Jenny tremble. It quivered with hatred.

'Oh no! No, it wasn't,' shrieked the other hoodie as she wriggled and sobbed. 'You said it was just to frighten her,' shouted Elizabeth.

The screech of tyres outside indicated the police had arrived.

'This way!' Jenny's voice shook, as she led two large policemen into the cottage. Their eyes grew larger as they saw the two men on top of the two dark clad figures. 'There were reports of a shot.'

Dan nodded, 'You'll find the bullet in the back of the television somewhere. These two broke in and were armed.' His voice sounded controlled and authoritative. 'If you would like to take charge of this one, I will show you my warrant card.'

The policeman bent down to take over, as Dan let go, and stood up. As the policeman went to look at Amanda she turned and spat in his face. He cautioned her for assaulting a police officer as he put on the handcuffs. The policeman frowned, 'Where's the gun?'

'Safely disarmed officer,' Jenny's voice quivered with tension.

She pointed to Amanda, her nostrils flared and her eyes darkened, 'She is responsible for the two murders in this village.'

The policeman lifted his head and a puzzled frown creased his forehead. 'That's a strong accusation. Exactly who are you?'

'Formerly Major Jennifer Maltravers, British Army.' He made no further comment, but his eyes flicked across her face. Other police cars quickly arrived including an armed unit.

62

After several hours as daylight dawned, the last of the police left. Jenny, Dan and Clayton sat down in the front room, each cradling a glass of whiskey. For several long minutes they lounged back in the chairs as exhaustion crept over them.

'What a night,' Dan's eyes crinkled with a mixture of tiredness and amusement. 'Every time I arrive in Peaklow they're always seems to be an unexpected drama waiting for me. 'Come on then explain. How do you know Amanda committed both murders?'

Jenny gave a self-satisfied smile. She remained certain that her supposition was correct. 'Elizabeth says one thing and then does the opposite. She had a strong opinion against Kevin, and expressed her dislike of him, whenever his name was mentioned. Although she had been having an affair with him for some time, she denied it emphatically. Despite her appearance and the personality she showed in the post office, she could be persuaded by men and women. Underneath her façade, she was a gullible woman, and was easily manipulated by the strong fanatical character of Amanda.

She couldn't resist men and was promiscuous. Sadly,

I suspect she was lonely and wanted to be loved. Anyway, to make matters worse she came directly under Amanda's influence, which turned out to be evil. She looked after Amanda's house whenever she was away in Birmingham, so the room could easily be used for meeting Kevin. Going up the steps to her flat would be obvious, so it was easier to meet him at Victoria House. It became simple when he started to work there.

On the night Kevin died Amanda had rung Elizabeth to say she would be away. Elizabeth would take the opportunity, they must have gone to bed together, and shared some wine.

'It's only a guess, but I would think the flame between Kevin and Amanda never died. I never found out what happened between them to cause the breakup of their relationship. For some reason, Amanda delayed her departure, and came back and saw the light on. She must have crept along the scaffolding to discover what was happening in the house.'

Jenny smiled, 'Lindy once told me that Elizabeth made a lot of noise when she was having sex. On one occasion when she visited the flat above the disused shop, which of course is next door to Elizabeth's flat, she could hear her. Anyway, perhaps Elizabeth heard noises and sent Kevin out the window to investigate.'

Dan smiled, 'All this is pure supposition. There is no evidence to substantiate it.'

'I agree,' Jenny grinned and exhaled a long slow breath as she relaxed. 'The next part requires a bit of guesswork and imagination. There were no lights on the scaffolding, so Kevin must have climbed out of the window in the dark. He would have noticed the open gate.

Automatically he would close it. From the light of the room, Elizabeth must have seen Amanda creep along the boards, and push him.'

'Why didn't she ring the police?' interrupted Dan.

Jenny slowly shook her head from side to side, 'To reveal that her only real friend in the village was a murderer and that she'd been in bed with Kevin would be too much for her. She crept away from the house hoping no one would see her. Amanda must have listened or spied, so knew the pair were Kevin and Elizabeth. She didn't know whether she had been seen, but planned to involve Elizabeth, and get her hooks into her so it wouldn't matter.

Amanda then quickly arranged the untidiness on the scaffolding and put leftover wine in the flask.' Then left to go to Birmingham. I'm assuming her car wasn't parked outside Victoria House. Perhaps it was at The George as she might have popped in to see her brother John.

'Do you think it was Amanda and Elizabeth that caused the break-in here?'

'Yes, that would be my guess. They were dressed the same as tonight. I would have never suspected it could have been Elizabeth when you consider her normal dress sense. Her appearance as an old spinster belies the truth. Tonight, when she left the Manor pub I went after her, but I can't run that fast. She sprinted down the road with ease. It took me by surprise, but also made me think.'

'But why Amanda?' asked Clayton.

'As soon as I became convinced Elizabeth had run away from the gallery that night, the next logical link would be Amanda, as they have been the best of friends for ages. Then it fitted together. Kevin's death at Amanda's House and her husband murdered.'

'You're going to have a hard job to convince me and the police about her killing Nicolas.'

Jenny sipped her whiskey and then let out a loud sigh, 'Jacqui had been my favourite supposition for the person who killed Nicolas. I hope she can forgive me for my thoughts. As she suggested I tried to work out who could have done it. I went to the scene where Nicolas had been shot.

'If Tony didn't shoot Nicolas and someone else had been there, he would have pointed a finger at them, but he believed only himself and Nic were there. The only way Jacqui could have been the murderer, without Tony knowing, was if she had been hiding in the bushes and nipped out and fired when he collapsed.

'How can you be so sure of Amanda and not Jacqui?'

'John inadvertently gave me the clue earlier. He went from the pub along the edge of the fields to Amanda's house.'

Dan scratched his head in puzzlement, 'How did he get over the walls and the ditch? 'When they were young, they built stiles and a bridge. A personal route for John and Amanda. If Amanda went the other way to the caravan site, she could have got there before Nicolas, who had stormed out and gone around the long route via the road. I don't know why she hid and listened, but then she saw her opportunity.

Tony fell unconscious on the ground. She could reach the gun. Nicolas must have been leaning over Tony to make sure he was still breathing. Amanda always wears a scarf, my guess is she used that, to hold the gun. Before Tony recovered, she left and returned home by the same route. No one would have seen her. No one apart from John knew the route across the ditch and the walls existed.'

'Had it been because Nicolas punched her?' queried Dan.

'It could have been,' she paused and pursed her lips, 'or more likely he suspected her. Perhaps he worked it out from the time she took to get to Birmingham the evening that Kevin was killed. He might have asked some questions and become suspicious.'

Dan grimaced, 'It will be hard to make any of the accusations stick unless one of them confesses. Elizabeth will go to pieces, but whether she would confess to what she saw is a different matter.'

Jenny smiled, 'Ironically the only firm evidence of a crime is tonight.'

'Yes, that's true,' Dan nodded, 'although they did have a key, which could complicate it. The police will focus on the gun, but it will still be a tough investigation.'

Clayton added, 'Do you think they will get away with it all?'

'The police will question them, and as they will now know what they are looking for they might find some new evidence, but unless they do, it will be difficult to build a case...' and his voice trailed off.

63

Jenny plodded slowly across the churchyard. A cold and damp day in the summer made the graveyard, sited on an exposed slope behind the village church, a chilly place. Moving slowly, she crossed to the far corner, with its new grave, where the flowers still fresh from the funeral covered the small mound.

Too soon after the death for a memorial stone, but words had been left on paper. Faded and hard to read, she only glanced at them. Closeness couldn't be her prerogative. 'I'm so sorry Amanda,' she knelt on the damp soil and bowed her head, 'I didn't want it to end like this.'

Jenny had only arrived back in Peaklow about an hour before. The day after the arrests of Amanda and Elizabeth, she had left Peaklow, as she couldn't face the people of the village. It had been good to see her friends in Essex, but it had made her realise that she didn't want to live back there.

The idea had formed of being an itinerant and nomadic artist. She could rent a house or shop for six months and then move. In that way, she would never become involved in local matters again, and could still enjoy the wonderful scenery, but without commitments. Dan had driven her back to Essex after the arrests and had returned to duty.

She had arrived back in Peaklow today, to pack up the cottage and gallery. Many of the paintings would need to be destroyed because of smoke damage. Her intention had been to quietly arrive, deal with the cottage and gallery and then to depart. A kind invitation from Gerald and Gwendoline, meant that she could stay at Stanton House again for a day or two, until she had completed her packing.

Away from the mainstream of the village, she could relax in their company. Her mind drifted back to her first dinner invitation at Stanton House. The word from the former headteacher of the local comprehensive rang in her ears. Beware of two families from the village. Oh, how she wished she'd listened to him, instead of dismissing his warning.

Struggling back to her feet, she peered down at the grave, and her thoughts went back to her time in the village. The wind swirled and blew fresh rain into her face, but she didn't move.

When she had first arrived at Peaklow her horrors had been fading, but now they were back. Time to move on and try again. The incident with the gun in her cottage had brought back the old images. She had relived the terrible night in Afghanistan so many times. It would never leave her. The screams of the patients and the gunfire in the field hospital. They were intent on murder. She was armed. That night she used her gun to kill.

She stood head bowed facing away from the church and the road. The wind and driving rain swept away noises, but she stood in silence to think about this lively beautiful woman. That is how she would for ever be remembered in Jenny's mind. From the day she'd started painting her portrait, that shining vibrant face with the wonderful hair would never leave her. It had been hard to believe it was the same woman who had come into her cottage armed with a gun, intent on killing her, having failed to achieve those ends in the arson attack. The gentle smile on the portrait, contrasted with the foul mouthed and spitting woman venting her anger at the police.

'Thank you for coming to pay your respects.' The voice startled her, and tension gripped her stomach as she recognised it.

Jenny turned to face him, 'I never wanted it to end like this.'

Lionel's shoulders drooped and he sighed, 'It's in the family and something every parent dreads.' Jenny tilted her head to one side and her brow crinkled in confusion.

Lionel picked up the quizzical look, 'In modern day terms it is called mental instability. My wife and I feared for so long about John. A loner until about eight or nine, then obsessed with looking after Amanda.' The pain in his face was evident and anxiety deepened the lines across his forehead.

Jenny reached across and patted him gently on the arm in a gesture of sympathy. 'John continued to watch over Amanda in adult life.' His voice was husky with emotion. 'It is humbling. We shouldn't have been worried about John. It had been Amanda, but we never realised. Only John understood and that's why he became so possessive. When you look back through my ancestry the pressure on people ended in suicides.'

'Is that how she died? Jenny whispered.

'I don't know the details and I didn't ask.'

'She collapsed mentally when taken into custody, but she had always been a clever lass. She fooled them, and had only been there two days, when she ended it.'

'I liked Amanda.' He inclined his head gravely to acknowledge her words but remained silent.

'What has happened to Elizabeth?'

'She told them what happened, but the police are unsure whether she will be fit enough to face trial. Initial assessments indicate an unstable character. They are taking it from there.'

'Poor Elizabeth. The more I knew her, so it became obvious she had serious problems.'

Lionel nodded, 'She always claimed we were distant relatives of hers. I thought it fanciful, but now I'm not so sure. I spoke at length to Clayton as he was there on that last night. You were perfectly right in your suppositions. Amanda killed Kevin and Nicolas. The police found evidence in her house. The relationship with Kevin continued and had never ceased. They carried on for years with only one person knowing.'

'I presume, John.'

'Yes, he knew but would never tell. He also knew of the dark depressive and evil thoughts she had. He could coax her out of the moods, but he recognised paranoid intentions.'

'A remarkable man and brother.'

'Yes, he certainly is. All these years we worried about him, but now he has been released from the burden of Amanda, he is a changed man.'

Jenny took a deep breath, 'My presence in the village must be hard for you and your family. I shall not be staying and have only come to pack my things. It was my intention to come and go unseen and without fuss.'

'You have not shown a single fault since you arrived in this village.' Lionel's sad eyes searched her face. 'You had no option but to defend yourself. My family and I would regret it, if you left. Terror gripped this village and we were frightened. You and your friends dealt with what the police couldn't.

Once poor Amanda had committed that first act of pushing Kevin off the scaffolding to his death, she wouldn't turn back to her normal life. She had to be stopped, there is no doubt in my mind.'

'But it turned out so sad in the end,' Jenny looked down at the flowers not wanting to see the pain in his eyes.

'I knew early on, but I wrestled with my conscience and couldn't tell the police.' Jenny gulped, as a shadow of alarm raced through her body. She jerked her head up and stared. What did he mean? 'The night I dined alone at the Manor. I came back past Amanda's house. Earlier, she had rung to say that Nicolas would not be going to Europe for his meetings, and she would journey to Birmingham to meet him.

As I came past the house I checked as I always did and stepped inside the gate. Despite the wind I could hear footsteps on the scaffolding. Kevin's body lay on the ground. The light caught his face and I could see he was dead. Ignoring the noises and movement on the scaffolding I went home. Outside the back of my flat I saw you walk past. I hoped and prayed you would find the body. You would deal with the circumstances in a proper and professional manner. During the night I couldn't work out the delay. Only later I found out that you didn't find him until the morning.'

His words shocked Jenny and she remained silent. How had he managed to turn his back on what had happened? Did he suspect, even then, that Amanda was responsible? How had he managed to keep control over the last few weeks? Poor man. What a burden he had been carrying.

'I do feel so much for you, your wife and John,' the words sounded so inadequate and trivial given the torment he must have suffered.

Lionel bowed his head in acknowledgement. 'Please reconsider your decision to leave the village.' He then turned and walked away. After a few paces he hesitated and swivelled round to face her, 'By the way, I've shaken hands with Tony. The feud between us is over. He is a changed man.'

Jenny could believe that. What must Tony have been thinking with a case against him for murder that seemed watertight. Standing motionless, she waited for Lionel to leave the cemetery.

64

She wished to avoid further accidental meetings. Other people in the village may not take such a benevolent approach as Lionel. At one time she had been determined to stay, once the crimes had been cleared up. Now they had, she suffered an inordinate amount of guilt to be at the centre of the disruption of a quiet village. Not wanting to bump into anyone else, she made her way quickly to her car and drove to Stanton House.

She spent a pleasant and relaxed evening with them, during which she explained her strange reaction about returning to the village. She remained convinced the locals saw her as a catalyst for the troubles that had happened. Although they disagreed, she wouldn't be swayed from her opinion.

To avoid more meetings in the village, she decided to leave Stanton House about five o'clock in the morning and go to the cottage and gallery to pack. By ten o'clock before the village got going, she would return to Stanton House. It would take only a couple of days and then she would travel back to Essex. As the following day was Saturday, she was convinced her plan would work, because hardly anyone came into the Square early.

The strategy worked and she successfully returned to Stanton House for the day. To make the least nuisance of herself, she set up her paints and easel on the lawn, with the idea of painting Stanton House as a small present for Gerald and Gwendoline's kindness over the months. Gwendoline popped out to confirm that she would be there that evening as a few friends had been invited. Jenny would be comfortable with Gerald's friends.

At about five o'clock as she finished painting for the day she went back into the house. Henry wanted a chance to speak with her, but had broken his ankle and so couldn't come that evening. Jenny agreed to go with Gerald over to Henry's house for a few hours. It was good to see him again and they spent some time talking about painting.

Gerald parked the car back at Stanton House, 'I expect some of the guests will have arrived by now. It's an informal buffet, so shall we join them in the dining room.' Jenny would have preferred to change but nodded her agreement. It was only going to be a small gathering because she couldn't hear any voices. As Gerald opened the dining room doors wide, so there was a big cheer from inside.

A gasp of astonishment leapt from her lips and tears welled in her eyes. All the faces she knew from the village were there, including Tony and Jacqui, Lionel and his family as well as Lindy. There were many other faces she knew, but weren't sure of the names.

Lionel, with John next to him, raised his hand and everyone went quiet, he stepped forward, 'Everyone has come tonight to try to persuade you to stay in our village.' There was a round of applause. A huge smile covered her face as tears trailed across her cheeks.

Then a voice behind her spoke, 'And if you are staying I want to come here as well.'

'Oh, Dan!' he stepped forward and kissed her on the lips. Making the assembled crowd cheer even louder.

THE END

Enjoy this book?

Thank you for reading my book. If you have time I would appreciate a rating or review. They are a great help to me in developing and writing my books.
You can find more information about my books on my website:

T M Goble's Website

www.tmgoble.com

Action Thrillers
Detective Murder Mysteries
Standalone Murder Mysteries
Historical Fiction
Contemporary Fiction
History of Peak District Literature
Seasonal Recipes

I occasionally send newsletters with details on new releases, special offers and other bits of news relating to my books.

Printed in Great Britain
by Amazon

22770970R00209